con

D1012587

"Parsley, sage, rosemary, and . . . murder. *Assault and Pepper*, the scintillating first book in Leslie Budewitz's new Spice Shop Mystery series, will add zing to your reading."

—Barbara Ross, author of the Maine Clambake Mysteries

Death al Dente

"Seldom does a new author hit all the right notes in a first book, but Leslie Budewitz does. Convincing characters, a believable plot, the right dash of romance, and a deft use of words all come together to create a seamless and satisfying read."

—Sheila Connolly, *New York Times* bestselling author

"Small-town charm and big-time chills. Jewel Bay, Montana, is a food lover's paradise—and ground zero for murder! A dizzying culinary delight with a twisty-turny plot! I'm totally enamored of Leslie Budewitz's huckleberry chocolates, Shasta daisies, and Cowboy Roast coffee."

—Laura Childs, *New York Times* bestselling author

"An intriguing sleuth who loves gourmet food, family, and her hometown, plus recipes to die for distinguish a delectable mystery." —Carolyn Hart, *New York Times* bestselling author

"The first book in a delicious new series. Leslie Budewitz has created a believable, down-to-earth heroine in Erin Murphy, who uses her sleuthing skills and the Spreadsheet of Suspicion to catch a killer. The supporting cast of characters, from Erin's mother, Fresca, to her cat, Sandburg, are charming. I'm looking forward to my next visit to Jewel Bay."

—Sofie Kelly, *New York Times* bestselling author

Assault
and Pepper

LESLIE BUDEWITZ

BERKLEY PRIME CRIME, NEW YORK

THE BERKLEY PUBLISHING GROUP
Published by the Penguin Group
Penguin Group (USA) LLC
375 Hudson Street, New York, New York 10014

USA • Canada • UK • Ireland • Australia • New Zealand • India • South Africa • China

penguin.com

A Penguin Random House Company

ASSAULT AND PEPPER

A Berkley Prime Crime Book / published by arrangement with the author

Berkley Prime Crime Books are published by The Berkley Publishing Group.
BERKLEY® PRIME CRIME and the PRIME CRIME logo are trademarks of
Penguin Group (USA) LLC.

For information, address: The Berkley Publishing Group,
a division of Penguin Group (USA) LLC,
375 Hudson Street, New York, New York 10014.

ISBN: 978-0-425-27178-0

PUBLISHING HISTORY
Berkley Prime Crime mass-market edition / March 2015

PRINTED IN THE UNITED STATES OF AMERICA

Cover illustration by Lesley Worrell.
Cover design by Ben Perini.
Interior text design by Kelly Lipovich.

For Lita

*Let others debate whether variety
or humor is the spice of life.*

I know it's friendship.

Acknowledgments and
Historical Note

A writer setting a story in a real place must ask indulgence from readers who know and love it. I have attempted to be as accurate as possible, while portraying a city in flux—as they always are—the city where I imagine Pepper Reece and her friends at work and play.

The removal of Seattle's Alaskan Way Viaduct—the elevated highway above the waterfront—and its replacement with a tunnel began in 2012 and is scheduled for completion in 2016. At this writing, proposals are being considered for a south entrance to the Market on the site once home to the Municipal Market, destroyed by fire decades ago. But nothing ever happens exactly as planned, so my portrayal and the city's evolution may not be perfectly in sync.

The Spice Shop occupies the Garden Center Building. To keep the herbs and spices safe from heat and light, I have replaced the large plate windows along Pine Street with clerestory windows and given the shop a side door—both changes not likely to be approved in real life, given the Market's listing on the National Historic Register. While most of the Market is owned by the city and managed by the Public Development Authority, a few buildings remain in private ownership, including this one, although not on these pages. At this writing, all Market shops mentioned are still in business in the locations described. Alex and his restaurants are fictitious; sadly, so are Café Frida and the Diego Lounge.

The Market was saved from urban renewal by Seattle voters,

led by the Friends of the Market and visionary architect Victor Steinbrueck. His *Market Sketchbook* remains a treasure. I have also drawn inspiration from *Soul of the City: The Pike Place Public Market* by Alice Shorett and Murray Morgan, and *An Insider's Tour of the Pike Place Public Market* by Michael Yaeger, illustrated by Sarah Clementson.

As a college student and later as a young lawyer, I shopped and ate in the Market weekly, but there's no substitute for inside knowledge. Thanks to Mercedes Yaeger of Market Ghost Tours for sharing her insights and experiences as a child—and adult—of the Market. Her book, *Seattle's Market Ghost Stories*, is a treat. Thanks also to the other merchants who chatted with me, and to Emily Crawford of the PDA and Detective Renée Witt of the Seattle Police Department for answering questions. Of course, I made the mistakes all by myself.

For Pepper's loft, I added upper floors to the Pittman Automotive building at the corner of Union and Western, which currently provides rooftop parking on Western and houses an antiques market on the Alaskan Way side. For spicy detail, Pepper and I both refer frequently to *The Spice and Herb Bible* by Ian Hemphill and *The Spice Bible* by Jane Lawson.

Lita Artis and Ken Gollersrud provided critical ground support and hospitality. Thanks to Lita and to Katherine Nyborg for reading a draft and sharing their perspective as longtime residents of the Emerald City.

My writer friends, at home and away, gave me their ears, examples, and encouragement. It's a pleasure to work with other professionals—and a joy to propose an idea they instantly love, as both my agent, Paige Wheeler, at Creative Media Agency, Inc., and my editor, Faith Black, at Berkley Prime Crime, did. Thanks to Robin Barletta at Berkley Prime Crime for jumping into the project with enthusiasm, and to all of you for helping bring this magical place to life—and ink.

And as ever, thanks to Don Beans, aka Mr. Right, always willing to wander any Market street or alley, eat any food, and talk about it all the way home.

Inventory—Aka the Cast

THE SEATTLE SPICE SHOP STAFF

Pepper Reece—owner
Sandra Piniella—assistant manager and mix master
Tory Finch—salesclerk and artist
Zak Davis—salesclerk and musician
Reed Locke—part-time salesclerk and college student
Kristen Gardiner—part-time salesclerk, Pepper's oldest
  friend

THE FLICK CHICKS

Pepper
Kristen
Laurel Halloran—restaurant owner, caterer, houseboat
  dweller
Seetha Sharma—the newest member
Gabe Halloran—Laurel's teenage son and honorary
  member

MARKET MERCHANTS, RESIDENTS, AND FRIENDS

Angie and Sylvie Martinez—aka the orchard girls
Yvonne Winchell—grows the best flowers in the Market
Jane Rasmussen—founder and former owner of Seattle
  Spice

Doc aka Damien Finch—the mysterious newcomer

Sam and Arf—a man and his dog

Jim and Hot Dog—Sam's friends

Marianne Finch—Damien's wife

Ken Griffey—Damien's partner

Alex Howard—restaurateur Pepper may or may not be dating

Fabiola the Fabulous—graphic designer

Keyra Jackson—Tory's sculptor friend and neighbor

Jen the Bookseller and Callie the Librarian—Pepper's former law firm employees

Vinny—the wine merchant

SEATTLE'S FINEST

Officer Tag Buhner—on the bike beat, Pepper's former husband

Detective Cheryl Spencer—homicide

Detective Michael Tracy—homicide

One

An herb is a fresh or dried leaf. A spice is a dried plant part—a bud (cloves), bark (cinnamon), root (ginger), berry (peppercorns), seeds (fennel), or even stigma (saffron). The same plant may provide both—fresh or dried cilantro leaves are the herb cilantro, while the dried seeds are the spice coriander.

"WHAT DOES AUTUMN *TASTE* LIKE? HOW DOES IT *SMELL*?"

Even as I asked, the questions seemed utterly ridiculous. This was already shaping up to be one of those glorious September days in Seattle that make you think the weather will never change, that the sky will always be a pure cloudless blue, the leaves on the trees a painter's box of green, the waters of Elliot Bay calm and sparkling.

I've lived here all my forty-two years, and I still get fooled.

But as the owner, for the last ten months and seventeen days, of the Seattle Spice Shop, it was my job to think ahead. Fall would be here in less than a week, by the calendar. And by my nose. I really could sense the difference right about this time of year. The annual run on pickling spices for the last cukes would soon give way to cider mulling mixes. And before long, our customers would be asking for poultry seasoning and scouting for Christmas gifts.

"The taste," I repeated to my staff, gathered around the butcher block worktable in our mixing nook, "and smell of fall."

Sandra fanned herself with a catalog from the kitchen shop up the hill and peered over the top of her reading glasses—today's were leopard print. "Fall, shmall. It's seventy-six degrees out." Spot-on to most Seattleites, but my assistant manager is one of those native Northwesterners who thrive in a narrow temperature range. Anything above seventy-two and she sweats; below forty-five, she shivers. And complains, cheerfully. A short, well-rounded woman of sixty with smooth olive skin, pixie-cut dark hair, and lively chocolate brown eyes, she came with the place, and I say daily prayers of gratitude that she stayed.

"Apples," Zak said. "Applesauce, apple butter, spiced apple cake. Plums in brandy. Plum pudding. Fruitcake." Zak had been my first hire after I bought the shop. Six-two and almost thirty, with muscular shoulders, he'd seemed an unlikely candidate for employment in a retail spice shop in Seattle's venerable Pike Place Market. But I'd been desperate and he'd been earnest. And he pleaded for a weekday job so he could rock the nights and weekends away with his band.

Plus he's my ex-husband Tag's best friend's nephew, and I have to admit, Tag Buhner isn't always wrong about people.

"You have fruit on the brain," Sandra said. "Been flirting with the orchard girls again?"

Zak blushed, a sweet look at odds with his shaved head, fierce dark brows, and black goatee.

The orchard girls, two sisters with shiny black hair, full red lips, and curves in all the right places, had caught the eye of every straight man under thirty-five in the Market since they took over the family fruit stand this past summer. Their looks and the location of their stall—they usually draw a prime spot across from us on Pike Place, the Market's long, cobbled main street—guarantee plenty of attention.

That their fruit is the freshest and their jams the tastiest doesn't hurt.

"Our tea is the essential fragrance of the Market year-round," I said, pointing my pen at the ornate brass electric teapot that resembles a Russian samovar. We'd just resumed serving the hot black Assam tea spiced with cardamom, allspice, and orange, although the iced tea dispenser would stay out a few more days.

"That, and fresh fish." Zak had recovered from his embarrassment. The fish merchants near the Market's main entrance put on a comedy routine to rival the Marx Brothers', tossing whole coho salmon like softballs, teasing customers, and welcoming both locals and wide-eyed tourists to the heart and stomach of Seattle.

Zak filled his mug, emblazoned with a Z, and snatched a hazelnut cookie from the box. It wouldn't be a staff meeting without treats from the French bakery.

"We need three or four new blends," I said. "For our home cooks. Zak's zeroed in on the harvest aspect of fall. But I'd like something to rub on those fish, or a slow-cooked chuck roast. To warm up the salty mist and stave off the chills, until we get into the familiar tastes of Christmas."

My staff turned thoughtful, summoning their own ideas of fall. They say the sense of smell is the most intimately linked of all our senses to memory, and I believe it. One whiff of a familiar scent, even one we haven't encountered in years, can transport us to a time and place long forgotten, even before we consciously recall the memory.

Our task was to find common elements and translate them into balanced blends of herbs and spices to evoke a positive sensory experience for our customers.

The Wednesday morning staff meeting is one of the few times we're all in the shop together. Such a satisfying sight.

Actually, we were one person short. I checked the

clock—a large, copper-rimmed metal ticker—next to the front door. As if on cue, the door opened and a blond cloud swept in.

"Right on time for the eight-seventeen meeting," I said with a grin. Kristen Gardiner and I have been best friends since childhood, when our families shared a creaky, turn-of-the-century house on Capitol Hill. She still lives in the house, a classic Seattle Box built by an ancestor, although now it glows with an attic-to-cellar makeover that would color any decorator in the Emerald City green. She helps out in the shop a few mornings a week, and she is never, ever on time.

"I'm so sorry, Pepper. One of the girls forgot her lunch and I had to—"

I held up a hand. "You're fine. We're brainstorming fall blends."

"Something pungent and flavorful." Reed spoke without glancing up from his task of running a rubber stamp of the shop name over small white paper cups. Shoppers who drop in for a sample of tea often end up buying herbs, spices, or other goodies they'd forgotten they needed. Or that they didn't need, but the fragrance and possibilities set their taste buds and imaginations awhirl.

"It's so neat how you can trace geography and history through spices," he continued. "When I open a jar of chili pepper cocoa, I'm in the world of the Aztecs. Ask me for a curry, and I'm halfway to India." Maybe five-six, an inch shorter than me, slight, with shaggy black hair and hooded eyes, Reed Locke is a history major at Seattle University. Wednesdays, he comes in early before dashing off to classes. His father runs an acupuncture clinic nearby, so he practically grew up in the Market.

We all turned to the world map on the wall, where colored pins mark the origin of every spice we carry. Many spices have migrated and become integral to cuisines and economies far from their genesis. The map also hides an ugly water stain on the plaster that paint didn't cover. Spice has added flavor to the Market since shortly after its founding in 1907, when our main competitor opened a shop, still prospering. In the fervor surrounding the campaign to save the Market from redevelopment in the early 1970s, hippie chick Jane Rasmussen threw her lot in with capitalist competition and started this shop. Why she thought the Market could support two separate spice merchants, I don't know— but she'd been right, running this one for forty years until she sold it to me and retired to an island in Puget Sound. Our building once housed a nursery, and in spring, we honor that heritage by carrying seed packets and potted herbs.

I like to think of myself as the caretaker of one piece in the Market puzzle.

"A curry is a good idea," I said. "Can we add a pinch of a chili or some other pepper, for our pungent mix? Put a chutney on the menu, and you've got Zak's harvest touch, with an international accent." Heads bobbed. "Okay, now we need a savory combo, and a comfort blend. Everyone's sense of comfort varies, but we're after something that evokes that feeling of coming home after a walk in the rain, or spending a Sunday afternoon reading by the fire."

"If we're spicing to feel warm, we'll be using the same stuff until April," Kristen said. She wrapped a black-and-white Indian madras scarf around her neck, tucking the ends into her apron, black with the shop name in white. "It's freezing out there."

Sandra rolled her eyes.

"We'll trot out our pie spice mix, of course. It's perfect for coffee, or oatmeal—"

"Or pie," Zak said.

"For the comfort blend," Tory said, "you want something earthy. Familiar, but not boring. A mix that makes you want to cook just so you can taste it."

Tory Finch had also come with the shop. Twenty-eight,

with a shapely figure, even in her black shop apron, and light brown hair in a chin-length blunt cut. She met my gaze, her golden brown eyes a touch less guarded than usual. Painter by night, spice girl by day, there was little question which she regarded as her real work. But when she spoke at our meetings—which wasn't often—everyone listened.

Every business needs at least one employee like that.

I nodded, with a glance at Sandra, my master mixologist. "Something for dips and sauces or to give a little oomph to chicken. Add depth to sautéed spinach or roasted squash." Labels inside the metal tins would include a recipe or two, with more on our website.

A tiny smile tugged at Tory's mouth, shiny with her usual pale pink lip gloss, and she reached for the second stamp to help Reed with the cups.

"And for the savory," I began, breaking off at the sound of angry voices outside. Zak strode to the door, and I dashed after him, confirming with a quick pat that my phone was in my apron pocket.

"I told you, again and again. This is *my* corner. When you gonna listen, old man?" Sam, a Market regular, jabbed his forefinger and pointed at the sidewalk where Pine Street meets Pike Place, the Market's cobbled main thoroughfare. Though he stood on the street, Sam towered above the man pacing on the sidewalk. Sam's wiry black hair, flecked with gray, peeked out from under a black wool beret that matched his long, flowing coat, and his beard stubble looked like coffee grounds against his dark skin. Beside him, Arf the dog, a tall gray-and-brown terrier mix, stood at heel, his emerald green nylon leash slack. Dogs aren't officially allowed in the Market, but you'd never know it.

"Hey, guys." Zak extended his hands like stop signs.

"Everybody cool it," I said, stepping in front of him and sizing up the situation. No fists were being thrown; no one appeared injured. "What's the problem?"

"He's got my corner." Sam stood as tall as Zak. The other man barely topped my five-seven.

"These are public streets," I said. "Anyone can be anywhere." Technically true, but that doesn't keep the regulars from staking their claims. Aggressive begging is illegal, as is blocking foot or vehicle traffic. But I'd rarely seen a problem—and never from Sam. Trouble usually comes from outside.

Sam's chin jutted out. He lowered his head apologetically, gnarled fingers tightening the dog's leash. I glanced at the other man, who'd shown up a few weeks ago and often stood on this corner or across the street. Sam, who had to be sixty, called him "old man," but it was hard to judge his age, with the khaki rain hat he wore every day tugged low over his forehead and his thin shoulders hunched inside his olive green raincoat. It hadn't rained in weeks.

"You're Doc, right?"

He punched his hands deeper into the coat's big pockets and nodded. Though I don't have children—by the time Tag felt "ready," the batteries on my biological clock had run down—Doc's response made me feel like I was separating squabbling toddlers.

"Sam, since Doc's the newcomer, why don't we show him a little Market hospitality and let him pick which corner he'd like today. You take that one." I pointed across Pine. "Tomorrow, you switch."

A long silence before Sam said, "Yes, Miz Pepper," a touch of the South in his deep, shy voice.

"That okay with you, Doc?" He raised his head briefly, then lowered his golden brown eyes, terror-stricken. He didn't speak.

"If either of you misses a day, just keep alternating. And if there's a problem, talk to me."

"I've called the police," a woman's breathless voice said.

Pooh. Yvonne Winchell sold the freshest flowers in the

daystalls—customers had come in all week carrying bouquets of her colorful dahlias, sunflowers, and others I couldn't identify—but I'd never met such a worrywart. The Market is safe and clean; still, put thousands of diverse people in a small space seven days a week and things do happen. This was minor.

Behind her, one of the orchard girls watched us.

"No need," I said. "Everything's under control." Yvonne stared intently, then ducked back under the shed roof that covered the long rows of daystalls, the long wooden tables with built-in benches rented by farmers and craftspeople.

"C'mon, Arf," Sam said.

Both man and dog were clean, if a bit scruffy, so I suspected they had regular shelter somewhere. I fumbled in my pocket for a liver chew, keeping it hidden in my hand. Arf perked up, his long gray and caramel ears flopping back as his nose rose. "May I?"

"Yes'm. Whachew say, dog?" he said as Arf licked my hand. Man and dog headed for the opposite corner, and I turned back to Doc.

He wasn't there. After all that, where had he gone? I scanned the sidewalk, in case he'd thought I'd sent him across Pine to the corner by the Triangle Building. But there was no sign of him.

Had he ducked into the Spice Shop for a spot of tea? We weren't open yet, but we did sometimes hand out samples of hot tea to help keep the street folk warm.

I glanced inside. Not there, either.

Tory stood in the doorway of our salmon pink stucco building, one hand braced on the forest green frame, the other covering her mouth. Anxiety shaded her usually placid face.

A metallic whizzing followed by the scrape of rubber on a hard surface commandeered my attention, and I spun toward the sounds.

"Damsel in distress?" said a familiar baritone.

Double pooh. Why couldn't this have been Tag's day off?

"We took care of it, Officers," Zak said from behind me. He knew how I felt about Tag's tendency to jump right on any dispatch to the Market and wheel his trusty Seattle Police Department bicycle into my neighborhood. I recognized the irony—Zak's protectiveness mirrored Tag's. Not that there was anything romantic between me and my employee. He's just that kind of guy.

So, alas, is Tag, and he hadn't quite given up on romance between us. Despite his affair with a meter reader. (I couldn't bring myself to say "parking enforcement officer.") Despite our divorce.

"A couple of street guys got into a shouting match," I said. "They both wanted to camp on the same corner, but I got 'em to agree on taking turns. No trouble. Sorry to take you out of your way."

"Your shop's never out of my way, Pepper." Tag balanced his bike, one long, lean leg stretched to the pavement, the other foot on the pedal, ready to take off at a moment's notice. Behind him, his partner, Jay Olerud, wove figure eights, eyes scanning the crowd. How they manage to stay upright on the cobbles and curbs, swerve in and out of traffic, and speed up hills and down wearing guns, radios, and other gear, all the while sniffing out trouble, I can never understand.

There's a lot I don't understand about Tag. Including why he still seems so keen on me. I ran a hand through my spikey dark hair. When my job as a law firm HR manager fell victim to the senior partners' shenanigans, leaving me unemployed only a year after my divorce, I cut my ties to the corporate world and cut my hair. My morning routine now means sticking my head in the bathroom sink, toweling it dry with a washcloth, and rubbing a handful of goo over the remains. Bed Head R Us.

And for some reason, Bike Boy thinks it's hot.

He grinned. I reddened. Why does the man always look like he knows what I'm thinking?

"No trouble," I repeated.

"You're sure about that," he said, fingering his radio. At my nod, he keyed a button and reported in to dispatch. His china blue eyes bored into me. "That changes, you call me."

I gave him a mock salute and turned away before he took off. Those tight shorts reveal things I really didn't want to see.

SANDRA and Tory—both true spice artists—and I worked most of the day creating the new blends. I had one advantage: Not knowing what didn't work made me open to almost any combination.

And after years in law firm admin, I am an organizer par excellence.

We tossed out ideas, using the framework we'd laid earlier, and Tory fetched the jars of herbs and spices. Before I bought the shop—when I was a curious customer who slowly graduated from sipping tea to buying premixed combos, then on to preparing my own—I'd walk around the place, astonished by its beauty. By the bounty of jewel-like colors, intriguing shapes and textures, alluring smells. The vibrance of it all still stuns me.

The variety intimidates some shoppers. They buy cinnamon in the grocery store, where only one jar says "cinnamon." That way, they don't have to choose between ground, chunks, and sticks, from Sri Lanka, Indonesia, and Vietnam, or a blend—particularly nice if I do say so myself.

"That's two parts to one and one, plus one-quarter part Aleppo pepper. Are you getting this, boss?" Sandra nudged me with an elbow, and I broke off my reverie and wrote down the proportions. She slid the mixing bowl across to Tory and me, and we each dipped out a sample.

I closed my eyes, the better to taste with, and sniffed. "It needs to be—darker, if that makes sense. To balance the hint of sweetness." Turns out herb and spice tasting is a lot like wine tasting, with some of the same vocabulary. Although I've never heard anyone refer to cumin's "legs."

"She's right," Tory said. "Try the other Aleppo, the smokier one."

We agreed on the pungent and savory blends before turning to names. We planned to continue the pattern that Jane, the prior owner, had begun, using historic names and geographic features of western Washington and a subtitle describing the flavors. Not exactly inspired, but I hadn't hit on anything better. Last spring, we'd highlighted the bays of Puget Sound: Elliot, Skagit, Shilshole, and Anacortes. A lot of local features bear handles derived from the languages of coastal tribes. The words trip up newcomers, but before long, they rattle off Duwamish, Nooksack, Snoqualmie, and Skookumchuk like natives.

Plus the tongue twisters amuse tourists, and I'm all for that.

Job done, we took a quick break. I left the nook—a raised corner of the shop, set off by pony walls to let us keep an eye on things—just as a regular customer came in. Once a paralegal at my old law firm, Jennifer now works at a mystery bookshop.

She thrust her list at me and waited, a sly look on her face.

"Sumac. Pomegranate molasses. Cumin, allspice, cinnamon, coriander, rose petals." I raised one eyebrow, pretending to be stumped. "Marjoram and oregano, and three kinds of pepper. Hmm. It's got to be Middle Eastern." The sumac gave it away. A bright, lemony flavor and a rich, dark red, it's essential to *Fattoush*, or Levantine Bread Salad. And the other ingredients make a classic *Kamunah*, or cumin blend. With a few variations, it could be found in Baghdad, Beirut, Tel Aviv, or Istanbul. Or so I understood— I had not yet taken my own Grand Spice Tour.

"Yes. And the cinnamon, caraway, and anise are for a Lebanese pudding made with rice flour."

God bless gourmet clubs. I weighed and measured, working my way down Jen's list, while she chatted about last month's French feast. Meanwhile, Sandra got back to work, but where had Tory gone?

I frowned as I labeled the white pepper. The front door flew open and Tory barged in, Zak two steps behind. She looked furious; he looked flustered.

Uh-oh. Workplace spat—or romance gone wrong? Had I missed the signs? Wordlessly, Tory returned to the mixing nook. I packed Jen's purchases in her canvas bag, and she headed out. A pair of women came in, and Zak tended to them.

The door opened again. "Hey, Yvonne. What's up? The girls watching your stall?"

She nodded. "I just, uh, need a pick-me-up." She gestured to the tea cart, then crossed the shop and poured a cup.

"Yvonne," Reed said. "Go see my dad for that bad leg. Acupuncture's great for pain."

"Voodoo," she said.

Zak twisted the lid off a jar of my favorite Hungarian paprika and the sharp scent filled the air. Yvonne sneezed.

"*Gesundheit.*" "Bless you." The automatic responses echoed around the room, and she left as quickly as she'd come, still limping and sneezing.

Back at the worktable, I puzzled over how to approach Tory about Zak. Ordinarily, I'd just pull an employee aside, report my observation, and ask if she needed help working out a problem. But you've got to tread carefully when the relationship you're probing might be more than professional. Tory and I got along well, but without the friendly jibing Sandra and I shared or the almost motherly feeling I had for Reed. She focused her attention on mixing, blending, smelling, and tasting, giving me no opportunity to speak.

I transcribed our tasting notes. Had Tory's visible distress this morning stemmed from concern for Zak's safety? But while the spat between Sam and Doc had gotten loud, it never presented any real danger—not to me, and certainly not to Zak.

"Any idea what's up with her?" I said to Sandra when Tory stepped away to fetch another jar of sage.

She shook her head. "That girl is as private as a Swiss bank account. She's worked here two years, and I read her about as well as ancient Cyrillic."

"Me, too. She pours her passion into her art. But I've never seen a painting. You?" Her expression said no. "I wonder if Zak is breaking through her reserve."

Sandra sealed the last of the plastic bags that held today's samples. We'd try them all again tomorrow before making final decisions—it takes a blend anywhere from six to twenty-four hours for the flavors to round off. "Maybe. Though he loves to flirt with the orchard girls and sweet-talks every female customer."

"That's our Zak."

But something had shaken my least flappable employee. I just hoped it was none of my business.

Two

Average number of rainy days in Seattle: 155 days a year. Average number of sunny days: 58. Everything else: shades of gray.

I SNICKED THE SPICE SHOP'S WORN BRASS LOCK SHUT, turned, and raised my face to the last glorious rays. People in other parts of the country think it rains every day in Seattle.

Let 'em.

The Market is tucked smack into one of Seattle's hills, with Western Ave on—go figure—the west side. First Ave lies uphill to the east, with Pike Place, a curious L-shaped street, and Post Alley sandwiched between. From Western to First is a steep vertical rise. Happily, my loft is on Western and my shop is in the middle, on Pike Place. So I rarely have to trek the whole thing at once.

Right now, I made my way up Stewart to First, a good climb, carrying a special order for a restaurant customer and test bags of today's blends.

Thinking of Alex Howard, proprietor and chef of the First Avenue Café, brought a smile. Proverbially tall, dark, and handsome. Not to mention successful, intense, and almost flamboyant. A media darling. We'd been out a few promising times.

No, I didn't mind delivery duty one bit.

At the corner, a woman stepped into view and started across the street. Tory. Two or three feet behind her came a man in an olive green raincoat. He appeared to be talking to her, reaching out his hands.

It was Doc. She shook him off, glancing over her shoulder, and kept walking.

You don't beg with both hands. You plead with both hands.

What did he want from her?

I hurried up the hill. She reached the corner just as a Metro bus screeched to a halt, and was gone before I could catch her.

Doc stood, hat pulled low, staring as the bus zoomed away.

"What do you want with T—with her?" I stopped myself from blurting out her name. Over the years, I'd had to intervene several times when downtown denizens hassled my young female employees. Bad enough that he knew where she worked and what bus she rode.

Doc did not reply.

"Leave her alone," I said. "If you've got a problem with Sam, or with the arrangement about the corners, you talk to me, not my staff."

He ducked his head till it almost disappeared between his shoulder blades. Without a word, he trudged down the hill.

I was breathless, not from exercise but from anger and protectiveness. From not knowing whether Doc posed a threat to Tory—or to any of us. He didn't look like much, but that was no guarantee.

When Doc reached Pike Place, he headed back toward the heart of the Market, to my surprise. Most of the street men—homeless or not—hang out at Victor Steinbrueck Park, a grassy lawn on the Market's north edge punctuated by a pair of fifty-foot cedar totem poles. The park is named for the visionary architect who saved the Market from destruction by progress. But now that I thought about it, Doc didn't seem the type to join that crowd—he was more of a loner. Plus, Sam and Arf usually spend the sunset hours there.

I shook off my apprehension. No point worrying without facts.

Several nights a week, Alex Howard presides over the kitchen at his flagship restaurant, the First Avenue Café. He owns the whole building, keeping his corporate offices on the second floor and his apartment on the penthouse level. We met when he grew frustrated with an inconsistent supply of Grenadian nutmeg for his jerk chicken and asked me for help. His charms were undeniable, but I resisted. After thirteen years of marriage to Tag, I'd seen the light: Charm is overrated.

But Alex had kept calling, and now I stood at the Cafe's side door, delivery bag in hand and hope in my heart.

A prep cook answered my knock. "Hey, Pepper." He took the bag and yelled, "Alex!"

I'd arrived in that brief twilight between prep and service. I peered into the dining room, fully set but unoccupied—except for the hostess, passing slowly between the tables, adjusting a chair, realigning an errant napkin. Each wooden surface—tables, chairs, floor—gleamed.

Even a glimpse of its casual elegance made me feel underdressed. I'd taken off my apron but still wore my retail uniform: black yoga pants, black T-shirt with the shop logo, black T-strap climbing shoes perfect for Seattle's hills and the Market's wobbly streets.

The kitchen's stainless steel pots and surfaces shone. The *mise-en-place* was all in place—mounds of chopped shallots, parsley, and other ingredients exactly where each cook needed them. The scene hummed with invisible energy, something like how I imagined a high-wire act would be.

Or a high-voltage electrical wire. I've never worked in a restaurant kitchen, and frankly, the idea terrifies me. The precision, the juggling, the unpredictability—amid all those knives and all that heat. And all that testosterone. No, thanks. Supply and delivery are close enough for me.

"Pepper Reese!" Alex bounded into view and bussed my cheek. "Family meal's just wrapping up. Curried clams with chickpeas and spinach over rice. A variation of one of tonight's specials."

I followed Alex downstairs to the prep kitchen, humid and fragrant. "A bowl for my friend," Alex called to a line cook. He pulled out two wooden folding chairs and reached for a basket of grilled naan.

I dug spice samples out of my jute carryall. "We'd love your impressions of the flavor balance, recipes, anything you want to suggest."

"We'll try them out and I'll give you a call."

A woman in white slid a bowl in front of me and I inhaled the sweet-sharp fragrance of a perfectly balanced curry. Remembering what Reed had said this morning about the geography of spice, I closed my eyes and conjured up the map. Hot, saucy. Southern India, with a Pacific Northwest accent.

Scuttle says some chefs begrudge every bite their crew takes and offer barely edible fare below stairs. Not Alex. "How can I expect a waiter to rave about my Dungeness crab cakes if she's hungry?" he'd told me. "If she's never eaten them, or she's ticked off that I fed her watered-down gruel? My cooks need good hearty fuel if I expect them to work their tails off."

His chair angled toward me, Alex rested his elbows on his knees and watched me eat. In the restaurant, he was all energy. Dark curls glistened on top of his head, the sides well trimmed but not too short. His brown eyes sparkled. He was like a long, sleek cat, pulsing with energy, ready to pounce into action.

Fascinating, and a little bit unnerving.

He rattled off the night's specials—they made me envy the paying customers—then stood. "Gotta run. Eat all you want. See you Sunday?"

I nodded, mouth full of curry. Chefs sweat over hot stoves all weekend. No Friday nights at the movies or Saturday dinner dates. I swallowed, and he swooped in for a kiss. A long, warm, luscious kiss.

Oh, I thought as he dashed up the stairs to take the reins of his domain. *Is this what fall tastes like?*

OUTSIDE, the last sunlight set the peaks of the Olympic Mountains aglow in orange and pink, trimmed in deep purple. I felt the same glow inside. From the curry or the kiss?

Who cares?

I'll be the first to admit, downtown living isn't for everyone. But I adore it. Tag and I had shared a sweet bungalow in Greenwood, a few miles north of downtown. When we split, it had been time for a serious change. I hadn't known, of course, that a year later, the law firm where I worked would implode in scandal.

And I hadn't known I'd find solace—and employment—in bay leaves.

Best. Thing. Ever.

No chill in the air, despite the twilight. Sandra might be sweating and Kristen freezing, but as far as I'm concerned, fall takes all the prizes.

A few last office workers shuffled past me to their bus stops or the light rail station. I strolled down Virginia to Pike Place. The totem poles in the park stood as silhouettes in the fading light.

A couple stood at the railing, arms around each other, watching the sun set over the water and the mountains beyond. Nearby, half a dozen teenagers laughed and joked.

"Miz Pepper."

The sound of my name took me by surprise. Sam, Arf beside him, broke away from a group of men huddled by the fountain and the *Tree of Life* sculpture.

"How you doin', Sam? Sorry, boy." I held out a hand for Arf to sniff. "No treats this time."

"Oh, he gets plenty. Market folks is good to him. You need a escort? Gettin' on to dark."

"Thanks, Sam. I'm fine." His offer reminded me of the encounter I'd seen earlier. "But I do have a question for you. The man you tussled with this morning, the one they call Doc."

His brows furrowed but he nodded to me to go on.

"He's fairly new around here, isn't he?" Another nod. "Causing any trouble? Other than wanting your spot."

"Why you be askin' that, Miz Pepper?"

"I know some of the men"—I gestured toward the group by the totem pole—"take an interest in protecting the women who work in the Market, like you do, and I wondered if you've seen Doc helping anyone that way."

He shook his big head slowly. "No, can't say as I have. He ain't here every day. And he don't stay down evenings. Don't know where he goes. I ain't seen him around, at the shelters or getting a meal. You want me to keep an eye on him?"

"Thanks, Sam, but no. It's nothing." I rubbed Arf's head with my cupped hand. "You two have a good night, now."

Despite refusing Sam's offer, I had a hunch he'd be watching Doc anyway. Poking around. Some of us are like that.

Three

Fueled by Alaskan gold, Seattle's population quintupled between 1889, the year of statehood and the Great Fire, and 1907, when the Public Market opened. Takes a lot of food to feed 200,000 people.

THE BUILDER WHO HELPED ME FLESH OUT THE LOFT'S bones called the mezzanine above the bedroom "retreat space, for yoga or meditation." Apparently some people exercise in their yoga pants. The cold steel steps zing my bare feet in the morning, but it's the only place in the loft that lets me peek over the Viaduct to the Sound. If I think tall. This stretch of the Viaduct is scheduled to come down soon, with all that traffic moving to a tunnel. They say it's for earthquake safety, but the changes would revamp the waterfront and give us downtown dwellers killer views.

Plus higher taxes and, no doubt, pressure from developers. My next-door neighbor, a city council member, has his finger on that pulse and keeps us all informed. I settled into a canvas director's chair, hand-painted by a Market artisan, to meditate on caffeine and morning mist.

The weather was clearly changing. Well, "clearly" wasn't the right word. Not today. Vapor from the Seattle Steam plant collided with cool air rolling in off the Sound to create a bewitching white cloud.

A fog horn blared and an outbound ferry glided into view. I grabbed the binoculars, but the air was too dense for me to make out the name.

As a child, I'd lie in bed and strain my ears to hear the fog horns, usually falling asleep first. One of my earliest memories is standing at a ferry rail clutching my grandfather's hand on one of his visits from St. Louis. I might have been destined for my business, but I was not, as most people assume, named for it. Grandpa nicknamed me after the legendary Cardinals third baseman Pepper Martin, known as a ball of fire.

I like to think I've mellowed since then.

I sipped my coffee, an Ethiopian Longberry Harrar, and ran through what we needed to accomplish that day at the shop. First, repeat the taste tests and settle on our descriptive subtitles so we could get the info to our brilliant graphic designer. Then choose the recipes. Plus the usual daily business of working with our walk-in traffic and commercial accounts.

Would yesterday's clash between Sam and Doc be a one-time thing? I hoped so.

But why had Doc been pestering Tory? Slim chance that I could get her to spill any details, even with careful questioning. She'd shift her shoulders slightly, set her chin, and tell me—without a word—that she could take her of herself.

I watched another huge green-and-white ferry chug into view—coming from Bainbridge Island, judging from the angle. They truly are iconic.

Enough in-home sightseeing. Time to get spicy.

I crossed Western, bypassed the elevator entrance, and trudged up the Market Hillclimb—my version of a cardio workout—to the Main Arcade. Emerged near City Fish—home of the famous flying fish—and exchanged greetings with the fishmongers. (And yes, that's what they call themselves.) Passed Rachel the brass pig, Market mascot and piggy bank for the Foundation, which funds housing and social services. Waved hello to the couple who run the Oriental Mart in the Corner Market. Bought a strawberry-banana smoothie at the Creamery and a blueberry bran muffin at Three Girls Bakery, one of the oldest Market tenants. Most retail shops were still closed, although I spotted a few merchants bustling around inside.

A half-dozen delivery trucks idled on Pike Place, men with hand trucks unloading cartons and crates. The aromas of fish, fruit, and fresh bread mingled with the sharp but mouthwatering smell of cheese making.

Have I mentioned I love this place?

I crossed Pine, my attention on the mess inside my tote as I dug for my keys. My feet slowed as I neared our door, on autopilot. "Eureka!" My fingers closed around the keys and I reached for the lock.

And froze. A truck clattered by on the cobbles. Up on First, commuter buses offloaded passengers, and out on the Sound, ferries blew their whistles.

While I stared at the man known as Doc, crumpled in my doorway, a paper cup stamped with our logo beside his open hand.

Four

Seattle's Public Market houses a year-round farmers' market, bakeries, meat and fish markets, produce stands, and specialty food stores. Two hundred plus craftspeople rent daystalls, operating alongside more than 200 owner-operated shops and services and nearly one hundred restaurants. The Market is also home to more than 350 residents—all in nine acres.

—Market website

MY SHOUT BROUGHT PEOPLE RUNNING, PEOPLE WHOSE phones weren't buried at the bottom of their tote bags or knapsacks, like mine. "Help is on the way," someone assured me as I knelt beside Doc, holding my breath and his wrist, praying for a pulse. A nurse on her way to the Market clinic nudged me aside but, when she got no better result, turned her kind face to me.

"He's gone," she said, her voice almost too soft to hear amid the chit and chat and scrape and squawk around us. In the distance, a siren screamed, but whether bound for here or some other unlucky locale, no telling.

I nodded. Years ago, at the law firm, a client stumbled into my office in search of the restroom, keeled over, and died. The image of his red face matching his red tie, contrasting sharply with his white shirt and hair and his classic navy blue suit, had stuck with me.

In contrast, Doc wore his usual olive green raincoat and scarred brown shoes. His eyes had lost their sheen, the dull, sandy skin around them pooched and pocketed like a Shar Pei's after an all-nighter. And yet, despite the world of difference from that long-ago client, he was just as dead.

The nurse pushed herself up, fingers pressing lightly into my upper arm. I shook her off. It seemed indecent to leave him, to stand back and join the small crowd staring at this odd, dead man. The merchants, farmers, and craftspeople of the Market call themselves a family, and family doesn't make one of their own into a curiosity, even a newcomer.

I'm a newcomer, too.

His hand lay half open, fingers gently curved, as if still holding the cup. The fingers were pale, nails well trimmed and scrubbed clean.

Amazing what goes through the mind at moments like this. My family was never traditionally religious, though both my parents were active in peace and justice causes during my childhood. My mother helped found a soup kitchen in the basement of St. James Cathedral but rarely attended Mass, entering the nave only to hear chamber music. Once I went with her to hear the Tallis Scholars sing and wondered, as I stared up at the gold-and-white-trimmed vaults, how their voices could climb so high and who was up there listening.

My father had chosen to study Zen Buddhism. Whether because of or in spite of his experiences in Vietnam, he never said. If asked, no doubt he'd smile and ask me quietly what I thought. Friends had wafted through the big house on Capitol Hill, day and night, to sit in meditation in the third-floor ballroom. Where Kristen's great-grandparents had held formal dances and her grandmother learned swing and defied convention by inviting a black jazz band to

entertain soldiers during the war, we heard rhythmic breathing, mantras being chanted, and the rolling tones of a
Tibetan bell. Kristen and I had helped our mothers melt the
used candle ends and remold them, adding sandalwood or
lavender oil. A mere whiff of Nag Champa Incense takes
me back.

Later, when Kristen's mother discovered yoga, we heard
the soft gummy sounds of sticky mats being rolled onto the
maple floors, punctuated by groans as stiff joints responded
to gentle coaxing from the teachers who came and went.

All my life, the medieval harmonies my mother loves
have slipped into my consciousness when I least expect
them. When my heart's been ripped open, when the stakes
are highest. They swirled around me now as I tried to summon the sacred peace of the Cathedral and the ballroom
studio, and wrap it around the man we knew as Doc.

I stayed there until another hand touched me. "Pepper,"
Tag said. "Let the EMTs take over."

He led me down the sidewalk, out of the way. Just yesterday, Doc and Sam had argued on this spot and Tag's
partner carved ruts in the road dust with the fat tires of his
mountain bike. Now navy-blue-clad EMTs tumbled out of
the red Medic One ambulance that had clambered down
Pine and idled noisily beside my shop. I hoped the parking
brake held. The crew, two men and a woman, fell into a
routine, tasks so well defined that they barely needed to
speak to communicate.

"What are you doing here?" I finally thought to ask. "And
where's your partner?"

Tag jerked a thumb over his shoulder, and I turned to see
Olerud, off the bike, notebook in hand, surrounded by half
a dozen Market folks. "You know we work First Watch."

I faced my ex squarely. "But why the police, for an old
man's heart attack?"

Eyes hidden by mirrored sunglasses, he shrugged one
shoulder. "Control the crowd. Preserve the scene. Do

whatever these guys need." He cocked his helmeted head toward the EMTs. One knelt by the body, repacking a box of equipment, while the others unloaded a gurney.

I glanced at the group gathered around Olerud. Misty, the baker, talked with her hands, but I couldn't read her lips or fingers. Yvonne looked gray and weary, as always. Talk was, she'd had a hard life. Health problems and a divorce from her mechanic husband, before I knew her. The orchard girls, Angie and Sylvie Martinez, wrapped their arms around each other and concentrated on the good-looking officer. The new manager of the cheese shop—his name escaped me—folded his arms across his chest, brows furrowed. Behind him, the nurse listened attentively.

"What I don't get," I said, "is how he got my tea. We don't open for"—I peered at my Bazooka pink Kate Spade watch, one of my last splurges before losing my comfy salary—"oh, pooh. I should have been inside half an hour ago. Where are my keys?" I slid my bag off my shoulder and rummaged inside. They must have gotten tossed back into the depths when I saw Doc. I glanced reflexively at his body, still stretched out on my sidewalk, the EMTs standing guard. What were they waiting for?

"There they are." My key ring—silver-plated with OFF WE GO! engraved on the fob, a birthday gift from my law firm boss, made ironic when we all got fired a few weeks later—lay on the ground next to the body. I took a step forward. Tag's arm shot out and blocked me. I looked up, stunned. Behind him, an unmarked car inched down the cobbled hill and stopped at an angle, blocking the road. A white woman about my age, in a stylish but practical black pantsuit, climbed out the driver's side and picked her way down the slope. Detective Cheryl Spencer probably had a closet full of nearly identical black suits. Her partner, Detective Michael Tracy, got out on the passenger side.

The light sweat I'd worked up on my jaunt up the Market steps froze on my skin. In my years of marriage to a Seattle police officer, I'd met hundreds of officers and detectives. This long-running duo had racked up a great record, despite their contrasts—the tall slender blonde and her black male partner, inches shorter and verging on stocky. They'd heard the jokes about their last names, and no, they didn't think it was funny.

Homicide cops are like that.

Tag's attention shifted to Pike Place, where the black CSI van had parked. A woman waved in acknowledgment, then helped her partner unload their gear. A white van marked KING COUNTY MEDICAL EXAMINER arrived. A man got out and suited up.

"You think this is a crime scene." I glared at Tag in anger and disbelief. "On my doorstep."

He glared right back in his "Don't question my authority" mode.

"This is my shop." I pointed at the door, my voice rising. "I must have dropped my keys when I checked on him. I'm going in and you are not stopping me."

"Pepper," Tag said. He'd dropped his arm, but not the controlling tone. "We can't touch anything, even your keys. We have to treat it as a crime scene until we know what happened. Any suspicious death, we do that. You want to know what happened, don't you?"

I let out a sharp breath, not meeting his eyes. It was protocol, not distrust. Still, I hated that he was right.

"If you don't let me have my keys, how am I supposed to get in?" I also hated that he brings out my whiney side.

"Looks like someone's already in." Detective Spencer peered through the front windows, shaded by deep soffits, still the original forest green. I followed her gaze toward the mixing corner and the silhouette of a seated figure.

"Nice to see you again, Pepper. Sorry about the circumstances," the detective said, holding out her hand.

I took it, nodding. "I'm always the first one here. From this angle, I can't tell who that is."

"And knowing you," Tag said, "no spare key."

"In the loft," I said, tired of the constant tug-of-war between us. "That I can't get into without my keys." The spare loft key was in the shop. "Hold on." I rummaged in my bag and yanked out my phone.

Spencer approved my plan, so I called inside and asked the early arrival to meet me at the side door, on Pine Street, but as the detective instructed, not to step outside or touch the door frame or exterior. As we headed up the hill, the EMTs slid Doc's body onto the gurney. His coat flopped open and a dark lump of cloth fell onto the sidewalk. Both Spencer and Tracy stepped forward for a closer inspection.

But I didn't need to. I'd seen it, on this very corner.

Sam's black beret.

SPENCER was going to want to know why Tory was in the shop so early. I admit, I was mighty curious, too.

The detective had not been in the shop before, at least not during my shifts. I pointed out the key features, including our private restroom and tiny back office. She strolled the aisles, hands clasped behind her, head tilted slightly, as though examining specimens in a curious museum. In profile, her otherwise straight nose bore a slight bump, as if once broken.

I leaned against a double-sided bookcase—we'd nearly quadrupled our cookbook and reference offerings since I took over—and watched. After opening the door for us and being introduced, Tory had returned to the mixing nook. She sat on one of the built-in benches, head back, eyes closed. She did not respond visibly to the news of Doc's death. She was too old to be my daughter, but my heart longed to reach out and my arms ached to embrace her in what Kristen calls "Universal Mother Mode."

Spencer stopped at the tea cart. Both the samovar and insulated iced tea jug were empty. First thing every morning, I start the day's tea. I glanced at the wall clock. No point getting anxious—no chance of opening on time today.

Through the glass in the front door, I caught a glimpse of Tag stretching yellow tape around our entrance. My gut cramped and I hoped hoped hoped it said CAUTION or DO NOT ENTER, and not CRIME SCENE.

Nearly six feet in her low-heeled black shoes, her blond bob falling slightly forward, and her hands still clasped behind her back, Spencer continued to study our tea cart.

What about that cup of tea Doc had been clutching? Had there been spilled tea on the ground? Or had he been bringing an empty cup back for a refill? That made no sense. I closed my eyes, remembering. Had I given him one yesterday? I didn't think so—no chill on the morning. I couldn't picture a cup in his hand during the spat with Sam, or when he'd been following Tory to the bus stop.

Sam. I'd think about him later.

Had Doc shoved an empty cup in the pockets of his oversized raincoat? But why? We never begrudge a paper cup. Customers who pick up a sample while wandering the store often take a refresher before leaving, but no one brings them back for refills later.

Detective Spencer turned to me. "What do you call this thing? There's a word."

"Samovar. The real thing is Russian, runs on coal. This one's electric. More like a big coffee urn than a true samovar."

"Ah. Like at that old Russian tea shop. Miss that place. They served those little turnovers—what are they called?"

"Piroshky. You can get really good ones up the street." That reminded me of the blueberry muffin I'd bought on the way here and no doubt dropped alongside my keys. Pigeon food by now.

"But they don't serve that beet soup." She wiggled her fingers as if to summon the name. "Borscht. You ever make that?"

Cut the chitchat, Cheryl, I wanted to say but didn't. She didn't care about my cooking. She wanted to put me at ease, get me talking, by pretending we were old friends.

"So where do you make the tea?" she asked.

I pointed to the big double sinks in the corner, behind the front counter. Directions are a bit skewed along Pike Place, so it's hard to say north or west with any precision. The front counters do double duty as display cases. Floor-to-ceiling shelves line the side walls, crammed with jars of tea and spices. In the center of the ceiling hangs a crystal chandelier I found in the antiques store in my loft building and a pair of Indian silver chandeliers from the import shop Down Under, the name given to the Market's lower level. The effect is internationally eclectic, and pretty cool, if I do say so myself. A beam of sunlight shining through a clerestory window struck a crystal and sent shots of color dancing around the glass-filled shop.

"Every morning?" she asked.

"Except on my days off. Then whoever's running the shop that day, usually Sandra Piniella, makes it."

"And are the pots empty by the end of the day?"

She could reach out and touch one. But I knew from living with Tag that cop training is better than any grandmother for teaching you to keep your hands in your pockets. Of course, that hadn't kept him from putting his hands in other places they didn't belong.

"If they aren't empty by closing, we dump them out. See for yourself. They're empty now."

"So how," she said, "did he get one of your teacups if you weren't open and hadn't made tea yet?"

"Not a clue. He had a heart attack, right? Or some other illness?" Market residents are mostly low-income and have clinic access, but they don't all use it. And it's a shameful fact that the street people, homeless or not, often die from treatable conditions.

"Probably. But until that's established, we have to investigate."

What Tag had said. Spencer looked into the mixing nook. "Any idea how he got the tea?"

Tory opened her eyes slowly, as if she felt Spencer's attention shift to her. Her golden brown eyes reflected the light as she returned the detective's gaze with a slow shake of her head. "No."

"When did you get here?" Spencer asked. "And which door did you use?"

"Seven o'clock. Front door."

An hour before my usual arrival, and an hour and a half before her scheduled time. She could have made tea for him, in the microwave in the back office. But after he'd harassed her last night, I doubted she'd have taken any pity on him. And why would a beggar be on the streets before the crowds?

I opened my mouth, but Spencer spoke first. "Did you see him milling around when you got here, or spot him through the front door?"

A silence, followed by another "no."

Spencer gestured toward the table where Tory sat. "What are you working on that brought you in so early?"

"Sketches."

That caught me by surprise. I had never seen Tory drawing in here. A sketchbook lay open on the nook table, an artist's pen beside it.

Reaching over the pony wall, Spencer muttered a quick "May I?" and picked up the book without waiting for an answer. She studied the drawing in progress, then flipped back through more pages covered with black lines forming squares and rectangles, patterns both familiar and unrecognizable.

"I'm not getting it," Spencer finally said. "Explain, please."

A spark flashed across Tory's face. "They're studies. For a series of paintings." She glanced at me, as if uncertain of my response. "Of the shop."

Both Spencer and I looked again. This time I got it. Abstract oils, I surmised, recalling the slight odor that sometimes clung to Tory. With all the colors and shapes in the shop, and the ever-changing light, it was a natural subject.

And I had never known.

Spencer laid the sketchbook on the table. "Good luck with it. Pepper, you'll need to use your back door for customers until CSI finishes out front."

"How long will that take? And you'll let me know when you figure out what happened?"

"Sure," she said, answering my second question first and waving her hand as she headed for the exit. "My guess, they'll wrap up by late morning, maybe noon."

Fat chance, I thought. Everything official takes longer than it should. The medical examiner would conclude Doc died from natural causes but no one would bother to tell us. Spencer and Tracy would be on to something else by then, reducing Doc to a leaf on the *Tree of Life* in the park, the sculpture honoring the men and women who had lived and died on the city's streets.

I followed Spencer up the short flight of steps to the back door and outside. A white-suited CSI detective—I knew their rank, from Tag—was packing a case by the door, the frame now filthy with fingerprint powder.

"Thanks again, Pepper." Spencer and I shook hands a second time, so very businesslike.

They walked down the hill, the CSI guy to his van and Spencer to chat with Tracy. The ambulance and ME van had left. No sign of Tag or Olerud, or my Market neighbors. Delivery trucks had resumed their routes on Pike Place. The sounds of engines idling and hand trucks squeaking up and down curbs rivaled the squawks of pigeons and gulls. A trio of young women in Crayola-bright dresses crossed Pine, nibbling croissants, sipping iced coffee, and chatting. They detoured around the CSI officers without missing a beat.

Just another day in the life.

Five

The use of perfumed oils, or a blend of cassis and cinnamon, to prepare a body for burial dates back millennia. The practice slowed bacterial decomposition, but made the spices more costly.

AFTER BUYING THE SHOP, I TOOK A BUSINESS TRAINING class the PDA—the Pike Place Market Preservation and Development Authority—held for tenants. It covered a lot of ground. But no amount of planning prepares you to find a dead body on your doorstep.

Had you asked me yesterday, I'd have said that after thirteen years as a cop's wife, nothing would rattle me. Early in our marriage, I'd listened patiently while Tag shared graphic details of his encounters with the worst of man's—and nature's—inhumanity to man, until finally realizing that talk might be good therapy for him, but if I ever wanted to sleep through the night again, he ought to talk to someone else. He agreed—his caddishness emerged later—but even so, there were times when the job followed him home and weaseled its way into our dinner conversation.

So when I closed the door behind Spencer and went to

help Tory fill the samovar, I was startled to see my hands shake.

I measured out our custom tea blend before speaking. "Why didn't you want the detective to know that Doc followed you to the bus stop yesterday?"

Watching Tory's face was like watching grass get longer. You know something is happening, though you can't actually see the change.

"I don't know what you're talking about," she said, making a decision. But she did know, and she knew I knew. Not that I'm a mind reader, but when I was the staff HR rep at the law firm, half the women I worked with didn't want to tell me what was bothering them while the other half couldn't wait to recite every excruciating detail. The trick was to get the first half to trust me enough to talk, and the others to trust me enough to shut up.

It's a rare woman who doesn't open up to her employer once in a while, but in nearly a year, Tory and I had never had a truly personal conversation, let alone an intimate one.

And the polite firmness in her low, calm voice said the door to having one now was closed.

A knock on the front window distracted me: Sandra trying to get my attention. I gestured to the side door and wiped my hands on my apron.

Sandra was puffing her way up the hill when I stepped outside, bracing the door with my foot and raising my face to the sun. This promised to be an un-Septemberly warm day.

"First I ask my aging knees to carry me down the hill. Then I ask them to carry me up. What the heck, they're asking me, and not so nicely, is going on?"

Zak cruised in behind her, so I filled them in together, repeating the story for Kristen a few minutes later. I left out the part about seeing Doc follow Tory, since I wasn't sure it meant anything.

"I wonder what his story was," Sandra said. Her dark eyes

dampened, seeming even larger than usual. "Who's missing him." It isn't uncommon for relatives of the lost or missing to circulate through the Market, pictures in hand, searching. Reunions are rare. Some folks don't want to be found.

Zak said nothing, but I spotted him giving Tory a surreptitious glance. *What*, I wondered, as I had yesterday, *is up between them?*

Ten minutes later, we opened for business, the first batch of tea chilling and the second abrew. I washed the fingerprint powder off the door and frame, glad to be wearing black— one drop of water and the stuff turns to India ink. Zak wrestled a petunia-filled concrete urn he borrowed from the Inn up the hill into place as a doorstop, and we welcomed our first customers.

And told "the story" for the first of many times. "An elderly man seems to have taken shelter in our doorway and had a heart attack. The police want to make sure they haven't overlooked anything." My version might not have been entirely true, but it wasn't untrue. And one thing an HR professional learns quickly is that not everyone needs to know everything. Tell them enough to satisfy their curiosity so they can get back to work.

And shopping.

After the first few customers panted in the side door— their complaints good-natured, but still complaints—I stifled the urge to call the police and demand our front door back. Calling would not make it happen any faster, and would only give Tag another reason to swing by and play Tough Cop.

Instead, I thanked each customer for making the extra effort to visit us and offered a small bag of cinnamon sticks, on the house. I rattled off our story in a kind-but-reassuring tone, and asked how we could help them. In a few minutes, the staff had the patter down and we stumbled back into the groove. Our tea scented the air, along with whiffs of ginger, curry, dill—whatever the customer ordered.

From time to time, I had wondered what the heck I had done, buying the shop. And why, if retail was my destiny, it couldn't have been in another precinct—one Tag would never transfer to, because he loves the bike beat too much. But I adore my shop. To me, the Market has always been the heart of the city—and its stomach. I'd never imagined working here and living so close, and yet it feels like a dream come true. With my loyal staff hard at work, customers trudging up hill to find us, and the phone and online ordering busy as ever, the dream was sweet, spicy reality.

At ten after ten, Tory, Sandra, and I gathered in the nook to retest the spice blends. Tory appeared placid. But then, she hadn't seen Doc's lifeless body.

And as my mother had told me in my angst- and drama-filled teenage years, it isn't necessary to share every emotion you feel with the entire world.

"Made a tasty lamb stew last night with this one," Sandra said, pointing to the pungent blend. "Great idea to use that smoky pepper. Mr. Right fell in love with me all over again."

That brought a wee smile to Tory's face, and a grin to mine. Sandra always refers to her husband of the last ten years as Mr. Right, to distinguish him from the oh-so-wrong first husband. Mr. Right claims to have married her for her cooking, but they are true lovebirds.

"I'd like to tweak the savory blend," I said. "I tried it in sour cream drop biscuits last night and it lacked zip."

"I sprinkled it on scrambled eggs this morning, and the flavors got lost," Sandra said. "Let's try increasing the oregano."

"Maybe double. And add a touch of lavender."

Tory was gazing up at a shelf full of antique British tea tins I'd found in a secondhand shop out on the Olympic Peninsula. Seeking inspiration for a painting, or daydreaming?

"Did you get a chance to try these, Tory?"

She jerked her attention back to me, eyes wide. It was obvious that she hadn't heard a thing until I said her name.

"We're discussing some fine-tuning," I said. "Let's all try them now."

A short time later, the air redolent with lavender, we'd reformulated the savory blend into a classic Herbes de Provence and given a group blessing to the others. I hadn't heard from Alex. Like most chefs, he was a night owl, but he knew we had a tight timeline. Maybe a quick call—I could use a little comfort, even if it came through the phone.

The sound of bicycle shoes clicking on the wooden floor broke my reverie. Misty the Baker leaned her bike against the inside stair rail and picked her way down the steps, more concerned than I about her shoes—the plastic cleats were noisy but harmless. She raised a good-sized white paper bag.

"Figured you could use something tasty about now. Macarons and sablés."

Cookies, in the vernacular. We hugged and I peeked in the bag, then handed it to Sandra, who promptly plucked out a chocolate sablé for herself and spread the rest of the meringue and butter cookies on a tray.

"Find anything out about the old man?" Misty said. "The cops quizzed the bakery staff, but nobody knew him."

I shook my head. "Natural causes, I'm sure. But it is weird, right on our doorstep . . ."

"Kinda creepy." She shuddered. "But you're brave. You won't let it bother you."

Brave was the goal. I filled her sports bottle with iced tea and thanked her for the cookies. I got the best of that trade.

My pal Laurel Halloran, chef, caterer, and a stalwart of the Flick Chicks movie club, had offered recipe suggestions for this season's spice blends. It was too late to catch her before her lunch rush, so I called the deli to make sure she'd be in for a while.

"You bet," she said. "I'm so behind on paperwork, I should stay here all day."

"Why do we call it paperwork when we do it all on the computer?"

"Beats me," she said with a laugh. "You know where to find me."

Only after we'd clicked off did I realize I hadn't mentioned Doc's death in my doorway.

But first, it was time to check in with our designer, who'd come up with some rough ideas for labels.

Plus I could use some fresh air—perfumed with the fishy, salty, diesel-y scent of the city. I tossed the sample blends into my bag. CSI still had my keys—Spencer had said they'd rush the forensics and get them back to me ASAP, but that could mean anything. I fished the spare loft key out of my desk drawer and tucked it into a zippered pocket in my tote.

I wanted to ask Tory about her sketches, but she was busy helping a woman new to the city stock her condo spice cabinet. The chance to make a good sale and win a loyal customer outweighed my nosiness.

I walked down to Pike Place to check the sidewalk on the corner outside my front door.

No new bodies had turned up while I wasn't watching. Just flowers, piled up against the salmon pink stucco exterior. A dozen or more bouquets, some fresh, others a little brown around the edges, like they'd been picked from the garbage instead of the garden. A hand-lettered cardboard sign read, DOC—RIP. I felt a brief pang of shame for not having created a memorial myself.

A few feet beyond the door stood a contingent of half a dozen denizens of the Market, men rarely seen in more than twos or threes. Tall, gaunt Jim, the left side of his face clear, the right scarred and bubbled as if by a burn. Irish Mick, who could be Italian for all I knew. A younger—meaning under forty—man called Hot Dog. Two men whose names I didn't know.

And lurking in the back, Sam and Arf. I had never seen Sam hatless. He looked uncomfortable without the beret, shifting from one foot to the other and barely glancing at me.

"Thank you, gentlemen. It's kind of you to remember Doc this way."

"Could be any of us," Jim said, and agreement rippled through the gathering. "We acknowledge our own."

Judging from the pile of flowers, others in the Market had contributed, too. I looked over my shoulder at Yvonne, the closest flower seller to the Spice Shop. The Market Master assigns daystalls based on seniority and dependability, meaning Yvonne usually got this one, on a prime corner. In mid-March, she offers the first tulips, and in fall, the last dahlias, zinnias, and sunflowers. She glanced at me while a customer debated between two bouquets. Several of the bundles by my door bore her signature red and tan raffia, and from the color on her cheeks, I suspected she'd left one herself.

I turned back to the men, their eyes on me.

"Hope it don't hurt your business none," Jim said. "Old man ain't got no business interfering even after he's dead."

Another man chuckled.

"We'll be fine," I said. "When the yellow tape comes down, we'll rearrange the flowers out of the way, where folks can see them. You fellows stay here as long as you want."

They murmured thanks. I touched Sam's arm lightly.

"Miz Pepper," he said softly. And I knew from the sadness in his tone that whatever Sam's problems, he had not harmed Doc. But they might have argued about the corner. This had been Sam's morning for it. Had Doc taken Sam's hat, to boot?

Their feud had been one of territory. When you don't have much to call your own, you get pretty protective of what you do have. And if there's a spot in this world where you like to sit, for whatever reason, it becomes pretty important, too. I got that. Why that spot was in front of my shop, I didn't get.

Get a move on, Pepper. Before you lose it.

TOOK more time to make my way one block from the Spice Shop to the Market entrance than to walk the eight blocks to my designer's studio at First and Cherry. The first delay had been the two women standing at the bottom of Pine, staring, confused, at my blocked-off door. I pointed out the side door propped open, thirty feet uphill. The slope wasn't steep by Seattle standards, but their expressions were dubious.

"You want us to hike up that hill?" one of the women asked. "I don't remember a hill when we were here last summer."

"There's been a mishap," I said, not bothering with the details. "But we have a small gift for every customer today, as our thanks. A bundle of cinnamon sticks. Plus samples of our custom blend tea."

"I don't care for cinnamon," she replied in a Texas twang. "We'll go somewhere else." She flounced away. Her companion gave me a quick, apologetic smile and scurried off to catch up.

I shook my head. The yellow tape signaled a situation out of my control, but some people are oblivious to the obvious.

The Market family enveloped me. The dim sum seller, the produce hawkers, the ancient Chinese lady who teases small children by chasing their feet with a paper snake on a string. The guys who throw fish, the doughnut makers, the men who run the newsstand.

"We're not sure what happened," I repeated over and over. "But we're fine. Thank you."

The questions, the sad eyes, the expressions of concern

for Doc and for me were proof that the Market—a city within a city—is by and large a safe place peopled by folks who treat each other as family.

I left the Market at First and Pike, near where Rachel the brass pig, the flying fish, and the Market's iconic clock and red-letter sign welcome one and all. (The pig was modeled on a real sow who lives on Whidbey Island. I was there the day she was brought to the Market to see her namesake. Fortunately, donors were more impressed than she was.) As I strolled down First Ave, my throat swelled with love for my city. I left after college, spending a year and a half in California. But as much fun as it had been to share a two-bedroom apartment with three other girls in a complex where rats darted across the sidewalk from one ivy-covered patch of "garden" to another, or to get hassled by pale, scrawny guys who swore they'd be software millionaires in six months every time I tried to relax by the swimming pool, I preferred the gray and the rain.

The comforts of home.

I passed the Seattle Art Museum and peered up at the *Hammering Man* sculpture. At nearly fifty feet tall, his arm moving up and down all day—resting overnight and on Labor Day—he'd raised a few eyebrows when first installed, but quickly become a symbol, along with the Space Needle and the troll under the Fremont Bridge, of the city's quirky creativity.

To my right, the Harbor Steps led first to Western, then on down to Alaskan Way, aka the waterfront. The western edge of the world glistened as tour boats and ferries came and went. The giant Ferris wheel turned. In the working part of the harbor, colossal orange cranes plucked containers off the big barges like chopsticks picking up grains of rice.

On my way to Pioneer Square, I thought more about Doc. How long had he been in Seattle? What brought him here? Seattle is a city of people from all over—families like Kristen's and my mother's, who have been here for generations, are rare. Some folks, especially Easterners, chose the Pacific Northwest because it's as far as you can go without leaving the lower forty-eight. Some came for the tech industry and, before that, for aerospace. Others came for the vibrant arts scene—from the funky to the sublime. Some came for the coffee and some for the wine.

Where had Doc fit in? What, as Sandra had asked, was his story?

Would we ever know?

Another question: Why hadn't I told Spencer about Tory's encounter with Doc? Respecting her privacy—or his? Who cares if he violated the city's ordinance against aggressive panhandling? The man was dead.

If it turned out—and it wouldn't, I told myself—that Doc's death was not natural, then I'd speak up.

Till then, keep mum and carry on.

Our graphic designer's studio is in a historic building at First and Cherry, with limestone columns and arches, and a red brick facade. The Great Tunnel project, the same one changing my own neighborhood inch by inch and foot by foot, had triggered the eviction of more than a hundred artists from an old warehouse badly damaged by the 2001 Nisqually earthquake. A dozen modern-day pioneers had seized on this building and pooled their relocation funds to redevelop the space into artists' studios.

Like Cher and Oprah, Fabiola uses only the one name, artfully emblazoned on the wall opposite the elevator in two dozen different styles, fonts, and colors. Different materials, too: a cobalt blue lighted sign (LED—clean and green); a mosaic of broken china; paint on canvas; hammered tin; barbed wire. Narcissistic as the display might seem, it sends the message that this woman can work in any medium the project might warrant.

And she is her own best advertising. Today, she'd piled her dark hair, mahogany highlights glinting, on top of her head and speared the 'do with an oversized pair of emerald green glasses. Frames only—no lenses. Her blue-and-white floral print blouse sported a Peter Pan collar that reminded me of my grade school uniform, and short, cuffed sleeves trimmed with gold buttons that could have come off an old naval officer's jacket. Her above-the-knee skirt—cobalt blue with white dots—swung when she walked.

We all know someone who seems to embody our own aspirations with creativity, flair, and confidence. But then we catch a glimpse—an unguarded expression, a fleeting look that barely registers—and we're reminded that none of us is always perfectly sure of every move we make. I know that about Fabiola, and love her even more for it.

"Trade you shoes," I said. Cherry red leather Mary Janes with three straps and a narrow toe, and the littlest stacked wooden heel.

"Reecie," Fabiola said, peering at me through the photos and designs clipped to a wire clothesline strung above her long, scarred white worktable, "play a little. Give your shop a new leash on life."

You can never be sure whether she's fracturing a cliché on purpose or not. I'm not even sure Fabiola is the name her mother gave her, but no matter. She's fab, regardless.

(I don't use the name my mother gave me, either. Even my mother doesn't use it. I like to think she's forgotten it.)

"We've been over this," I said, settling on one of the industrial-look metal stools designers favor. "The change in ownership was a serious big deal. I can't risk messing up our image or the old customers, especially the irregulars, won't know we're still the same Seattle Spice Shop."

Especially now. My encounter with the Texan tourists reminded me how critical—and fragile—familiarity is to casual customers.

"But you're not the same. You're young and hip and your packaging should reflect that. Not look like a state tourism office campaign from the 1970s."

The collage of mirrors on the far wall reflected my

scrunched-up face, broken into bits and reassembled into a not-quite-recognizable, cubist-style whole. Fabiola and I replayed this debate with every design project. When to move away from the shop's old identity? How quickly, how completely to give it my own stamp? Jane had taken many of the shop's artifacts with her, and I'd rearranged, adding new furnishings and décor. More than one customer had been briefly confused, not realizing we were still the source they'd relied on forever until they recognized Sandra and tasted our distinctive tea.

Wasn't it about time to complete the Spice Shop's make-over with a new logo?

"Okay. Let's see what you've got."

"Yes!" She turned to the shelves beneath the mirrors, skirt twirling, and drew a fuchsia file folder from a stack. Expression somber, she raised it in both hands like a State Department security briefing book, or the communion host at Mass. She set it on the table, opened it dramatically, and spread out a cascade of images.

New labels for the tins were just the start.

She'd given us a crisp, graphic view of the Sound with the giant Ferris wheel and the mountains beyond, in primary colors accentuated with emerald green. A bold sans serif font that looked like an engineer's block print with a forward lean, as if it were in a hurry, proclaimed SEATTLE SPICE SHOP.

"We'll use that font for your website and all your printed material." That meant business cards, recipe cards, and shelf-talkers, which describe each herb and spice and suggest a few uses.

She'd even redesigned our aprons, and the stamp we use on our paper cups.

At that, I lost it. A rebirth, a death, a year of change. Two years plus of change. I couldn't explain my blubbering, but Fabiola isn't one to mind tears and snot.

What did I owe the past? What did I owe myself?

"Okay. I'll do it. The whole shebang. To celebrate my

first anniversary in the spice biz," I said, rummaging in my bag for a tissue and finally spotting a box on Fabiola's shelf.

To celebrate another step in running my own life.

"Celebrate yourself." She raised one foot in her chic Mary Jane. "They're on sale. The shop's right around the corner. Tell 'em I sent you."

Ten minutes later, I strolled back up First Avenue with Fabiola's file folder in my tote, next to my comfy black climbers, and tutu pink Mary Janes on my feet.

Change your shoes, change your life.

Six

The Travels of Marco Polo introduced Europeans to Oriental spices, but many doubted his eye-popping tales. Not Christopher Columbus, who carried an annotated copy on his own travels.

AT LUNCHTIME, THE MARKET HOPS. THAT'S WHEN OFFICE workers swing by to grab a slice of pizza at DeLaurenti's, a sandwich at Three Girls, or a guess-what at Piroshky-Piroshky. Then they pick up produce, fish, meat, and cheese for the evening, and the seasonings to make it a meal.

We hum extra loud on Thursdays and Fridays. When people have more time to cook—say on the weekends—they want to be more adventurous. And at the Spice Shop, "Adventure" is our middle name.

Or it would be when we had our new labels.

I tossed my tote and Fabiola's file on the desk in the coffin-sized office, snatched up my apron, and joined the crew on the shop floor.

"Move those to the front counter, where customers can enjoy them," I said at the sight of a giant bouquet of sunflowers stuffed in an old pickle jar on the mixing table.

"Nope. Those are for you," Kristen said, a glint in her gray-green eyes.

I reached for the flowers. No card.

"Mr. Howard brought them by," she said, wiggling her eyebrows and her hips at the same time. "Hoping to catch you."

A faint warmth crawled up my cheeks.

"Go sell something," I said, waving my hand. Embarrassed about a boy in front of my BFF, at forty-two? Heck, yeah. Never too old for that. I slid into the nook to admire the flowers before retreating to the office to make a quick call. Or rather, to leave Alex a quick happy voice mail.

Back on the floor, I tended to customers. "That's going to be a spicy dish," I told a twenty-something in a splashy red-and-yellow print dress carrying a recipe torn from a magazine. I grabbed a book on Indian cooking and flipped to a page showing bowls of creamy, herbed yogurt. "Cool it down by pairing it with a raita, a dipping sauce for fresh pita bread or pita chips. It's easy: grated cucumber, yogurt, chopped mint, and a touch of cayenne and cumin."

"Won't the spices make it hot?" Her long blond hair brushed her upper arm as she tilted her head.

"Use just enough for flavor, not enough for heat. With so much cayenne and cumin in the stew, putting a little in the raita will tie the two dishes together. You can get fresh mint from Herb the Herb Man across the street." Herb, another Market regular.

"Lord love the new cooks," Sandra said a few minutes later as our customer left through the side door, the raita recipe scribbled on a card tucked inside her shopping bag.

"First meal for her boyfriend's parents," I said. "If they like it, we'll be heroes."

The deli manager at DeLaurenti's had delivered a mouthwatering assortment of sandwiches, meats, and cheeses, refusing to let me pay. Tragedy evokes generosity. I poured a tall glass of iced tea, returned to the mixing booth, and pondered my choices.

Not for long, though. I was starving.

I'd finished a mini roasted pepper, basil, and mozzarella panini and was contemplating a second when Reed pointed out that the CSI unit had returned to the corner outside.

What now? And what about the makeshift memorial? By this time of day, the street men would have scattered to the park or their favorite panhandling corners. I doubted Sam would want this one today.

Sam. The hat.

Whoa, Pepper. You've got enough to do without asking questions here. Let it go.

But I got all fired up again when I saw the bike patrol officer standing guard over the CSI unit. They could do the job themselves without the ever-watchful eyes of one Officer Thomas Allen "Tag" Buhner.

He was there to watch over me and I was tired of it.

But snapping at him wouldn't make him behave. It would only convince him I'd gone over the edge and needed his intervention.

So I flashed him the smile I use to mollify difficult customers. "Hello, officers. Can I help you with anything?"

"Stay out of their way, Pepper."

I wasn't in their way. "Aren't the flowers lovely? Doc hadn't been part of the Market community long, but . . ."

A CSI detective brushing print powder on the door frame turned her head toward me. "They're no trouble, ma'am. We just need to redust a few prints."

I peered a little closer and noticed several other spots she'd redone on the front and side walls of the building.

"Does that rough finish interfere with your impressions?" The salmon pink stucco is one of my favorite features of the building. Art Deco with a Northwestern flair.

"Pepper—" Tag said, his tone a warning.

"Yes, ma'am, it does. The more uneven the surface, the harder it is to get a clear print. We're redoing all of these, then we'll take them back to the lab. We should be able to get you back to normal soon."

"Thanks." I could practically feel Tag breathing down my neck. "And when will I get my keys back?"

"Not my call," she said. "But I can't imagine it will be too long."

"Thank you. This has been a pain in the—an ordeal. I appreciate how helpful you've been." *Unlike you, Officer Buhner.* I walked past said Officer Buhner and strolled up Pine Street to my back door.

A few minutes later, the CSI detectives came in to print all the employees, me included, "for elimination purposes." I watched as they rolled each finger and palm, and noted every staffer's contact info. Happily, it didn't take long and customer traffic was light.

"I'm taking spice samples up to Laurel. Meanwhile, take a gander." I laid the fuchsia folder on the mixing table, next to the empty sandwich tray. "From Ms. Fabiola. Labels, and a whole lot more."

"Oo-ooh," Kristen said. "You finally said yes?"

She made it sound like a marriage proposal. "I haven't said yes to anything yet. Just tell me what you think."

"Yes, ma'am," she said, smirking.

"Smart-ass."

I left the shop and had almost reached First when I heard the wheels behind me.

"We need to talk," Tag said, handlebars wobbling as he kept the bike in balance.

"No, I don't think so."

"Yes, we do." He was on foot now, wheeling beside me as the light changed and I crossed the street. "Alex Howard came by while you were out."

I didn't ask how he knew. That flush returned to my cheeks.

"He's trouble, Pepper. Stay away from him."

"What do you know about it?" I whipped my head toward

him before he could respond. "That was a rhetorical question. Don't answer."

"I know some things you don't. And it's not good, Pepper.
You'll only get hurt."

And he knew all about hurting me. His wide rubber bike
tires made a soft whirring sound on the concrete sidewalk.
A young couple coming toward us dropped hands and
stepped apart to let us through.

"Is lecturing me really a good use of the taxpayers'
money, Tag? Shouldn't you be out doing something produc-
tive? Like solving crime?"

"Spencer and Tracy are on it. And don't harass the CSI.
They'll release your crime scene when they're good and
ready."

I stopped on a dime. "*My* crime scene? You do think it
was a crime, don't you? Doc's death, I mean."

Dang, I hated that self-satisfied look on his face.

"Why?" I went on. "He wasn't shot or stabbed. There
would have been blood. Yeah, there are other methods, but
what about the scene makes you think—"

"You know I can't tell you that. Police business."

For half a second, I had actually taken him seriously. For
a nano-blink, I had thought he was expressing genuine concern for me. But Tag Buhner wouldn't know genuine if it
bit him in the extremely fine, tight ass.

"Why did I even imagine you cared? I haven't owned the
shop a year but you want me to be a failure. Will that make
you feel better about cheating on me?" I hitched my bag
higher on my shoulder and marched forward.

"Pepper, wait," he said. "It's not like that."

It was exactly like that. And I wasn't going to wait around
for him to prove it once again.

"SO nobody knows who he is?"

I swigged my strawberry lime soda, the sharp fizz

striking my nostrils and threatening a sneeze. "Somebody, somewhere. But not in the Market." Laurel and I sat in the front window of Ripe, her gourmet deli on the Fourth Avenue side of the former bank building still known as "the box the Space Needle came in." In the nine years I'd worked in its upper reaches, I'd probably drunk or eaten something of hers, eat-in or take-out, three or four days a week.

"It's an injustice," she said. "In our so-called civilization, how can people fall through the cracks?"

"SPD will figure out who he is. Homeless doesn't necessarily mean anonymous."

"I'm sure you're right and he died of natural causes." Her voice said she wasn't sure at all. "But the family deserves to hear from someone who knew him."

Laurel's husband, Patrick, had been shot and killed two years ago when he heard a noise and stepped outside to check on it. Laurel and their teenage son, Gabe, had been away on a school field trip. A neighbor found the body. No arrests were ever made, but officials seemed to think the murder was linked to a corruption case Pat had handled as an assistant federal prosecutor. Laurel sold their Montlake jewel box and bought a houseboat on Lake Union, desperately needing change but not wanting to completely uproot Gabe. He'd taken to the boat like, well, a duck to water. So had she.

People tell you not to make a major change right after a major loss, but Laurel and I were both proof that conventional wisdom isn't one size fits all.

Her meaning took a moment to sink in. "But I didn't know him," I said. "Not really. Besides, SPD has a team that notifies the family. If they're in another city, the police request a notification by local authorities. It's routine."

" 'We're so sorry about your father/your brother/your son. He was a bum, he had it coming.' " Laurel's long, curly, gray-brown hair was tied back, as always when she worked, but a tendril had escaped. She shoved it behind her ear.

"They didn't treat you like that. They won't treat Doc's

family like that." Laurel and I had known each other casually for years, but after her husband's murder, I'd offered her an unjudging ear. She'd ranted and raved—still does, occasionally—but despite her freewheeling opinionating, I could scarcely imagine her pain. She'd hinted a time or two that someone higher up might not want the case solved, might not want a trial and all that it could expose, but I'd been married to a cop when it happened and she hadn't spilled the details of her doubts. In truth, I didn't want to know. I like believing that most people are good at heart and do the right thing.

"My bad luck he died on my doorstep, but that doesn't make me responsible for bearing bad news."

Her dark brown eyes glistened and she wrapped her strong fingers around my wrist. "Don't leave justice to the system, Pepper. It's too important."

We locked eyes and I sighed, hoping I wouldn't regret what amounted to a solemn promise. "Change of subject. Dish the dirt on Alex Howard." She knew I'd had dinner with him a couple of times and gotten all starry.

"He's big time. His restaurants are booked weeks out. He gets the celebrity photo shoots and the rave reviews." She gave me a crooked grin. "He's wickedly good-looking. But I can't say we run in the same circles."

"So why is Tag warning me off him?"

"It's Tag. Do you need a reason?"

I picked up my bottle. "Seems like more than not wanting me to date. But maybe you're right."

Someone called her name from the kitchen and she slid off her stool. "Trust me, I'm right. About Tag, and about Doc. You make sure those detectives tell you when they find out who his family is so you can get in touch. Nobody ever regretted going out of their way to be kind."

Famous last words.

Seven

Egyptian morticians stuffed pepper up Ramses' nose to guarantee him eternal life.

LAUREL'S WORDS FOLLOWED ME BACK TO THE MARKET. Did I honestly have a responsibility to the family I'd never met of a man I barely knew, just because he'd had the misfortune to die on my doorstop?

But I take seriously the point of view of people who've been where I haven't. Laurel knows what it's like to lose someone you love unexpectedly and get no resolution. No justice. No closure, in modern terms.

The haunting harmonies of my mother's beloved chants began to play in my head, a sure sign that I'd made up my mind.

The early-afternoon lull had settled on the shop by the time I returned. I made a few phone calls, updated our Facebook status, twipped through our Tweets, and flipped through Fabiola's fuchsia folder.

The more I saw, the more her ideas grew on me. But they also made me nervous. They screamed "Hip! Modern! Eat this, love this!" And that was great. But they were a *looong* step away from our image. Our tradition.

The flip side of classic is boring, and the dark side of tradition is stuck-in-a-rut. Which side you land on depends on your point of view.

And I wasn't so sure about upending our customers' view of us. Or my own.

"They're good," Reed said, shrugging one narrow shoulder when I asked the staff for their opinions. "But they don't, really, like, rock."

"Do-o-o it," Sandra said, drawing out the words in an urging tone. My face showed my reluctance. She tucked her hands in her armpits, flapped her wings, and clucked her way to the front counter.

"What do you two think?" I asked Zak and Tory, busy refilling the spices on the wall. The job goes faster with two—one to climb the rolling wooden ladder and fetch extra inventory off the upper shelves, and one to refill the jar, note the date, and confirm the records generated by our point-of-sale inventory software. With bulk supplies, you've got to have an idea how much you sell over a period of time, so we were developing a baseline. A total pain, but Jane had tracked inventory on a yellow pad no one else could read, so anything was a vast improvement over nothing. We hoped to have all the info we needed after a full year. *Soon. Soon.*

"Go for it," Zak said, tucking the caraway back in place. He almost didn't need a ladder to reach the shelf.

"Follow your heart," Tory said, voice soft, eyes carefully trained on the iPad inventory screen.

What message was she sending me?

"Back in a flash." Zak headed for the restroom.

"What's next?" I asked Tory, my foot on the bottom rung.

"Brown cardamom."

She still wasn't looking at me, and that wasn't like her. Not a lot of call for brown, also known as "bastard cardamom," except in the Indian community. Even there, green cardamom outsells brown. Jane introduced me to the spice through her Indian Butter Chicken, and I love grinding the rough, ribbed pods in my flea market brass mortar and pestle to release the smoky, woodsy flavor.

I handed Tory the dark brown jar, Jane's spidery script on the red-trimmed white label yellowed with age. Those labels we would never modernize, except when we couldn't read them anymore.

"You told the detective you didn't see Doc this morning. Did you see Sam?"

Her eyes widened, then quickly narrowed.

"He was here," I continued. "His beret fell out of Doc's coat when they picked up his body."

Tory stared at me, speechless. As if the shock of the death had just hit her.

"But—Sam," she said. "He couldn't—he wouldn't—"

"Brown cardamom," Zak said, taking the jar from my hands. "You know, I don't think I've ever sold that to anyone."

Eyes still on Tory, I said, "You can count on us."

"Boss," Sandra called, and I headed to the front counter. She clutched the phone in both hands against her chest, muffling our conversation. "It's Callie Carter. You used to work with her. Her toddler used her grandmother's antique nutmeg grinder to make rocks into gravel, and her mother's coming to visit next week. This is your department."

I glanced at the spice grinders in the glass-front display case and took the phone. Five minutes later, I'd sent Callie, a librarian at my old firm, pictures of two possibles and one likely replacement, and she'd promised to come down on Friday to check them out. We spent a few minutes catching up—she still worked part-time with several of our colleagues. I also suggested she take the original grinder to the cutlery shop up the street; the wizards there can mend all manner of abused kitchen toolery.

A deep masculine grunt at the side door caught my attention and I trotted over to check it out. Before I reached the top of the landing, a broad-shouldered brown-clad back popped into view, jerking a heavily laden hand truck up the outside step and over the threshold.

"Figures," the UPS man said, a teasing tone in his rough bass. "Biggest shipment of the year and your front door is blocked and I gotta haul it all uphill. Backwards."

"Like Ginger Rogers, but without the heels," I said.

His blank look said the joke went over his head. Too young, or too male? Or not a fan of old movies.

A few minutes later, stacks of boxes crowded the shop. I started unpacking a shipment of newly released cookbooks, resisting the temptation to cart the lot to the nook and drool.

"We can unveil the new designs for your anniversary," Kristen said.

"I'm beginning to feel like you're all ganging up on me."

She was sitting on the floor, dusting and realphabetizing the bookshelves. You'd think books would pretty much stay where you put them, but no. They travel. An Italian cookbook ends up next to the oregano and a book on French bistro style cozies up with tarragon. In high school, Kristen clerked in a now-closed bookstore on Broadway a few blocks from our house, and always says the adventures of our cookbooks don't hold a candle to the travels of *The Joy of Sex*.

Expanding our once-slim book selection had boosted the bottom line. Plus books make great displays. This shipment included *Salt: A World History*, by Mark Kurlansky, and *Salted: A Manifesto on the World's Most Essential Mineral, with Recipes*, by Mark Bitterman. September's Spice of the Month: salt. We'd pair books, shakers, cellars, and grinders with *fleur de sel* from the Camargue region of France, Maldon Sea Salt from Britain—both smoked salt and the very popular flakes—and of course, salts handcrafted from the icy waters of the San Juan Islands.

Head tilted, Kristen looked up. "For somebody who makes major decisions in an instant, you can move like a glacier on the small stuff."

A good friend is someone who knows all about you and should know when to keep her mouth shut, even if you did ask for it.

I found out about Tag's affair when he told me he was working an extra shift for a buddy, freeing me to join my office pals for a drink after work at a trendy—and pricey—new place. To see what was going on. On my way to the restroom, I spotted Tag and Miss Meter Maid in a corner booth all but plugging coins into each other. I kept my cool on the spot, but yelled and screamed for a few hours and moved out the next day. Filed for divorce the next week. "Don't rush this," he'd pleaded, but the discovery made sense of tiny, odd details: furtive expressions, last-minute changes in a long-established work schedule, and clothes I didn't think he'd worn coming back from the cleaners.

In less than a month, I'd closed on the loft. A year later, my job evaporated when the partnership voted to dissolve. The firm had been hit with hundreds of thousands of dollars in sanctions after two senior partners failed to disclose information in a medical malpractice case. In the fallout, the accountants discovered the IT director had embezzled two and a half million. And an entire unit, including eighteen of fifty-six partners, decamped for another firm.

I'd have voted a lack of confidence in management, too, but nobody asked me.

And then came the chance to buy the Spice Shop. Took me twenty minutes to decide.

A good friend admits when you've pegged her.

"You're right. How can choosing labels and logos be so hard?" Fabiola's designs were variations of a scheme she'd been suggesting since our first project together, last winter. We'd been introduced by one of the displaced younger lawyers who snared Fabiola's business after setting up her own firm representing "creatives." Hate the term; love the women.

And in truth, I loved her designs. But cute as they were,

the change would cost that proverbial pretty penny. I had to be sure.

Kristen read my mind. "You keep saying you're doing better than you expected for the first year, money-wise. And it takes money to make money." She stood, shaking her blond hair out of her eyes, and put her hands on my upper arms. "This place is worth the investment, Pepper. You're worth the investment. You've come alive since you bought it."

I blinked back tears and nodded. "I'll call Fabiola."

"And where did you get those shoes?" she called after me.

BY six ten, I was alone in the shop.

The Second Watch patrol—Tag and Olerud's afternoon-into-evening counterparts—had taken down the yellow tape. I cleaned up the doorway and fluffed the wilting memorial flowers for late passersby to enjoy. In the morning, I'd get a fresh bouquet or two. It would take some good Seattle rain to wash the last bits of black dusting powder away, though the stuff couldn't be good for the water supply.

Front door shiny and ready to greet the hordes on the morrow, I went back inside, leaned against the counter, and surveyed my domain. Kristen was spot-on: We were headed in the right direction, despite the cost of refurbishing the space and expanding the inventory. This was no longer Jane's Spice Shop. It was Pepper's.

Time for me to make that statement to the world.

I scooped up a ginger candy wrapper that had escaped Reed's broom and dropped it in the trash. As I did, my watchband caught on the rim of the can and popped off my wrist.

"Dang." I could barely see the shiny bubblegum pink band. The closer my fingers got, the deeper it slipped into the recesses of the trash bag. I plunged my hand in further.

No luck.

I grabbed another bag, snapped it open, and started transferring trash. Halfway down, my nose wrinkled. Flowers? What were they doing in here? My staff knew better.

Throwing decent flowers in the trash is universal bad karma. It's seriously bad karma in Seattle, where recycling is religion. Even our sample cups have to be recyclable or compostable. Putting "green waste" in the wrong container violates more rules than you could shake a cinnamon stick at.

Finally, I managed to extract my watch. It had settled into the folds of newspaper surrounding a bouquet of sunflowers nearly identical to the ones Alex had brought me. The ribbon said they'd come from Yvonne's stall.

After spending the day buried, they weren't exactly fresh as daisies, but freedom and clean water would perk them up. I swapped them for Alex's bouquet and wrapped my flowers in the discarded paper for the journey home.

I didn't know how they'd gotten there, but no city trash collector was going to levy a fine on me for wasting a perfectly good bouquet.

Talk about bad karma.

I thought briefly about dropping in on Alex to say thanks in person, but it was nearly time for him to start dinner service. The gushy phone message I'd left earlier would have to do.

After the crazy day, I decided to take the long way home, to stretch my legs and drink in the view. I swung up to Post Alley for a recommendation from my favorite wine merchant.

"How you guys doin' down there?" Vinny asked. Another merchant destined for his job. "Good thing you got a side door. Me, I'd be SOL."

I smiled and traded cash for a bottle of Oregon Pinot Gris. "Thanks, Vinny. Temporary inconvenience—we'll be back to normal tomorrow."

"Good, good. Say, who was that fellow anyway? Never saw him till a week or two ago. Funny for a guy to move here just before the weather changes, but I guess we got a little while before Rain Season starts for real."

True on both counts. It's common knowledge that some of the homeless travel the circuit, moving around the country with the weather.

"Hope so. The webs between my toes have dried up. It'll take a while for them to grow back. Cheers!" Webbed feet, an old Seattle joke.

I headed up the Alley, past the Irish pub that had revitalized the Butterworth Building, site of the city's first mortuary. Bad luck—the work of unhappy ghosts?—had driven out previous tenants, but the current incarnation seemed to have made peace with the past. No doubt the ghosts enjoy a draft of Guinness now and then.

Another sparkling day on Puget Sound as the sun ducked down toward the Olympics. The usual folks clustered in Victor Steinbrueck Park—teens hanging out, couples arm-in-arm at the railing, tourists catching their breath after panting up the hills. A few men lounged near the totem poles—Jim, Hot Dog, and another man I'd seen outside the shop. But no Sam and no Arf.

I returned Jim's wave and made the turn to stroll down Western. A step or two later, I heard raised voices and looked back.

"Get a job, freeloader," a tall white teenager with floppy blond hair yelled at Hot Dog.

"Who you calling freeloader?" Hot Dog raised his fists chest-high, the expression on his dark face hidden by the shadow of the totem pole. "Living off daddy's credit cards."

My arms were full with the flowers and a bag of produce, my shoulder tote extra-heavy with the wine and a loaf of bread. And my phone, buried in there somewhere.

The kid took a step closer. Two of his friends pulled him back. No doubt they saw what I did: He was younger and better fed, but Hot Dog had fought before. A couple standing at the overlook watched, alert. The woman dug in her purse. The man slipped his phone out of his pocket, handed it to her, and took a step forward, his attention on Hot Dog and the boy.

"Come on," one of the kids said.

"Let it go," said another. "It's not worth the hassle."

The would-be fighter hesitated, then stepped backward, his friends' hands on his arms. He finally acquiesced, glaring over his shoulder as they tugged at him, and the four headed up Virginia, away from the park. Hot Dog maintained his stance a good while, then sank onto a bench. Jim said a few words to the third man, who stood guard, eyes trained on the disappearing teens. The sightseeing couple resumed their ferry watch.

I sighed in relief and turned toward home, but not before Jim scurried toward me.

"Thing I like about you," he said a few moments later, a slight wheeze in his chest, "is you keep your eye on things. A spot of trouble doesn't scare you off."

"Thanks." Prelude to a shakedown for cash or food? Some of the men who walk women to their cars or downtown apartments try that. Sam certainly never had—not that I'd heard, at least—but I didn't know my new escort well. "Where's Sam tonight?"

"Sam?" A wheeze. "Heck, I don't know. He doesn't check in with me."

That didn't ring true. Not only had Jim been the clear leader at the makeshift memorial, he'd hesitated long enough to make me think he was bluffing. A slight flush rose on the unscarred left half of his face.

"Jim, this morning, you said something about Doc that puzzled me. If I remember right, you said, 'Old man has no business interfering even after he's dead.' What did you mean?"

Again, that hesitation, this time in his step as well as his voice. "Oh, just blowing smoke. Don't give it another thought."

I stopped. "You're blowing smoke all right—right now. Tell me what was going on with Doc, and what's up with Sam."

His deep-set eyes grew weary, and his tone became guarded. "You're married to that cop, aren't you?"

"I was married to Officer Buhner of the West Precinct Bike Patrol for thirteen years. Divorced for two. If you're afraid I'll tell him something you don't want the police to know, you'll have to trust my judgment. But if you try to harm me, I've got him on speed dial." If I could find my phone.

"Ah, shoot. Don't be afraid of me." He looked like a kicked puppy, disappointed in himself for having disappointed his owner. "I'm just an old man who likes my life and keeps an eye on his friends. Doc had Sam all upset. Sam, he—" Another wheeze. "Well, I'll tell you the truth. He doesn't always think straight. And sometimes, he gets—ideas."

He emphasized the word, making clear that Sam's ideas weren't always healthy ones. Delusions maybe.

"And how does Doc come into this?"

"Well, Sam likes his corner. He's convinced it's the best one in the Market. Now, it may be." He'd recovered his dignity and held out a hand apologetically. "I mean no slight to you."

"None taken."

"What matters is Sam thinks so, and we all let him have it, because it means something to him. And whatever means something to a man has got to be respected. You aren't a man anymore if you can't manage that. Or a woman, too, I expect." His cheek pinked, and I wondered how long it had been since Jim had had an extended conversation with a female. Did he have a long-abandoned wife somewhere? A daughter who prayed every night to keep him safe, and please God, bring him back to the family before he dies?

"And Doc threatened that," I said. Jim nodded solemnly. "But why?"

A long, slow wag of the head. "No idea. Man just showed up a week, ten days ago. Ignored the rest of us. Didn't want to talk—and I respect that, but we have our ways, and he didn't want any part of them or us."

Doc had violated the rules of the streetwise community. Sounds odd to call it that, but every society has its rules. Theirs include protecting the weak, those who—like Sam—can't always protect themselves. Doc either didn't know the rules, or chose to disregard them. Why?

And why stake his claim outside my door?

I'D been tempted to give Jim my strawberries from the Corner Produce or a chunk of bread from the French bakery, but realized in the nick of time that he would see the offering as an insult. He might eat in church basements or drop by the Market Food Bank for produce donated at the end of the day, but he was taking care of himself.

I sipped my wine while the grill heated, on the teeny little ledge the developer called "the veranda." You have to climb out one of the twelve-foot-high windows to reach it—why windows line the fifth floor of an eighty-five-year-old warehouse is a mystery lost to time. Five or six people could stand out there to get a breath and stare at the Viaduct, but access is strictly FOLI: First out, last in.

The only interior walls in the place surround my bedroom and the bathroom. We'd left the high ceilings open, the ductwork and brick walls exposed in classic loft style. For the corner kitchen, my builder pal had struck the mother lode: oak cabinets salvaged from the demolition of a country school out on the coast. An old zinc counter runs along the brick side wall, and salvaged butcher block tops the peninsula, where I do most of my cooking. I'd hunted down leaded glass windows that the builder attached to basic wooden boxes for upper cabinets mounted on the side wall. Extra shelves had been milled from wood the last tenants left behind.

I grated zest and juiced an orange, mixing orange, garlic, and cumin into creamy yogurt. The sliced chicken breast had taken a quick bath in my favorite citrus marinade. I slid the strips onto metal skewers for easy grilling. A bowl of greens stood ready.

Time to fire. I carried the plate of chicken out the window and carefully positioned the skewers on the grill. Some single people hate to cook—"All that fuss for one?" But why deprive myself of good food? It's easy to plan ahead—the extra chicken would go in a pasta salad or a chunky vegetable salad later in the week.

In the distance, Bertha—the world's largest tunneling machine—chugged on. While all this destruction and construction wreaked havoc with a woman's piece of mind, I honestly believed in the waterfront revitalization project. As a matter not just of safety, but of healing old wounds and making downtown and the waterfront neighbors again.

And I would have one freaking fantastic view—and maybe even a veranda I could sit on. A girl can put up with a lot for that.

"*Buona sera*, Pepperoni." My neighbor called to me. Our verandas are the same size, but while mine feels crowded with a few terra cotta pots of tomatoes, herbs, and flowers, his blooms like a jungle, flowering trees in giant pots, and who knows what else. He's not actually Italian—he's a gay, red-haired city councilman—but endearments in all languages spill from him effortlessly. "Smells delish, whatever it is. *Ciao!*" A plate of grilled salmon in one hand, he waved with the other and stepped through the window into his own loft.

My conversation with Kristen—and my encounter with Tag—had triggered too many memories of too much change. They poked at my jaw, my shoulders, my stomach. In HR, we referred to a handful of employees who were always in turmoil as the "Crisis of the Month Club." I had never belonged, despite recent evidence to the contrary. And I had no intention of joining now. Just as things were settling down, just as we approached my first anniversary as the Spice Queen of Pike Place, a man died on my doorstep. Maybe a crime, maybe not. But unsettling as it was, someone else's crisis had nothing to do with me.

I much preferred my personal club—the "Spice of the Month Club."

S for September and salt.

I slid the chicken off the skewers onto a bed of greens, and drizzled the plate with yogurt sauce. Added a sprig of fresh thyme for garnish. I might not be dining at Alex's fine table, but no reason to neglect the details in service for one.

A little Puget Sound finishing salt would be bliss. I grabbed my favorite glass shaker, a reminder of the diners we stopped in when my brother and I were kids and we made long, hot treks to St. Louis to visit my grandparents.

My collection of shakers, graters, mortar and pestle sets, sifters, and other kitchen paraphernalia had exploded in the last year. I'd hung gridwork panels on an open stretch of wall to hold the spice scrapers, egg beaters, and other gadgets that had to be seen to be believed. The modern version of Julia Child's pegboard.

The Flick Chicks had tested margarita salt last week when we gathered at my place for Mexican Movie Night. A double-header: *Night of the Iguana* to depress us about our love lives and *Like Water for Chocolate* to make us yearn for romance anyway. Not last week—this week. Two days ago.

Murder on your doorstep destroys all sense of time.

I set my salad on the dining table, a weathered round wooden picnic table Tag's mother had given me. A consolation prize after the divorce, for a nearly furniture-less woman reassembling her life. Two benches sat under it, but

I slid into a pale pink wrought iron chair I'd found at a sidewalk sale. It looked like a refugee from an ice cream parlor. A perfect match for my new shoes.

Laurel could be pretty insistent. But I wasn't going to do it. If I knew Doc's family—if he had one—then maybe I'd go barging in with sympathy and flowers.

But I certainly wasn't going to track them down and pick up the phone, both caller and recipient feeling as awkward as an elephant in a roller rink.

Kristen was right. I really had come into my own since buying the Spice Shop. I didn't mind one bit being the "life begins at forty" poster girl. If the cliché fits, wear it.

I glanced at my pink shoes, sitting demurely side by side at the front door.

It was time to fully live my own life, and no one else's. Not Laurel's idea of what I ought to do, not Kristen's or Sandra's.

Not even Fabiola's.

Eight

> The original Skid Road—the track used to skid logs
> down to the mill—was Seattle's Yesler Way, now the
> heart of modern-day Skid Row, a gathering place for
> the down-and-out.
>
> —Murray Morgan, *Skid Road: An Informal
> Portrait of Seattle*

I FORCED MYSELF TO TAKE MY USUAL ROUTE UP THE
Market Hillclimb Friday morning. No spooking me.

Detective Tracy stood outside my shop door, hands in
his pants pockets. His tan sports coat, buttoned against the
morning damp, pulled across his chest and stomach. There's
an art to looking rumpled before 8 a.m., and he has it nailed.

"Morning," I said through a bite of cinnamon-raisin bagel.
Juggling bagel, latte, and tote, I pushed several bouquets aside
with my foot. "Thought you police types travel in pairs."

"Detective Spencer is interviewing witnesses."

I straightened and eyed him sharply. "So now you know
this wasn't death by natural causes?"

His dark eyes gave nothing away.

The leaky windows in my loft—another upgrade await-
ing the end of Tunnel Mania—had tipped me off that

mornings were getting cooler, and I'd grabbed a raspberry pink fleece jacket on my way out the door. It matched my watchband and complemented my new pink shoes.

I fished in my jacket pocket for my spare key. "Voilà!" I said and held it up as Tracy dangled my key ring from two fingers.

He followed me inside, uninvited but not unexpected. I dumped my things in the office and walked back out, sipping my latte. Some tea and spice shops sell coffee beans, but I'd decided to leave that to the experts. And in Seattle, coffee experts abound.

Tracy was giving our shelves the same curious inspection Spencer had.

"Are you a cook, Detective?"

"My wife is." He continued to scan the rows of glass jars and other curiosities.

An image of a pretty, petite dynamo popped into my mind. Laughing, chasing two small children at a lakefront beach party, if memory served.

His gaze stopped on the samovar.

He turned toward me abruptly and slipped a notebook out of his jacket pocket. "Shall we sit?" He gestured toward the mixing nook.

"I can spare a few minutes." As if a detective with an agenda and a list of questions would give a fig that I had a shop to prep for the day.

"You've got an established work schedule, I presume. I'll need a copy, plus all time records that show changes— anybody work late, switch shifts, that sort of thing. Everyone gone when you left Wednesday evening?"

"What does my staff have to do with this? Doc was dead before we opened Thursday. And yeah, I'm always the first to arrive and the last to leave. Except Mondays, my day off. I usually come in anyway, at least part of the day." Still high season, still my first year. Still my baby.

"Except," he said, "when you're not." A long pause. "When your resident artist beats you to it."

Point. And if we were talking foul play, any of them could have seen something critical, whether they realized it or not.

"Do they all have keys?" A department-issue notebook lay open to a blank page, a black pen advertising a local hotel beside it.

"No. Just Sandra and Tory. Sandra's my assistant manager. She opens and closes on days I'm off. Tory's been here the next longest, and someone else needs to have a key, in case I'm out when it's time to lock up. You know, I might run to the bank, swing by the Market office, make a delivery." Reed and Zak handle most of our mail runs and downtown deliveries, but I like to visit the commercial accounts occasionally. Like Alex.

"And is it understood that employees may use the shop for personal reasons at other times?"

I frowned. "No, not really. A retail shop has no other uses." If Reed wanted to study here or someone wanted to use the nook for a meeting, fine. No one had ever asked. "But I don't have a problem with Tory coming in early to sketch."

His head bobbed ever so slightly, revealing a sprinkle of salt in his peppery, close-cropped hair. "You seem to have quite a bond with the Market residents and the people of the street."

My eyes narrowed. I had no idea what might have gone wrong, what—besides a heart attack—might have killed Doc. But why are the less fortunate everyone's first suspects?

"Some of them are very observant," he continued.

The relationship between the police and the street folks is complicated. Suspicions cloud both sides. Individual patrol officers often forge good working relationships with individuals. Homicide detectives, on the other hand, work where they're needed, lessening the chance of long-term connections.

But I wasn't keen on making those connections for Detective Tracy. I'd told Jim he'd have to trust my judgment, but that meant I had to control my judgment—and watch my tongue. "If you need to talk with them about what they saw, why don't you ask for Officer Buhner's help?"

"I'll do that. Thing is, the one I'm interested in seems to be missing."

I caught my lower lip in my teeth. He had to mean Sam. Beret-free Sam. "I'm sure you can track him down. You guys know all the shelters and housing programs. The camps. All the haunts."

He nodded. "Now, about that schedule."

My HR brain briefly debated my obligation to protect my employees against my obligation to cooperate with the police, but experience told me the work schedule wouldn't legally be considered confidential information. So I flicked on the office computer, and the printer spat out a copy. "Fridays are busy. They'll all be in at some point today. Reed comes in at one, and Zak leaves at two."

"I'll keep that in mind. Thanks for your time."

After he left, I scrambled to fire up the tea. Tory arrived in time to finish the job while I set up the cash drawer and did a last-minute walk-through. A box or two remained from yesterday's deliveries, and I tucked those out of the way.

I unlocked the front door and propped it open so the world could see we were back to normal. Sort of—normal does not include a mound of flowers and notes handwritten on scraps of paper or cardboard no doubt scrounged from recycling bins. I culled out the most badly wilted bouquets and rearranged the rest—in the sight line but out of the foot line.

A shame to risk the notes being blown away and trampled. I slipped them into my apron pocket. If Doc did have a family—well, I'd give the notes to Spencer or Tracy and let them decide what to do.

And then we were off and running, attending to the Friday rush and rattle. Sales had dropped a hair on Thursday—not too much to absorb, but business owners watch the trends, and I like mine moving up.

Judging by the jars waiting to be reshelved, Seattleites

were trending up on red, green, and especially black teas. They were planning weekend meals from every corner of our map, using every herb and spice from Aleppo pepper to wasabi. (We got your roots, your powders, and your tubes of paste, and not one of them is horseradish colored with spinach powder. On my honor.)

September is still tourist season in these parts. The PDA clues us in on the big draws—the annual Flower and Garden Show in February, Folklife, Seafair, Bumbershoot—and dozens of smaller festivals and gatherings. More than ten million people stroll through the Market's nine acres every year.

And though we couldn't see the terminals from here, I knew one of the nearly two hundred cruise ships that stop in Seattle had docked at the Bell Street Terminal, aka Pier 66. The giveaway? The wristbands and the clutches of women, a few men straggling behind, and their purchases. Cruise shippers don't bring in shopping lists or recipes. They buy products: lavender wands and sachets from Sequim, the town across the Sound that calls itself the Lavender Capital of North America, probably because that's easier to pronounce. (For the record, it's said Skwim. It's a Klallam word. Or Clallam. Or Cle Elum. You think spelling some English words is tricky—try the native languages.) Sea salt harvested from Puget Sound. Or our Seattle Spice Shop Tea, custom blended every week and sold for your tasting pleasure in bags or bulk.

And when we have them, our seasonal spice blends.

Today's tourists kept Zak busy, quizzing him about the shop, the tea, the Market, and more. He is a good ambassador, despite the unlikely appearance—or because of it. To the cruise ship crowd, he's proof that grandsons can grow up to be decent young men despite strange hair, terrible music, and tattoos peeking out of shirtsleeves.

Minutes before noon, I was straightening a display of tea mugs and infusers when Sandra hustled over. "Favorite cop alert," she whispered, and Tag, in uniform, strolled in as if he owned the place, slipping off his mirrored sunglasses in a gesture of extreme cool.

A cop's presence has a curious effect. Even among the upstanding, you can detect a touch of anxiety. *What's going on? Why is he here?* Tag, naturally, eats it up.

"Let's get a bit of sunshine," I said and headed for the side door. I made a mental note to be sure Zak returned the Inn's flowerpot doorstop before he left. Fridays are a gig night for him, so he works a short shift. "To what do I owe the pleasure, Officer?"

"Just—want to make sure you're okay." His china blue eyes showed concern. As I've said, he isn't always a schmuck, but it's not always easy to tell.

I crossed my arms and sucked in my lower lip. "Thanks. 'Preciate it. Glad to have the yellow tape gone—you know how busy weekends are down here."

He hadn't put the sunglasses back on, and for a split second, an uncharacteristic glimmer of hesitation crossed his face. I opened my mouth to ask what was on his mind when he spoke. "Well, then, good. Glad to know everything's good. You'll be fine." He slid the glasses on and kissed my cheek. "Later," he said, and strode down the hill, bike shoes tapping on the concrete sidewalk.

What the heck was that about?

I followed slowly, drinking in the sunshine and atmosphere. One of my favorite buskers often plays on the corner across Pine, and the strains of his fiddle danced on the air. Locals on lunch breaks smiled, tossed change in the beat-up black case open on the sidewalk, and kept moving. Tourists sauntered by, snapping pics with their phones. A few stopped to listen, forming an attentive semicircle. When he finished the piece—Stephen Foster's "Hard Times Come Again No More"—he bowed deeply, then flashed a grin, toothless as an eight-year-old.

To my surprise, several of Doc's compatriots had lined up along the Spice Shop's front wall, flanking the mound of flowers. Each man had his head bent, hat in hand. A show of respect or coordinated panhandling?

Only one logical response. I popped inside, filled a tray with paper cups of tea, and headed back out. I felt a bit like an altar girl—servers, they're called now. I'd ached to be one in fifth grade but my mother had refused to sign the consent form. Jim stood nearest the door, and his gaze barely met mine when he took the cup.

"Seen our friend today?" I asked. Sam loved the Market musicians.

A barely detectible shake no.

"If—when—you do, please let him know we're thinking about him."

A faint nod. I offered cups to all the men, then to passersby. Tray empty, I felt someone's gaze and followed the feeling. Across the way, Yvonne flushed and whipped her head back to her stall, fiddling flowers madly. Empty tray in hand, I crossed the street.

"Not sure if you've been giving the men your unsold flowers to add to the tribute or if they've been paying you, but either way, thanks. It's nice to see Doc honored."

"You shouldn't encourage them to hang around, giving them tea and crumpets."

I shrugged. A debate as old as Seattle's hills. Does acknowledging street folks and offering occasional generosity encourage vagrancy as some claim—those who deride tolerance and call the city "Fre-attle"? Or is it simply human kindness to show compassion for the less fortunate? The latter, in my view. The homeless are just like the rest of us. Except for that home thing.

Besides, they get their crumpets day-old from the Crumpet Shop in the Corner Market.

"And thank you for helping Alex Howard pick out that gorgeous bouquet. It made my day." This time we both blushed and she almost smiled.

After lunch, the Market Master dropped in. Part den

mother, part supervisor to the farmers and craftspeople, from the moment the morning bell rings, he's on the move.

"So sorry to hear what happened. I was out in the field yesterday—literally. Inspecting a potential grower's operation." He reached for my hand and embraced it in both of his. "Anything you need?"

It struck me how no one ever wants to say the D words: "dead," "died," "death." As if the words themselves are to blame for the sadness they bring—and the sense of mortality they trigger. We'd heard every euphemism in the book in the last twenty-four-plus hours, from "bought the farm" to "met his Maker."

A homeless guy might enjoy owning a farm. But if Doc was as unpleasant as the other street men suggested, it might not be his Maker he was meeting.

"Thanks," I said. "It's crazy to find someone dead on your doorstep. But we're fine."

"It happens from time to time." He squeezed my hands again, an earnest expression on his narrow, weathered face. "Anything we can do, you let me know."

Callie the librarian arrived with the broken grinder, five-year-old future geologist in tow. Zak took charge of the child while I inspected the tool. You stuck a whole nutmeg through a hole on the side of a two-inch cylinder, then pushed a wooden plunger that held the nutmeg against a small grater attached to another wooden handle. A trombone-like metal slide held the two pieces together. Gripping both handles, you slid the cylinder back and forth across the grater. Rather ingenious, and a genuine antique.

And seriously busted. One of my potential replacements was an excellent match and a bargain to boot, so she bought it. She'd also brought a list of herbs and spices to stock up on, so by the time she left, we were all smiling.

But it was nearly witching hour for Zak, so I decided to take the day's shipments to the mailing service myself, in the Soames-Dunn Building a few hundred yards north-ish.

I strapped two plastic crates crammed with small boxes and padded envelopes to our rickety orange hand truck and toddled up the street, leaving the crowded sidewalk to the foot traffic. Walking in the street has its hazards, too—the cobbles and vehicles the least of them. Most shops lack alleys and space is tight all over, so deliveries sometimes sit next to curbs for hours, alongside recycling bins, piles of flattened boxes, and other urban obstacles.

The Market opened in 1907, and most buildings date from the expansion in the teens and twenties. The Market Historic District is the only mixed commercial and residential district on the National Historic Register. Chain stores aren't allowed unless they started here, like the original Starbucks, which opened in 1971 in the Stewart Building, and the first Sur la Table, begun the next year right behind the Spice Shop, in a building that once housed the St. Vincent de Paul Thrift Shop. Both still buzz with caffeinated sightseers and locals.

A few minutes later, I pulled my cart out of the shipping service and paused in the Arcade to slip the receipt into my apron pocket. As I did, a sweep of dark fabric caught the corner of my eye and I glanced to the rear of the Arcade.

It was not unusual to see men and women in costume downtown, and a few of the more eccentric folk consider long black coats daily apparel, even on warm days. But if my vision was correct, that coat belonged to a man I wanted to see.

I shoved the cart up tight against the wall and dashed to the back of the Arcade, past the Soap Box and the Oyster Bar and their competing aromas. Bounded up the zigzag of ivy-draped steps for Upper Post Alley. At the first turn, I stepped aside for a thirty-ish man descending, stroller in hand, followed by a woman carrying a toddler. I hid my impatience behind a smile. Dashed ahead as soon as they passed by.

When I first started working downtown, the Pink Door

restaurant and cabaret was the only place of note in this stretch of Post Alley. (And even in the Market, a place with its own psychic tarot reader and a trapeze act is of note.) Since then, the old mortuary has become home to the Irish pub, and the alley boasts a tea room, a chocolatier, and the wine shop on street level, with housing on the upper levels.

And lots of doorways, all empty.

Breath a bit ragged, I hurried on. At Virginia, I looked both ways. Sam was nowhere to be seen.

Still searching, I headed up to First, scouted the block, then jogged down Stewart to Pike Place, circling back to the Soames-Dunn to reclaim my cart. How could a six-foot-plus black man in a long, dark coat and a good-sized dog simply disappear? Sam always said—joking or not, I never knew—that the beret made him invisible.

But the beret was in a police evidence bag.

Maybe the magic was in the coat.

Foot traffic had thinned enough for me to push my empty cart down the sidewalk. Jim, Hot Dog, and the man I'd seen last night at the park kept vigil outside my shop.

"Jim, I need to talk with Sam. For his sake."

The scarred half of Jim's face remained immobile, but caution filled his eyes.

"Hell, man." Hot Dog's words came out "Hey-el, menn."

"You said last night we could trust her."

Something unspoken passed between the two and I got the feeling, despite Hot Dog's words, that Jim was still wary of me. His Adam's apple bobbed, his eyes lowered. He hesitated, then spoke quietly. "If he's in the Market, and I'm not saying he is, you might find him Down Under, by where the bead shop used to be."

"Why there?" My brow furrowed. Down Under, the lower levels beneath the Main Arcade, is home to shops of all kinds, including my favorite import shop. Before it moved, the bead shop on that level had hosted a specter who liked to play tricks on the owners and rearrange the beads.

Strange place for Sam to hang out.

"But he ain't always in the Market," Hot Dog said. "Could be anywhere."

"Pioneer Square?" I said. On the other end of downtown, the Square is a perennial favorite of the street folks. It had been Skid Road when the term referred to logging, not the destitute.

No response. Jim and Hot Dog were telling me that they weren't really telling me. I understood. *Don't let Sam know we told you, and don't tell anyone else.*

First places first. I tucked the cart inside the shop and crossed Pike Place to the daystalls. Waved to Yvonne and trotted toward the wide stairs leading down to the Mezzanine level and Down Under.

But I hadn't gotten far when a flash of sunlight off bright metal drew my attention back to the street. A shiny blue patrol car glided to a halt in front of my shop and two uniformed officers exited. A second patrol car idled a hundred feet behind, the uniformed driver standing by her open door, eyeing the crowd. Her partner took up a sentry post at the bottom of the hill. A familiar unmarked car parked on Pine. Tag and Olerud circled on their bikes.

And Spencer and Tracy headed for my door.

Nine

> You are the salt of the earth, but if salt have lost its
> savor, it is good for nothing but to be cast out, and to
> be trodden under foot.
>
> —Matthew 5:13

"THEY ARRESTED HER," REED REPEATED. "I CAN'T BELIEVE
they arrested her."

We huddled together in the middle of the shop while
Spencer told Tory she was under arrest for Doc's murder
and Tracy on the handcuffs. Tory still wore her
black Spice Shop apron.

"I'll call Eric," Kristen called out. "He'll know what to do."

Tory shook her head no.

"Why not?" Kristen turned to me, eyes wide, worried
voice rising. "Why doesn't she want a lawyer? She didn't
kill him. Why would she kill him?"

"Call him anyway," I said, watching Tory. "She isn't
thinking straight."

With her perfect calm and salt-of-the-earth self-
possession, Tory always seemed to know exactly what she
was doing and saying. But now? It was all too strange.

"Don't you want your purse?" Tracy asked. Tory shook

her head no, hard, emphatically. Did she glance at me briefly, or did I just imagine it?

The uniformed patrol officers took Tory by the upper arm and led their prisoner out the front door. I glimpsed them tuck her in the waiting car, firmly but not unkindly.

A gaggle of cruise shippers had been in the shop when the police arrived, and they stood, agape. Oh, the wonders of the evil city, to report to the women in the bridge club and the church choir back home in Iowa or Indiana or another distant utopia. A few clutched bags of lavender or Puget Sound sea salt.

Spencer gestured. "You have customers, Pepper."

In other words, show's over, get back to business. But I was not so easily distracted. "Where are you taking her?"

"She's in good hands."

I gripped my elbows to keep from shaking. "What are you charging her with? She didn't kill Doc. She couldn't have killed Doc."

"Boss." Sandra touched my arm and tilted her head almost imperceptibly toward the customers.

I didn't care what they heard or saw, what gossip they shared back home. I only cared about Tory.

But Sandra was right. I breathed deeply and put on my pleasant HR face. "So sorry about the disruption. All just a mistake, I'm sure. Sandra will be happy to help you make your purchases and"—I scanned the tables quickly before spotting the obvious choice—"please accept a box of our custom blend Spice Shop tea bags, with our compliments. A tasty souvenir from your sojourn in Seattle."

"Keep the tourists happy," the instructor in my business training class had said. A variation on the old adage "The customer is always right." Still true. Even in a crisis.

Especially in a crisis.

"Don't give them those," Tracy said. I looked at him quizzically, and he took the box.

Sandra led the customers toward the front counter,

spinning tales of the Market's history. She had a nearly endless supply of such patter, some true, some questionable, and all entertaining. Reed skittled forward to help out.

Kristen emerged from the back room. "Eric says he'll send an associate with criminal defense experience, to make sure they don't pressure her to talk."

Good luck getting Tory Finch to tell you anything she doesn't want to.

I nodded numbly. Zak had already left for the day. Their relationship was a mystery. Would she call him? Should I? Later, I decided, when I knew more. No reason to worry him on his way to a gig when he'd be powerless to help.

Of course, if she didn't want a lawyer, she might not want a friend, either.

Too bad, sister. You work for me, you got me in your life. I'm done being kept at a distance. Deal with it.

I held the door, that bland smile glued on my face, and handed each of the half-dozen tourists a business card. "Take a right at the corner and head up to the alley, then take a left and keep going till you reach the Pink Door. Get a table outdoors on the rooftop. Tell them Pepper sent you, and I'll buy the first glass of wine."

"The pink door?" said a balding man, a good-sized belly stretching his red-and-white-striped polo shirt.

"There's no sign, but you'll know it the moment you see it."

A deeply tanned woman sporting a cap of snowy white hair put a hand on my arm. "Don't worry. It will all work out."

My throat tightened and my smile wavered. I bobbed my head and locked the door behind them.

Tory? But why?

I flipped our sign to CLOSED. "Why? Why arrest her?" I marched across the room toward the mixing nook, where Tracy had corralled my staff. He stood outside the nook, next to the samovar. "Why would Tory Finch kill a homeless old man living on the streets? Why would she kill anyone?"

Tracy shrugged. "The usual reasons. Some grudge she's nursed all these years."

I squinted. "What are you talking about? He just showed up last week."

"Wouldn't let her stay out with friends. Kept her from seeing some guy. Took away her TV privileges when she was eight and wouldn't eat her beets." He returned my hard stare with a look of studied disbelief. "You didn't know?"

"Didn't know what?" A small eddy began to churn in my gut.

Tracy's lips curved smugly. Whatever was coming, I wasn't going to like it.

"He was her father."

THERE are moments when a new piece of knowledge unlocks a door. Makes all the puzzle pieces snap into place and reveals the picture on the cover of the box. Like when I caught Tag with his girlfriend and understood in a flash that everything I had done to save my marriage had been a fool's errand, and that I had to leave to save myself.

This was not one of those moments.

The four of us stared at Tracy in silence.

"Her father?" Kristen said. "Her father lives on the street? Did he follow her to Seattle? Was he trying to get money from her, or a place to live?"

An almost microscopic twitch on Tracy's face said shut up and let him ask the questions.

"She's always nice to street people," Reed said.

"She grew up here," I said. While Tory kept her private life private, I did know that much. Earlier this summer, a customer had recognized her, and they chatted for a while, the other woman telling me they'd been classmates at Lakeside, an exclusive private school in Seattle's North End.

So not only had Doc probably not been homeless, he had probably been well off. Once upon a time, anyway. At least now I knew why he'd been so determined to stake out our corner. But why stalk his own daughter? What had he wanted from her? What had she refused to give?

As a cop's ex-wife, I realized they might not know yet. And they would reveal only what they thought was necessary to get information from us.

Two could play that game. I sure as heck wasn't going to tell them anything they could use against Tory unless I had to. She may have kept her distance; heck, she may have kept Lake Washington between us. But nobody works in HR as long as I did without developing an almost psychic sense of intuition.

One thing I knew for sure about Tory Finch: She would not involve anyone else in her problems. Wasn't the corollary that she would not blame anyone else for them?

And isn't murder the ultimate blame game?

"What evidence do you have?" I said, just as Reed spoke up. "How did he die?"

"Ah, see, now that's the interesting thing," Tracy said.

Here it comes, I thought. *Fishing*. I folded my arms and leaned against the nook's pony wall, determined not to rise to the bait.

"See, he was poisoned."

One of my employees gasped.

I knew what was coming before he said it. I knew now why the detectives had been drawn to the samovar like a hungry dog to a butcher's back door, and why Tracy wouldn't let me give away our signature product.

"With a cup of your tea."

Ten

It burns, it stings, it turns you into a virtual dragon! Yet thousands of YouTube users post videos of themselves taking the ever-popular, ever-stupid Cinnamon Challenge, a pointless attempt to swallow a tablespoon of cinnamon in 60 seconds without water. Don't be an idiot. Just say no.

DETECTIVE MICHAEL TRACY SLID A LONG WHITE ENVE-lope out of the inside pocket of his sport coat and handed it to me.

In old B movies, starlets recoil from a subpoena or war-rant, extended by an unseen hand, as if they could avoid legal process by treating the thing like a diamondback ready to strike. I'd listened to lawyers in the lunch room recount tales of witnesses who refused to touch dangerous papers, and Tag had once had to tase a suspect who tried to avoid arrest by setting fire to his house and running out the back door.

At the moment, I sympathized with the starlets and the suspect.

If the papers Detective Tracy handed me were any indica-tion, I was *"the possessor of premises believed to contain or harbor evidence of a crime, e.g., murder in the first degree, e.g., causing the death of one Damien Finch, street name 'Doc,' with premeditated intent."*

I felt like swearing. Tracy had gotten a warrant to search my shop for evidence of murder. Premeditated murder. Intent to kill.

"How'd you find out his name?"

"His wallet."

Duh.

First-degree murder. Accidental poisonings do happen, but if it's truly an accident, it isn't usually murder, is it? Manslaughter, if the circumstances make it a crime, and a terrible, horrible, regret-to-your-dying-day mistake if they don't.

What about a spice wizard who poisons her father's tea?

"Evidence of poison, the means to poison, or intent to poison or otherwise harm," I read. Was it getting cold in here?

"If you tell me what poison you suspect," I said, running through my mental list of potentially toxic spices, "we could speed up your search. I mean, overdosing on nutmeg can send you on a bad trip, but it won't cause any real harm. And some folks are sensitive to cinnamon or mustard, but even a megadose would only give them a serious stomachache. If they managed to choke it down."

"No, I don't think I can share that information," Tracy said dryly. "Ms. Piniella, if you'd be so kind, unlock the front door and allow my officers in." A minute or two later, officers guarded our doors, and a small cadre of detectives and patrol officers wearing rubber gloves stuck their noses in every corner of our business. They climbed the ladder and poked and prodded our jars and bags and boxes while the four of us fidgeted in the mixing nook.

Tracy told me I could leave, but I didn't budge. Then he suggested the others head home. Either he didn't antici-pate further questions for them, or he was willing to postpone the quiz in exchange for fewer eyes on the search. But Kristen had looped her arm through mine and refused to go, and the others chimed in that they were staying, too.

Now my employees leaned forward in their seats in the nook, radiating a blend of anger and determination, watching every move the detectives made. Retail keeps you sharp-eyed.

"Do you store spices anywhere else?" Tracy asked me.

"Yes and no. We blend and bag our tea every week at a certified facility in SoDo." South of the Dome—the long-gone Kingdome. "The tea and spices we use are shipped directly there. Everything else comes here."

"Does Ms. Finch have access to that facility?"

"No. Ms. Piniella and I take turns supervising production." I gave him the name and address of the place. Jane had used it for years. "Once it's blended and bagged, we keep it here." I gestured toward my ancient Chinese apothecary, bought long before I imagined owning a spice shop. It still emits faint whiffs of jasmine and ginger. But its open drawers hold tea strainers and infusers, the upper shelves designed for a Buddha figure now displaying teapots and mugs. Plastic bags of bulk tea and boxes of individual tea bags fill the lower shelves.

The nineteenth-century piece had belonged to an elderly widower on our block, and I'd admired it for years. After his death, his daughter said he'd wanted me to have it. Tag had groused—"What do you want with that piece of junk?"—but I'd insisted, and he and the old man's son-in-law had gingerly carted it to our house.

It seemed life had been preparing me for the unforeseen.

I followed Spencer and Tracy to my office, a glorified broom closet. Two people barely fit, so I leaned against the door frame, arms crossed, observing the search.

Don't you block my line of sight, I told Tracy silently. *This is my life you're pawing over and don't you forget it.*

A heavily varnished remnant of chipboard had been wedged between the walls to make a desk out of two dented black file cabinets, the shelves above crammed with reference books, food mags, and catalogs.

Many spices and herbs are imported, and it isn't always possible to buy directly from the grower. For some exotic varieties, especially those suited only to remote climates or harvested in countries where export is difficult, suppliers hold the key.

And while paper catalogs might be going the way of dinosaurs, like those old fossils, they have their uses—besides propping up a rickety table leg. To some of my commercial customers, no website will ever convey as much as a picture they can hold in their hands. Others like to take a catalog back to their kitchen to browse during slack moments.

Happily, the shelves were reasonably well organized, and it took Spencer almost no time to conclude they held nothing relevant to Doc's murder or Tory's arrest.

"She use the computer?"

Holy moly. Would they, could they?

"No reason she would." Tory had no responsibilities involving the computer and I'd never seen her on it, though I left it on during the day. She wasn't the type to sneak a peek at Facebook or Twitter when she should be working.

The last thirty-six hours intimated that I didn't really know what type she was.

"No," I repeated, shaking my head slightly. My business depended on that computer. And yes, I had a backup system, and our iPad cash register could function on its own, but having the hard drive seized would be a major PITA.

Tracy looked skeptical, but then, he usually does.

Spencer sat in my chair and riffled through my file drawers. I'd started my own filing system when I bought the business, and true to my HR roots, the files were all clearly labeled and organized.

"Supplier records, and leasing info and correspondence with the PDA in the top left drawer," I said. "Financial records in the bottom."

Spencer flipped while I peered over Tracy's shoulder. I detected a faint odor of a particular chile. "Thai for lunch," I said. "You eat in the Market, or that place down by SPD Headquarters?"

His dark cheeks flushed slightly and his eyelids twitched, as if to say, "*How the heck . . .*"

"This drawer is locked." Spencer tugged at the handle of the bottom right drawer.

"Of course it's locked. Those are personnel files. No one has access to them but me."

"Pepper," Tracy said firmly, "the warrant."

"The warrant does not specify confidential personnel information, and there is no reason to believe those files have any relevance to your investigation." I tried to channel the lawyers I'd worked with. The good ones.

"Everything related to Ms. Finch is relevant. We have a witness."

"I don't care if you have six witnesses. You go back and get another warrant. I've got an obligation to protect those files until a court tells me otherwise." I'd be violating the law myself if I handed them over voluntarily. Tory had no access to that drawer and it was hard to imagine how anything in a personnel file might relate to a charge of premeditated murder. It's not like anyone writes on their job application that they intend to kill their father at some future date, on the employer's doorstep.

I felt that old pain in my jaw. The sharp stabbing that said this might not be the most comfortable time to stand up for myself.

But I was through backing down. I met Tracy's cold glare with one of my own.

"We'll just do that then," he said as Spencer said, "She's right, Mike." He looked annoyed.

My jaw replied with a spasm.

Tracy scanned the office one more time. "Where did Ms. Finch keep her personal belongings?"

Apparently I took too long to respond. Apparently Tracy no longer trusted me, if he ever had.

"Her purse," he said, voice and eyes snapping like a peevish turtle.

How I longed to draw the line. To tell him no and mean it. To tell him no and believe I could get away with it, without facing charges of obstruction.

But the warrant gave them the right to search anywhere that they might find evidence of the crime or motive. And that included Tory's bag, stashed in our staff-only bathroom. I edged past Tracy into the tiny room and opened the cabinet above the toilet. The brown leather shoulder strap of Tory's olive green messenger bag flopped out.

"That one," I said.

Tracy stretched to loop a finger through one of the leather tabs on the front pockets and the bag came tumbling down. He caught it mid fall, but the main zipper was open and stuff went flying. He swore loudly and clapped the thing shut, capturing her sketchbook before it slid out.

I snared her wallet before it hit the floor and scooped a pink lip gloss out of the toilet. A sketching pen skittered to a stop between Spencer's feet. All three of us glanced around instinctively, but nothing else appeared to have escaped.

"Your fingerprints," Tracy said, blustering. "Now you've contaminated evidence."

"You'd rather it took a swim?"

"I don't have an evidence bag that big on me," Spencer said. "Play nice while I grab one."

Tracy's scowl deepened, but I put on my HR face. A small medicine cabinet hung above the sink and I started to tuck the lip gloss inside.

"Everything," he snapped.

"Tory wore pink lip gloss every day. She would hardly stash poison in it."

"Everything," he repeated.

"Here we go." Spencer returned carrying a large clear plastic bag. Tracy slipped it over the messenger bag and I started to drop the wallet and lip gloss inside.

"Bag those separately," he said. "Since Ms. Reece has interfered with the process."

Spencer complied, taking the wallet and lip gloss from me with a gloved hand, then filled out the peel-and-stick chain of custody forms.

"Thank you, Detective Spencer. You have been most kind." I swept my arm like an old-fashioned maitre d', pointedly ignoring Tracy, who huffed past me.

Back on the shop floor, patrol officers were labeling and logging evidence bags.

"They took all the paper cups," Sandra said in a low voice, "and all our custom tea."

"What about—" I spun halfway around. One gloved officer snapped open a large bag, while another lifted the samovar and gingerly slid it inside.

"Careful. It's fragile. And not cheap."

The officer holding the bag gave me a faint smile. "We'll do our best, ma'am."

My staff and I stood shoulder to shoulder, breath shallow, eyes darting as the detectives and officers finished poking, probing, packing, and labeling. The pile of evidence in their wheeled cart grew: the samovar and its mate, paper cups, both rubber stamps, Tory's personal mug, her messenger bag. All our trash cans and recycling bins. The tea, but no other inventory.

Odd, that, but it gave me hope that they would realize their mistake quickly and release Tory.

"Any medicinals?" Spencer asked. In the good cop–bad cop game, her role was obvious.

"Yes and no. We focus on the culinary, but many herbs also have medicinal purposes, in another form."

Her eyebrows furrowed. I gestured toward the shelves. "Oregano, for example. You've eaten it, cooked with it. But oregano oil, which we don't sell, is used as an antiseptic. Some mints are used in medicinal blends. Turmeric treats a number of conditions. Herbalists and naturopaths use cinnamon capsules to treat high blood pressure. I hear it works wonders."

She consulted a list, tucked it back in her jacket pocket. "That's everything, then."

"Ladies. Mr. Locke," Tracy said. "I'm sure we'll see each other again soon."

I smiled stiffly and latched the door behind him, then let out a deep, heavy breath.

My staff studied me, wide-eyed and wordless. A sense of gloom and despair filled the place. We had all worked so hard to make the transition from longtime owner to new, revitalizing the space and expanding the stock to make the Seattle Spice Shop into a sensory paradise where anything seems possible.

Anything but this.

"Group hug," Kristen said. I guessed no one but her felt like it, but we all joined in. Sadness permeated our huddle. It made me angry—but at what? Not Tory, who had to be innocent. Not Doc—no one deserved premeditated murder, if that's what it had been.

Not even Tracy. He was simply the focal point for a bad situation.

But he'd made Tory and me his targets, and that ticked me off.

"We'll get through this," I said, releasing the hold. "Sandra, can you blend a new batch of tea tonight? You should be able to get kitchen access despite the short notice, though we may have to pay extra for time on the bagging equipment."

She nodded.

"Great. I'll call Laurel and beg an urn and a couple of vacuum pots until we get our stuff back," I continued. Assuming we did. Assuming they found nothing incriminating.

"You bet. Mr. Right will help. We'll get her done if it takes all night."

"Great. Reed, can you scrounge up some trash and recycling bins? I'll get paper cups and napkins. I'm sorry, Kristen," I said, my voice cracking. "I know you've got kid stuff all day Saturday and I wouldn't ask if—"

Her eyes glistened, but there was nothing soft about her tone. "Don't you dare apologize to me. Of course I'll be here. Early."

And with that, a little glimmer of light bathed my heart.

AFTER the detectives left, I sent Reed and Sandra home, then slumped in the nook wishing a stiff drink would appear by magic. Kristen had refused to leave, though she dashes out of here most days to meet her girls when they get home from their after-school activities.

"They'll be fine." She dropped her phone in her apron pocket and shook off my concern for her family routine. "Eric will order pizza and pop and be a hero."

"I'm responsible for this," I said. "For Doc being on that corner."

"No, you're not. He wanted that corner." She slid onto the bench beside me.

"The question is, did the killer know about the dispute? It wasn't his day for the corner, so why was he there?" Plenty of people had heard me lay down the law for alternate days. I'd counted on the Market network to hold Doc and Sam to their word.

No question Tory knew.

The bigger question was why the police had focused on

her. That Doc was her father didn't prove anything. Nor did her early arrival, ostensibly to sketch.

Spencer and I had seen the drawings. But they didn't prove she'd been sketching the entire time, or even that she'd done the drawings that day.

I wished I'd had time to flip through her sketchbook before it had been spirited away.

And why had her father been in the Market?

She had denied seeing him the morning he was killed, but I wasn't convinced. If he'd come here to see her, he'd have been waiting by the door when she arrived, or knocked or peeked in. She'd also denied seeing him Wednesday at the bus stop, and I'd witnessed that encounter myself.

Tory would not lie without good reason.

They knew it was poison, and maybe even what poison, explaining the limited search and even more limited seizure. So they'd had time to test Doc's body. And they'd tested the cup.

The cup from my shop.

In the movies, CSI takes prints off paper—off nearly anything—but real-life forensics faces real-life limitations. I pictured Tory, Wednesday morning at this very table, stamping the cups alongside Reed. Who had unwrapped the roll, set them out, moved them around? They might have found prints from any one of us—even me.

"Who do I call?" I said with a start. "If Doc was Tory's father, what about her mother?"

Kristen looked at me in horror. Keys in hand, I dashed to the office and unlocked the file drawer.

"But what will you tell her?" Kristen asked from behind me. "You can't say 'they've arrested your daughter for killing your husband.' What if she doesn't know he's dead? Or that they think—" She wrapped her arms around herself, making a cocoon of her white sweater.

"We don't even know if her parents are together," I said,

flipping through the files. My breath briefly caught when I got to Tory's. Jane had never been good with the paper side of the business, and while I'd insisted on formal applications and created real files for Zak and Kristen, I'd overlooked the records for existing employees. Meant to audit the files and beef them up, but the task languished on my list. My bad.

Nothing but a W-4 and an I-9 form inside the manila folder.

"Dang it, Jane," I said. "Not even the basics." I reached for the phone and punched in Jane's number, wondering what to tell her. "There's been an accident"? An "incident"? Or just spill it?

But no spilling to voice mail. "Jane, it's Pepper. Call me. It's—important."

At least the W-4 had an address on it.

A knock sounded at the front of the shop. "What now? The cops can't be back already."

Kristen got there ahead of me and opened the door for Laurel, arms laden with a big brew thingy, two stainless steel insulated pumper pots dangling from her fingers.

"Am I losing it? I meant to call you. Did I?"

"Kristen called. We're keeping you company tonight."

My gaze swept from one of my best friends to the other. "I'm okay. Really."

"Yeah, you are," Laurel said. "But it's gotta be rough, worrying about Tory, wondering . . ."

"I'm not wondering," I said sharply. "She didn't do it."

"We know that," Laurel said in a soothing tone. "We know there's a terrible injustice being done—"

"In the name of justice," I said, despite my fear of where this was leading.

"And you've got to get her out," Laurel continued.

"But we can't help her if she won't let us," Kristen said.

"Hold on. You're both right. She's innocent." Of murder anyway. Guilty of poor judgment and perhaps of fueling a family feud. "But she did shake us off."

"Before she knew how much trouble she was in," Laurel said.

Before she'd been hauled down to police headquarters, left to steep in a tiny, blank room, subjected to repeated attempts at interrogation, then, I imagined, marched across the street to the King County Jail. I'd never been to the jail—by all accounts, a decent institution.

But when it came to certain institutions, aren't we all, like Mae West, *Not ready?*

Eleven

Some say variety is the spice of life.

"I NEED DINNER AND A DRINK," LAUREL SAID. "IF WE'RE going to work out a plan."

"Wait a sec. Yesterday, you badgered me to find Doc's family and offer condolences. Now we know his family is Tory, and you want me to help her."

"Don't you want to help her?" Kristen said.

"Help them both," Laurel said. "By figuring out what really happened."

"Whoa." I held up my hands. I'd already started asking questions, but Tory's arrest changed everything. Or did it? "If she didn't want a lawyer, she won't want my help."

"But she trusts you," Kristen said.

Tory had lied to me, at least once. Not your typical sign of trust.

But it might be a sign of someone in pain, reluctant to disappoint someone else. Of Tory not wanting to tarnish my trust in her.

I was sunk. In up over my pink shoes and my spiky brown hair.

"You have to tell Zak," Kristen said. "Dating or not, we know they're close."

"Sooner, not later," Laurel added. "He deserves to know."

"But he's working tonight—" My phone rattled on the wooden table. I glanced at the name and number. "Decide on dinner while I get this. Walking distance."

"Hey, Jane. I hate to call with bad news, but . . ." Back in my office, I sank onto the chair and told her the story.

A raspy intake of breath.

"Jane, are you okay?"

"Where is she?" Well past seventy-five, Jane walks with a cane, but she had never sounded old or tired until now.

"King County Jail. I don't know if they'll let me visit her, since I'm not family or a lawyer, but I'll find out tomorrow."

"I always knew I could count on her."

The non sequitur pricked my ears. I could almost see Jane tilting her crown of feather white braids and squinting her island blue eyes, but I'd lost track of her train of thought.

"Jane, what's going on? What aren't you telling me?"

Silence. Then she cleared her throat and spoke, her voice both soft and firm. "One reason I sold the shop to you was your background, taking care of employees."

I waited.

"The other reason was you see this as more than a business. You see with your heart, dear. You'll know what to do."

Much as I value Jane's faith in me, I really wished she hadn't said that.

Almost as badly as I wished for a margarita.

"THE citrus glaze on the pork carnitas," Laurel asked our server, "is that orange or lemon? And how's it spiced?"

"Chef uses *Sanguinello* blood oranges, ma'am, with a touch of lime and a dash of his own chile blend."

I knew that blend, had helped him source it.

"Hmm. Make sure that grilled asparagus is well charred. Brings out the earthiness. And I hope those chipotle mashed potatoes were made this evening—reheated potatoes taste like wallpaper paste." She'd donned purple-rimmed readers, and her eyes darted over the menu. "But I can't quite wrap my tongue around the idea of pickled vegetables with citrus-glazed pork. Let's substitute this tropical fruit relish you serve with the scallops." She pointed. He made a note.

Going out for dinner with a chef is always an adventure.

"The *Chile en Nogada*," I said, handing him my menu. He nodded swiftly, a flicker of relief in his dark eyes at the simple order. Shredded beef, sun-dried fruit, and nuts stuffed in a poblano pepper, pecan cream sauce, pomegranate seeds, and baby *haricots vert*—why mess with a combination like that?

"The sea bass," Kristen said.

"Bites," I called. She'd chosen *Lubina al Pistacho*, pistachio-crusted sea bass with a corn, cilantro, and jalapeño relish and a salsa risotto, my second choice.

Café Frida had opened a few months ago, and while I'd helped the chef locate some unusual herbs and spices, I'd only eaten here once. I'd come for drinks and appetizers with Alex and the head chef at his own south-of-the-border restaurant. Where the food was nicely done, but far more traditional.

They'd ordered one of almost everything, sampling and comparing notes. Figuratively speaking—the waitress recognized a spy mission when she saw one, and the chef came out to welcome us, forestalling any actual note-taking.

"Creative," Alex had said, begrudgingly, as we took our leave. His chef had barely uttered a word, and I wondered if he'd gone back to his own kitchen to revamp his menu. Or to reconsider it over a shot glass and a bottle of Jose Cuervo Reserva.

I sipped my passion fruit margarita. The place buzzed like a Mexican cicada.

At least there were no insects on the menu. "Sophisticated Mexican cuisine," it declared, beneath a line drawing of Frida Kahlo herself. On either side of the beveled walnut back bar, rumored to have come from a nineteenth-century brothel in Idaho, hung reproductions of her self-portraits. Café Frida was the latest tenant to test its pluck in this Belltown space, a few blocks from the Market. Judging from the crowd—and the noise level—it had struck the right note.

"Did you have to use your name to get us a table?" I asked Laurel, then took a sip of her mango habañero margarita. "Mmm. That's good."

"No." She drew the glass toward her protectively. "I used yours."

After the long, strange day, laughter felt good.

In addition to an area near the bar filled with tall tables for the drinks and appetizer crowd, Frida's owners had taken over the adjacent club space, serving up tequila, cerveza, tapas, and music. Some Latin music but mostly a cross-over paradise. The space had once been a haven of grunge, the Seattle Sound of the 1990s. Pearl Jam and Soundgarden had rehearsed in the basement, and I'd been an early fan, pawning my gran's silver tea service for Pearl Jam tickets. (I got it back before she noticed it was missing. It now holds center stage in my brother and sister-in-law's dining room. And the show was totally worth the risk.) After those glory days, the building had wasted away, along with much of Belltown. Tag regularly reported drug raids and calls to knife fights, until an influx of Microsoft millionaires and heavy-duty cleaning fluids turned the neighborhood hip again.

I had no idea who topped the bill in the lounge tonight and didn't care. After this week, I could hardly wait to take my happy belly home to bed.

Kristen tasted our shared appetizer: chicken meatballs, bursting with fresh corn kernels and cilantro, artfully arranged on a lime green plate, crema and molé carefully poured around them.

"Orgasmic," she said, mouth full.

Laurel wore her "Don't disturb me, I'm identifying the flavors" expression.

I stuck my fork in a meatball, cut it in half on my small red plate, and swirled the bite in sauce. Took a nibble. Took another, bigger bite.

"Holy molé," I said, mouth full.

Kristen wrinkled her nose at my bad pun.

Laurel swallowed and lowered her fork, resting it on her plate. Without a word, she pushed back her chair and left the table.

Kristen and I exchanged looks. "If she doesn't come back," Kristen said, "that leaves more for us."

I was reaching for another meatball, contemplating spooning up the extra sauce like a thick soup, when Laurel returned. A nanosecond later, the chef approached, our server close behind.

"Ms. Halloran," the chef said, bowing most elegantly. "Ms. Reece." He nodded acknowledgment to Kristen. "Ma'am. An honor to have you ladies in my restaurant."

"Chef," Laurel said. "The honor is ours. This dish is exquisite. The spices are strong but balanced, never over-powering the core flavors. Deft combinations, perfect textures." Her hands punctuated her words, fingers opening and closing like umbrella spokes.

Laurel freely expresses her pleasure over food, but she rarely raves. And she never gushes. Was it the tequila? Or the emotion of Doc's death and Tory's arrest?

No, I thought, itching for another meatball. *This food is that good.*

The chef beamed. He wiggled his fingers at the server,

who held out his order-taker dealie and showed him our ticket. "Ah. You've chosen well. I hope you will let me buy dessert for the table, as a professional courtesy." He turned to me for an answer.

I knew already I would be too full for dessert, because I intended to eat every bite on my plate and any scraps my companions dared leave behind. And I didn't care. I grinned and nodded like a bobblehead doll.

Our main courses went down as smoothly as the meatballs, gliding across our palates like well-aged mezcal. We barely spoke. Not that we shoveled it in—no. We ate respectfully, deliberately, in reverent silence.

"Well," I said after the server cleared our plates. "I'll be coming back here. And after your praise, I bet I won't have to beg for more of his business."

Laurel's eyes glinted, from more than the glow of the tin and glass star lights and wrought iron chandeliers hanging from the timbered ceilings. "When the news breaks," she said, "you're going to need goodwill in the food community."

The delicious food in my stomach became a sodden weight. "Tell me you didn't put on a show worthy of an Oscar."

"No." She wagged her head quickly. "This food is fabulous. I don't normally praise other chefs to their faces. It's not like we're competitors—I'm doing breakfast and lunch and everyday take-out with a gourmet flair."

Ripe's slogan.

"But why not give an honest rave?" she continued. "It can't hurt."

I grabbed my bag and left the table, shaking. Could Tory's arrest damage my business? The thought had not occurred to me. Why would anyone—commercial or casual customer—lose confidence in me because of accusations against my employee?

Or was Laurel right? Should I be out proactively reinforcing old relationships and building new ones?

I shoved open the red padded door to the women's room—a vestige of a prior decorating scheme—and entered a shrine.

A montage of Frida Kahlo paintings covered one wall, embellished with stone-studded silver crosses. Another wall bore a mural of her famous calla lilies and dense jungle foliage. Deep pink and red floral headdresses of the style she often wore had been mounted above the gilt-framed mirrors over the sinks, so that I seemed to be wearing one.

It went well enough with the stretchy green-and-purple peasant blouse I'd pulled on over my black yoga pants—a spare top I'd kept at the office—but looked out of place with my dark spikes of hair.

The stakes were bigger than I'd realized. *How hard are you willing to fight for the new life you've made?* I asked myself.

Doc's death and Tory's involvement could affect more than just my shop and my own livelihood. The recession had cut a lot of HR jobs, though I had connections. I could always find something. But I felt an obligation to the Market and my staff to keep the Spice Shop going.

To make sure Tory had a job to come back to, when we got this mess cleared up.

I took a deep breath and stared at my reflection. Funny how seeing yourself with a fiesta on your head changes things.

Not that I wasn't peeved at Laurel. When I resisted getting involved, she all but manipulated me into taking action.

Right goal, wrong approach.

"What would Frida do?" I said out loud. Behind me, a toilet flushed and a door unlatched. A woman I didn't know emerged from a stall.

A slow flush crawled up my neck. Our eyes—mine embarrassed, hers amused—met in the mirror.

"Frida," she said, dropping her handbag on a gilt chair covered in lush purple velvet, "would order another drink and eat cake."

I nodded at the mirror.

Sí.

Twelve

Others say laughter is the spice of life.

NOT ONE, NOT TWO, BUT THREE DESSERTS CROWDED our small table. Flan with fresh berries and caramel. A chocolate molé cake adorned with a crown of chocolate mousse and dark-flecked ice cream. And a sponge cake—*très leches*—resting in a swirl of fruit reductions that reminded me of those gigantic all-day lollipops kids get at carnivals.

"They make their own ice cream," Kristen said in a hallowed tone. "Coconut and black pepper."

"What are we waiting for?" I sat and picked up a fork.

I have never seen a group of men share dessert the way women friends do. Sure, a man will split a piece of pie with his wife and tolerate her taking a sip of his postprandial brandy. But to let another man stick his fork into the same food over and over? Horrors to them; part of the fun to us.

The rhythm of forks going back and forth between dishes dispelled the tension between Laurel and me. Or maybe it was the sugar and milk, so sweet and soothing.

The sounds of guitars being tuned and amps being checked wafted into the restaurant from the lounge.

"The address Tory put on her W-4, three years ago, was in the U District," I said, "but the bus she got on Wednesday after work goes to Capitol Hill. So she moved. But where?"

"That fits." Kristen waved her empty spoon. "I saw her walking out of QFC on Fifteenth a few weeks ago, carrying bags."

"Which way did she go?"

She tightened her lips and shook her head. "I had the kids with me. I didn't notice."

I couldn't believe I didn't have a current address for one of my employees. That was bad management in about six different ways and probably a serious IRS violation. No matter that I distribute paychecks and W-2s in person.

"Monday morning, everyone is filling out job applications and new forms. We are redoing the personnel files and doing them right."

A guitar riff interrupted me.

"Let's get another drink and watch the show," Laurel said, scooting back her chair as if her heels were on fire.

"Long day, long week. I don't think—" But my protests fell on empty chairs. My friends had taken flight. Resisting the temptation to lick the cake plate, I whispered to it instead. "Thank you. We'll meet again soon. Promise."

The lounge was nearly full, but Laurel and Kristen had lucked out, snaring a table up front. I slid into my seat.

"Mexican coffee," I told the server, glancing over in time to see Laurel hand her a small white card that read RESERVED.

The room lights dimmed and a spot picked out the lead guitarist as the first notes rang.

Holy molé. Zak.

My jaw cramped as I glanced at my girlfriends, their eyes trained on the stage. Here I thought we were hanging out, drowning our sorrows, and they'd planned this to force me to get involved. To prove how much Tory's fate mattered. To tell Zak about her arrest tonight.

My chest tightened. I didn't know whether to be mad at them for pushing me, or glad that they cared so much.

We were all here because we cared about Tory.

"How did you know he'd be playing?" I leaned toward Laurel, sitting closest to me.

"Kristen called him while you were on the phone with Jane. It was obvious he didn't know about the arrest."

I didn't have to tell him tonight. We could just enjoy the music. But stalling wouldn't be fair—to him, or Tory.

My drink appeared and I raised it to my face, eyes closed, breathing in the earthy scent of fresh Mexican cinnamon—misnamed, as most of it comes from Sri Lanka. My mother's one conventional domestic habit in my childhood had been to greet us—my brother, me, Kristen, and her sisters—with milk and cookies after school. The house on Capitol Hill had radiated an aroma of yeast, sugar, and cinnamon that no amount of remodeling could dispel.

Relax, a voice inside me said, followed by the voice of this afternoon's cruise ship tourist: *Don't worry. It will all work out.*

The music took me back, brought me forward, swirled and hipped and hopped around me. A little grunge, a little alternative, a little hip-hop, with a nod to Seattle's storied jazz scene, all blended together perfectly.

"Did you know Zak could play like this?" I leaned across the table, but the music drowned out my words.

For a woman who considered herself committed to her employees, turned out there was a lot I didn't know.

The band played way past all our bedtimes, but was so much fun I didn't mind. Still, I understood when at midnight, Laurel called a cab. The cooking starts early at Ripe. Another round in front of us, Kristen and I settled in until the band's last number. The lights rose and the crowd funneled out. Zak hopped off the stage and headed for our table, snagging a chair on his way. He twisted the lid off a bottle of water and looked at me expectantly.

"It was great," I said. "Honestly. Stupendous. The music in here is as good as the food in there."

He broke into a grin, took a long swig, then rolled the frosty bottle over the back of his neck. "When Kristen called, I hoped Tory would come with you. You've probably figured out . . ."

And the sweet tone in his voice told me he would never forgive me for keeping secrets. The house music was a touch loud for the conversation we needed to have, but I dove in anyway, hating every word I had to say.

"Zak, I'm so sorry." Alarms went off in his soft eyes, and I put a hand on his illustrated arm. "Tory's been arrested. They're going to charge her with Doc's murder."

Despite the low light, I saw him blanch, then color in anger and confusion.

"Wednesday morning," I continued. "When Doc and Sam were arguing, you knew who Doc was, didn't you?"

He dropped his gaze. "She thought we shouldn't tell you. I disagreed, but her family, her decision."

"Why was he in the Market? What did he want from her?"

He raised his big bald head, looked me in the eye. "She wouldn't talk to him and wouldn't tell me why. It goes back years."

Tracy had suggested as much, but surely the reasons were deeper than those he had tossed off. There was little end to the harm a parent could do to a child. *Not that.* The thought jolted me. Surely Tory would not have such strength and self-possession if she'd had an abusive childhood.

Zak spoke firmly. "Not what you're thinking. He never hurt her physically. I asked and she swore it. And you know Tory doesn't lie."

I let that one go and tightened my grip on his arm. "Help me help her, Zak. This is real trouble."

His Adam's apple throbbed.

"I'll need to talk to her friends and neighbors," I continued. "But I don't even know where she lives."

He took a long drink of water and wiped his mouth on his arm. "Up on Twelfth, in one of those old apartment houses. All the tenants are artists and they divvied up the attic into studio space."

The lounge was nearly empty now, the rest of the band well into tear-down.

"Gotta go." He scribbled an address on a cocktail napkin and shoved it into my hand. Two steps and he turned back, bent down, and kissed my cheek.

"Thanks, Pepper. With you on her side, I know it's all going to work out."

Thirteen

Pepper is hot. In fact, it's the most popular spice worldwide, accounting for more than twenty percent of the global spice market.

THE NIGHT LOOMED DARK AND QUIET—AS DARK AND quiet as the heart of a city gets at 1 a.m.

Eric came downtown to scoop up Kristen and dropped me off in front of my building. After one of those days that felt more like forty-eight hours than the standard twenty-four, all I wanted was to brush the chile-tequila-coffee medley out of my mouth and hit the hay.

"Where have you been, so late?"

My new pink shoes might have had springs in them, I bounced so high. "You scared the devil out of me." Tag had grabbed the door before it closed and now gripped both knob and door, as if I might try to shut it on him. I squinted at my watch. "What are you doing here?"

He was alone. No bike, no uniform—just one fiercely protective off-duty cop, hiding in the shadows like the criminals he loves to chase.

We all like someone watching out for us. But not when it's the wrong someone.

"Oh, never mind. Come on in. It's late and I'm tired, and I don't want to stand out here arguing."

He followed me up the wide stairway, trudging over worn planking yet to be refinished, under industrial fluorescents that hummed and winked. I'd long stopped asking the developer when he intended to make the promised upgrades. At least the umpteen Simple Green baths my neighbors had given the stairwell had banished the industrial perfume of engine oil and moldy sawdust.

Inside my loft, I slipped off my party pink shoes, dropped my bag on the kitchen counter, where it gave an ominous thunk, and got out tea. Chamomile, that herbal tonic of insomniacs, tastes like dried grass clippings to me, but our nighttime blend, heavy on jasmine and lavender, softens the edges nicely.

"Wow."

I snapped the infuser shut. Tag stood by the door, surveying my domain. I'd forgotten he hadn't seen the place since it was little more than a shell and he'd made an excuse of carting over a few things he was sure I'd left behind by accident.

"So that's where Mom's old picnic table went. You swipe it from her trash?"

Same old Tag. His mother, Phyllis, knows fun and funky furnishings delight me, though her own style runs to Bauhaus, Danish modern, and Frank Lloyd Wright. Phyllis adamantly—and rightly—refused to take sides in our divorce, but she keeps in touch. We shared a delicious afternoon at the Pink Door earlier this summer when she came down to check out the changes I'd made in the shop. I knew she approved when she ordered a bottle of Prosecco at lunch.

"It was a gift. As you know."

"Sorry. Truce?" He held up his hands. I nodded and raised my tea in question. "Coffee, if you don't mind. I'm on shift in an hour."

I got out a second mug and the French press and ground the beans. The aroma alone was enough to wake me up.

"Building's a firetrap," Tag said. "But it suits you."

It hit me like a grandfather clock striking midnight that in all the day's drama and trauma, I had never considered calling Alex. He was not the kind of guy you turned to for comfort.

Neither was Tag. Not at the moment, anyway.

I flopped on to the couch, surrounded by a sea of pillows, and propped my bare feet on the timeworn pine packing crate, a combination coffee table and blanket chest. Tag perched on the edge of a blond oak midcentury rocker—one I'd rescued from a neighbor's trash and re-covered myself, back in the bungalow days.

"You knew, didn't you?" I said. "That Spencer and Tracy suspected Tory?"

He stared at his coffee, avoiding my gaze. A fine white scar on the inside of his wrist pulsed faintly. His tell—so subtle no run-of-the-mill crook would ever spot it.

"You couldn't give me a hint?" I continued.

He slammed the mug on to the crate and stood. A big, fat drip rolled down the side. "You know better than that. You were a cop's wife for a long time."

"Too long," I said. He'd begun to pace but stopped to glare, angry but guarded. "Too long not to know you could have told me if you'd wanted to. You could have suggested they arrest her somewhere besides the shop. Do you know what kind of damage that can cause a business?"

Tag had a way—they might teach it in cop school—of making himself appear even taller than his six-two. He used the trick now, and I steeled myself to stay seated, to not let him intimidate me.

"You couldn't have kept that a secret, Pepper, and you know it."

The contempt in his voice stabbed my heart and my jaw. *Don't react. He wants you to react.* In HR, I kept secrets every day. Still knew things I'd never told.

"You'd have felt sorry for her," he went on. "One glimpse

of those golden brown eyes of hers and you'd have spilled your guts."

"No, Tag. You're the one with the weakness for golden brown eyes." Mine are hazel. I rose and opened the door.

He marched past me to the landing, where he paused for a look back. "You can't fix everyone's problems, Pepper. Don't even try."

His feet thundered down the wooden stairs. I stood in the doorway until I heard the front door of the building slam shut.

I dumped the now-cool coffee into a schefflera plant in need of a boost. Outside, lights whizzed by on the Viaduct like fireflies on speed. All around me, things were coming down and things were going up. On the pier, the Great Wheel stood, still.

I carried the empty mugs into the kitchen and headed for my sanctuary. Two corner walls of exposed red brick give the bedroom warmth, while light reaches the caramel interior walls from French doors opening to the living room. I fluffed the pillows against the black tufted leather headboard and turned down the black-and-white "orange peel" quilt, both vintage finds Kristen and I had snared on an island excursion. Grabbed a book from the bedside stack and climbed in.

Spice lore and history fascinate me. Jane left a few references at the shop; I keep an eye out for others, old and new. For my birthday, Kristen's youngest gave me her favorite volume about that intrepid Siamese cat, Skippyjon Jones, *Lost in Spice*.

Once or twice, I'd chosen a book from the library's online catalog without reading the blurbs and ended up with a hot romance. The Flick Chicks still razz me about the spicy movie choice that turned out to be pure porn. We had to stream *Julie & Julia* instead.

And then there were the Brother Cadfael mysteries by Ellis Peters. A loyal fan, my mother downloaded them all on the Nook my father bought her for the move south, and rereads them regularly. On her visit home last spring, she unearthed her collection of paperbacks from my brother's basement and presented me with the dusty box as if it were the lost Ark of the Covenant. Maybe I could learn a thing or two from the elderly crusader turned monk and herbalist. He always solved the crime. Always served justice, though he didn't always serve the law.

Don't even try, Tag had said.

What would Cadfael say? No medieval proverbs came to mind, just the wisdom of Yoda.

Do or do not. There is no try.

SATURDAY mornings, my mother shops and my dad golfs. Or fishes. Or drops by the dojo to spar with other ex-pat retirees and local kids. Or he stays home puttering with an extra cup of coffee.

In short, my father loves retirement. I dialed the number.

"Chuck Reece," a deep baritone said. Took me a minute to realize the voice was live, not prerecorded for playback in a later time zone. Costa Rica's an hour ahead of Seattle, or as he puts it, an hour ahead and a light-year behind.

"Dad, it's me."

"How's my baby?"

"Running fine," I said, knowing he meant both me and the 1967 Mustang he'd left in my care. Costa Rican roads require sturdier transportation.

Don't ask me what else we talked about. I only knew I needed to hear him. But I did not tell him about the murder or Tory's arrest.

And when we hung up ten minutes later, calm reigned. Like I'd been blessed by monks and warriors, and sent out into the world to wage peace.

The image was apt, as a host of winged things battled in my stomach on my approach to the shop. But all was quiet on the western front. No detectives, no CSI techs, no dead bodies. One or two bouquets, smelling not so sweet. I scooped them up and glanced around for a green waste bin. One stood open across Pike Place, where the day's featured farmers were setting up their tables and canopies on the cobbles, sorting potatoes, kale, and the first winter squash: the familiar deep green acorn, dark orange mini Hubbards, and warty gourd-like varieties that resembled lab accidents.

The frilly red-tinged kale tempted me, but it signaled a change of seasons I wasn't quite ready to concede. So I picked out a pint of blueberries, popping a few in my mouth as I crossed the street and unlocked my shop door.

Inside, the scents greeted me like old friends—sharp mingling with sweet, pungent paired with musk. My heart swelled with fondness for the glass display cases showing off antique spice gear, teapots, and other treasures. My eyes brimmed with joy at the sight of the open shelves, jars of all sizes mixed with colorful tins, new and old. In the grocery stores, uniform jars stand side by side like soldiers ready for inspection. Standardization has its value, but part of our shop's appeal is its funk and charm. I'd worked hard, with help from Kristen and the rest of the staff, to accentuate that over the last few months. My spice shop might not have the same century-long history in the Market as our competitor, but it has been here more than forty years. My whole life.

When I left Tag, I vowed to do only what I wanted to do, to surround myself only with things I loved, as I'd done here in the shop. To never again deny myself because of someone else.

But that didn't mean refusing to help others. I'd gone into HR to be of use, to put my skills to work protecting the people who did the real work.

In the law firm, as in most of the corporate world, that meant keeping a distance from the support staff I was responsible for. Make sure they got their regular evaluations, that their chairs fit and their keyboards didn't cause carpal tunnel, that they knew what their health insurance covered and what was excluded, that the vegan legal assistant got a cubicle far away from the carnivore who ate her daily hot roast beast sandwich at her desk.

And stay out of their personal lives.

But I ran the show now, and we weren't going to do it that way. Not anymore.

I set my latte on my chipboard desk and punched on the computer. Outside IT whizzes had scoured the law firm's databases during the embezzlement investigation, but computer forensics were Greek to me. The object: Spot what shouldn't be there.

After twenty minutes of fruitless clicking and scrolling, it dawned on me that Reed would breeze through this stuff. Why not wait till he arrived? I sighed in relief, then checked the shop's e-mail and posted a Facebook update showing off the squash at the farmers' stalls—with suggestions for tasty seasonings.

My phone signaled a text: *I'm at the front door—open up!*

"So I told Eric the whole story," Kristen said, skipping "Hello" and "How are you?" "And he says you were absolutely right to withhold the files until they get a warrant. They can't charge you with obstruction or whatever because you did what the law required you to do, as an employer."

Exactly what I'd told Tracy.

"But he thinks Tory's in real trouble. Bail will be high and she won't be able to make it. Plus she told the lawyer he sent that what's going to happen is going to happen, and there isn't any point trying to change the path of a wave. Whatever that means. Sounds like some goofy homemade Zen koan."

I stared at her. "Why?" Was Tory that naive?

Or that guilty?

Kristen shrugged, her eyes warmly sympathetic.

No doubt Tracy would arrive with that new warrant at the least convenient moment. We had to be prepared. "So here's what I want you to do," I said and set her to work copying every page in our personnel files, starting with Tory's. And in case his warrant stretched to our computer, I made sure our cloud-based backup was current and downloaded a copy of all our files to a flash drive.

Then I dashed to the newsstand for the morning paper and scanned it for Doc's obituary.

Nothing. Only the briefest news account of the death on my doorstep and an arrest. No names mentioned.

"Pepper, I just heard." Misty the Baker bounded onto the street, her chestnut braid partially protected by a flour-covered shower cap, her ticking stripe apron permanently stained with splotches of gluey residue. "When I saw Sam's beret fall out of the old guy's coat, I thought it had to be him. But Tory? I can't believe it."

Nothing to say to that. We hugged wordlessly.

I was brushing flour off my pants, staring at the phone in my other hand, when a bicycle pulled up beside me. "Go away, Tag," I said, not raising my head.

"I only want what's best for you," he said.

"No." I stopped brushing and reading, and looked straight at him. "You want what you think is best for me. But what's best for me is for me to decide what's best for me."

At the moment, of course, I was trying to decide what was best for Tory. I pushed the contradiction away.

"Pepper, wait." He dismounted and pushed his bike beside me, wheels and shoes clattering. The Market buzz starts early on Saturdays. I detoured around a young couple debating whether to shop or eat first and a chef I knew by sight carrying a large wicker basket chock-full of farm-fresh chard.

I glanced at my watch and broke into a trot.

"Pepper!" Tag called behind me.

"Pepper!" Another voice caught my attention and I stopped. Angie—or Sylvie? Hard to tell the orchard sisters apart.

"Tory didn't kill that old man, did she? She couldn't."

The girl's eyes were wide and worried, her olive skin blanched to the color of unripe wheat.

"She was so kind to all the street folks," she said, meaning the downtown residents and the homeless wanderers. Her sister appeared behind her. "She took one of them to the doctor once, and helped hand out Christmas gifts last year."

More details I hadn't known. Tory had also distributed hot tea with me on cold mornings. But past generosity didn't mean she hadn't slipped something poisonous into another cup of tea.

But I had no idea what that poison might have been.

A few feet away, wearing her usual haggard expression, Yvonne stood at the weathered wooden table in her stall tying up mixed bouquets and bundles of sunflowers.

I hoped the sunshine and foot traffic would burn through the pall hanging over us. Gloom and despair did no one any good—least of all Tory.

I dropped my phone in my pocket and squeezed the sisters' hands. "I'm sure it's all a mistake. Think of her every time you sell a jar of jam, and she'll be back here before you know it."

The first customers of the day were Detectives Tracy and Spencer. Tracy handed me the warrant, not quite suppressing his satisfaction. Spencer studied the makeshift tea service we'd put together, using Laurel's BrewMeister and vacuum pumps. I skimmed the warrant, then read it again slowly.

"The only personnel file listed is Tory's."

"Judge agreed with you that the others aren't relevant," Spencer replied. "Since you keep them under lock and key, and no one else had access."

"Maybe she's not a model employee after all," Tracy said. "Disciplinary notices, warnings."

They'd be disappointed on that front. The paper in my hand shook as I read further. "But why the computer? We need it."

"Judge agreed since it's available to any employee, we need to check for evidence. She had a key to the shop, and she did come in early." Tracy's voice held a note of triumph.

Score one for him, Tory had no job-related reason to use the shop computer, but I couldn't swear she hadn't used it without my knowledge.

I glanced at Kristen, who nodded almost imperceptibly. The original personnel files were back in place, the copies safely in her bag. "Follow me," I said, making a show of finding the special key on my ring and unlocking the drawer.

"I hope it's helpful," I said, extending the slim file to Tracy.

"You better not have tampered with evidence," he said. "I don't think you appreciate the seriousness of this matter."

I didn't give one hoot what Detective Tracy thought. Detective Tracy could go ahead and arrest me for all I cared.

He slipped the file into an evidence bag, packed up the computer, and nodded curtly before backing out.

"And I thought we had cramped quarters," Spencer said.

"You know what the Market's like. No space too small to be used for something."

She held my gaze. When she spoke, her tone was not unkind. "My partner comes on a little strong sometimes. But he's a good cop, and he isn't out for blood. He only wants to see justice done."

Me, too. But justice is what justice does.

Fourteen

It's a poor man who can't see the beauty in the sun and the wind and the rain. And it's a sad man who can't love his neighbor and always finds cause to complain.

—Traditional American folk song

MY STAFF STRAGGLED IN, BURDENED BY THE SAME GRIM, anxious mood that I'd encountered earlier. I sent Reed to the bakery, hoping caffeine and sugar would perk us all up.

Sandra's husband made a rare appearance, driving her downtown to haul in the new tea supply. He kissed her tenderly and gave her a big thumbs-up before heading home. Mr. Right, indeed.

I left the others to manage the shop and dashed home for my personal laptop. I hadn't dared bring it in earlier, for fear that Tracy would seize it, too. I got it set up and downloaded the backup shop files, so we could access our basic records, including the mailing list for our inaugural Spice Club shipments. A sweet plan: Once a month, we would select a small batch of herbs and spices to be used individually or in combination and send them, with recipes, to club members around the country. We'd already received several hundred subscriptions, and I wanted Sandra to double-check the numbers and confirm that we had enough spices, tins, and mailing supplies on order.

Our first shipment would include sample-sized packages of our fall blends. If they were going to arrive on time, we needed to hop to it.

I circled through the Market and environs, dropping off standing orders and last-minute requests. I steeled myself for quizzing about Tory and Doc, but to my surprise, the comments were brief.

"You think you know your people," the kitchen manager at the Pink Door said, shaking his head. He stuck his nose in a bag of Saigon cinnamon. "Perfect. I'll poach the late-season pears we found this morning and sprinkle this on, with roasted pecan syrup and a dollop of mascarpone."

"Sucks when an employee goes bad," said the grill cook at my favorite breakfast joint, a Market institution offering three floors of great food and views with the motto "Almost classy." "Glad you got my special pepper in. Gotta have it for the Sunday sausage."

Then it was a detour Down Under, a shortcut to the Hill-climb. I hopped down to Western, dropping off cinnamon for my Ethiopian baker friend, then swung by the Middle Eastern restaurant. The owner—a doll and a marvelous chef—thanked me profusely. He'd changed his menu recently and hadn't figured out yet how much spicery to keep on hand.

No one held the murder or arrest against the shop, thank goodness, contrary to Laurel's conjecture. But 'twas early days. If the charges went forward, Tory and Doc would be news for months, and my customers might view things differently.

They were wrong about Tory. I knew it. I rubbed my jaw beneath my right ear.

They had to be.

AFTER the last delivery, I hopped a bus and chugged up to Capitol Hill.

Seattle adores its neighborhoods. Each has its own distinct character. Even so, there are always pockets between communities, blocks that seem out of place, like this stretch of Twelfth Ave. Too far from Seattle University for the coffeehouses and funky shops that crop up near colleges, and too far from the Pike-Pine corridor to share in its recent hip revival. The neglected rental properties had not benefitted from their proximity to streets where classic older homes, small and large, testified to the Hill's history as one of Seattle's oldest and best-loved enclaves.

As I stood on the spidered sidewalk, staring at the sagging concrete steps and the bare bulb dangling between two front doors, their white paint peeling, I had a hard time imagining my put-together, casual-chic employee living here. But for young artists, low rent and studio space make a few creature discomforts tolerable.

An embroidered dish towel curtain fluttered in an open window. My kind of place.

"Hello," I called. "I'm Tory's friend." No response.

I picked my way up the steps. A few decorative tiles stuck to the risers, gray mortar exposed where pieces had gone missing. Choosing the left-hand door at random, I pushed the bell. Silence. I reached for the knocker, then noticed it was painted on—shadows, flaking gilt, and all. *Tromp l'oeil.* I rapped my knuckles on the peeling wood and called out again.

The other door opened a crack. A slim woman of about twenty with dark brown skin and a dozen waist-length cinnamon braids threaded with brass, copper, and silver beads peered up at me.

"I'm Pepper Reece. Tory Finch works in my spice shop."

The steely edge in her eyes softened. "The police have already been here. They had a warrant."

"Are you her roommate?"

Her braids clattered like pipes on a wind chime as she opened her door wider and motioned me in. "Neighbors.

We traded spare keys, just in case. But I never imagined this. My name's Keyra Jackson."

And I never imagined that an apartment in this decrepit manse could be so astonishing. Keyra worked with found objects. Trash. Bits and pieces scavenged from backyard scrap heaps and the industrial recycling center. She didn't look big enough to lift the truck fenders she'd made into bird wings, let alone wield a welding torch with precision.

"Are those bike parts?" I said, nodding at a pipe-and-board shelf unit crammed with odd clocks and lamps.

She handed me a bottle of ginger beer, brewed in the Market. "Yep. My specialty."

"A box grand?" The piano's surface gleamed, but when I pushed a chipped, dingy key, a painful twang sent the room's metal artwork into a discordant series of echoes.

"Rosewood. Biggest found object ever. Still trying to figure out what to do with it that won't forfeit my security deposit." Once a duplex, the building had been reconfigured so each side held separate first- and second-floor units. The doors had been relocated, stranding the piano.

Keyra had watched officers carry bags of evidence down from Tory's second-floor apartment, but had no idea what they'd found. "They said they were looking for evidence of poisoning. But even if Tory were a killer—which I don't believe—she's too smart to leave stuff lying around."

My thoughts exactly.

I followed her up the narrow stairs to Tory's place. Yellow tape warned, DO NOT ENTER. I brushed aside a wisp of hesitation. After all, Keyra had a key, and Tory needed our help—whether she was willing to admit it or not. Keyra opened the door and we scrambled underneath the tape.

As in Keyra's rooms, age-burnished woodwork set off plaster walls the color of antique crocheted lace. There, the resemblance ended. The younger artist had filled every nook, corner, and cranny with curiosities and, when those were full, hung bike wheels from the ceiling and dangled metal bits and gadgets from the spokes. "Visible storage," she called it.

Tory's place, in contrast, was almost minimalist. Jute rugs anchored each room. Classic carved walnut chairs and a matching loveseat slip-covered in creamy muslin created a tone-on-tone feel.

Except for the walls, a virtual crayon box. The abstracts I'd glimpsed in Tory's sketchbook had been studies of form and line. These pieces were the finished product, the real deal. Dozens of canvases—some framed, some flat, others wrapped—leaned against the walls. Recognizable objects or vistas were less about themselves and more about the play of color, line, and shape.

"I had her half convinced she was ready for a show," Keyra said. "In quality and quantity. She'll be the new artist of the year someday."

"Why the reluctance?" I asked, but Keyra shrugged.

This vivid joy and wild bliss from the woman who dressed year-round in tans and grays. Who wore the black-and-white shop apron like a mask. Was the limited color palette of her clothing a disguise? Did she see herself as muted and bland? Or simply save color for the canvas?

A twinge of guilt speared my jaw. Invading the privacy of a very private woman felt like a sin. But I wasn't the first—and unlike the searchers before me, I was here for her sake.

Tory's bedroom continued the tone-on-tone color scheme. On top of the antique oak dresser stood three photographs—the only personal touches other than the paintings.

In the first, a young girl sat on one of the marble camels at the Volunteer Park Art Museum. Every Seattle child has a similar picture, although the original statues are now protected inside the museum while modern kids ride concrete replicas outside. Even at three or four, Tory had radiated self-possession. She reveled in pure joy—no "Say Cheese!" smile for the camera.

The second photo was of Tory and Zak at the foot of a giant willow. He beamed at her and why not? Her head thrown back, her eyes dancing, her features were transformed.

In the third, Tory stood between a man and a woman. Doc in his late forties, a full head of hair the same color as Tory's. This past Wednesday morning on the street, Doc had refused to look at me, but I'd glimpsed the worry in his eyes. Now I knew why they had seemed so familiar.

But it was the woman who drew me in. She bore that same self-contained look as her daughter, and yet it was impossible not to see utter love and devotion in her eyes and the way her slim hand rested on the girl's shoulder.

I picked up the frame and opened the back. "Tory, age 7," written in fine black felt-tip. A woman's hand.

"Do you know her parents? Or where they live?"

Keyra's braids twirled as she shook her head. "I asked about the furniture once and she said it had been her mother's, in a way that made me think her mother had died. She never mentioned her father."

She pointed to a small desk that held cords and a printer. "They must have taken her laptop."

In the bathroom, I peered into the medicine cabinet and under the sink. Did the same in the tiny kitchen, but it's hard to know what you're looking for when it isn't there.

"How long were they here?" I asked.

"Not long."

Searching for something specific, quickly, without leaving a mess—or that nasty black fingerprint powder.

A rickety staircase out back led to the third-floor studio the four renters shared.

"They searched upstairs, too, but they didn't take anything," Keyra said, hugging herself.

Tory occupied the south dormer, lit by a single uncurtained window. The patterns of light shining through the diamond-shaped, multipaned glass echoed the abstracts she'd sketched in the shop.

Her brushes lay neatly on a paint-spattered table next to her wooden easel. On the easel itself stood a canvas, eighteen by twenty-four. If I read the underpainting right, we were gazing through a mullioned window onto a wooded ravine, shapes between the trees suggesting future shrubs, a distant view still blank. A more traditional landscape than the evocative-but-playful pieces I'd seen downstairs. Sadder. Deeper.

Keyra's puzzled expression said she knew no more about the place than I did.

A landscape of the memory, or of the heart?

JANE sat across from me, her back to the window. She'd told me once that the view of Puget Sound from her island home brightened every day. "Like Johnson said of London. When you're tired of looking at water and mountains, you're tired of life."

So here we sat at Maximilien in the Market, at a table for two set with white linen napkins and gleaming silver. But she had turned her back on the panoramic views, not even glancing at their reflection in the antique mirrors that lined the bistro's dark walls.

"Thank you for meeting me, dear. I know how hectic Saturdays are."

Jane's call had come as I was promising damp-eyed Keyra I'd do everything I could for Tory. She was calling from the shop, disturbed to find me not there. I'd hustled to meet her at her favorite table in her favorite restaurant. She'd already ordered oysters—untouched—and a bottle of her favorite white wine—half gone.

I gave the waiter my lunch order and sipped the crisp, dry Bordeaux that Jane had chosen, notes of citrus and flowers opening beautifully.

"I couldn't sleep a wink, wondering what to do." Jane's voice quavered. "What to say. I'm afraid I wasn't completely honest with you."

No surprise there.

"It's about when I hired Tory. Do you remember—I imagine she still comes in—Marianne is her name. About your height, a little fuller-figured. Always impeccably dressed. High cheekbones. Expensive highlights." She gestured, expressive fingers drawing a full, poofy bob ending in a point near the chin.

I squinted, trying to picture the woman. No luck. "What's she got to do with Tory?"

Jane fiddled with her fork, shuffling it from one side of her plate to the other, her knuckles swollen. "I've never been sorry I hired Tory. Excellent employee. Reliable. Keeps herself to herself, but nothing wrong with that."

I reached over and stilled her hand with mine.

"So I suppose I didn't check her out as fully as I should have."

A sudden chill struck me, and not from the air or wine. "Jane—"

Our waiter appeared at my elbow and I paused while he slid Jane's oysters aside and replaced them with her entrée.

"*Le confit de canard pour Madame.*" Duck. Jane is a creature of good habits.

"And for you, the *tartine*. Herbed goat cheese, Yukon gold potatoes, sliced Anjou pears, and fresh arugula on pastry." A rectangular French pizza, of sorts.

The service *chez Maximilien* is never rushed, and I've never minded—not in this atmosphere, with these views, or this wine list. But, knowing Jane needed the semblance of privacy, I sent our waiter mental "hurry up" messages as he refilled our wineglasses, clasped his hands, and smiled before turning away.

I leaned forward. "Jane, what does this woman Marianne have to do with Tory?"

Anguish filled her blue eyes and the fork trembled in her crooked fingers.

"I think she's her mother."

IN a flash, I'd pulled out my phone to see what I could find online about Marianne Finch, but the waiter's apparition at my elbow put the kibosh on any lunchtime research. I should have known it was a phone-free zone.

So here I was, tromping down Fifth Ave toward James, punching the tiny buttons.

Holy cow.

If Google was right, Tory and I had a lot to talk about.

If you didn't know better, you might think the King County Correctional Facility a low-rise office building. Home to lawyers and accountants. Or a nice, safe insurance company.

Not hardly.

"Oh, Tory. Help me help you," I muttered after wending my way through the security checkpoints, keenly aware that I was not the only person in the waiting room talking to myself.

Finally, a guard ushered me into the visiting area. Tory sat on the other side of a Plexiglas window. She did not rock a red jumpsuit the way she did her usual outfits. But while she looked a darned sight better than the other inmates, time inside had eroded her usual serene expression. The vee of her left hand massaged the front of her throat.

We picked up our handsets. A sign reminded me that calls could be recorded. Wasn't that a violation of privacy laws? Or did privacy vanish once you were arrested for murder?

"Everyone at the shop is worried about you. Jane, too. Has Zak been here yet?"

"I didn't want to see him."

"Tory, honey." The wall between us might as well have

been solid brick. "He told me about the two of you. I should have guessed. He cares about you. He believes in you. We all do."

Phone to her ear, she stared at her lap.

"They'll appoint a lawyer to represent you. Monday, probably," I said. Her head bobbed slightly. "Unless your mother hires one for you."

That got her attention. "I don't have a mother. I mean, she's dead. Fifteen years."

Then who, what? "So who is Marianne? The woman who got Jane to give you the job?"

Tory's brown bob spun. "She didn't get me the job. She told me Jane had an opening, but I'm the one who went in and applied. I got that job on my own."

I wanted to shake her. To ask why she was so stubborn, so foolishly insistent on doing things for herself. On pushing people away.

My walk-and-scroll session on the way here had not started out well—Google knew next to nothing about Tory or Marianne Finch. But then I'd hit pay dirt, sort of. With a name like Damien, it had to be him.

I hadn't had time for in-depth research. First came those annoying pseudo-directories that crop up on any name search. They rarely list any info other than a name and address, a school or professional license, and invite you to "Be the first!" to rank and review the subject.

Still, they provided an explanation for Doc's street name, and an office address on Pill Hill. And an unexpected opening into Tory's secrets.

"Tory, was your father actually a medical doctor? And if Marianne's not your mother, who is she?"

Her face slammed shut like a bank vault. "It's complicated."

"I'm listening."

She stared at the wall behind me. I stared at her.

"Look, I know your father came to the Market to see you.

I saw him following you, and Zak said he kept trying to talk to you. What did he want?"

"He wanted . . ." She shook her head. "It's no use, Pepper. I didn't kill him, but no one will ever believe me. Even Marianne. She's known me my whole life, raised me half of it, but I'm the only one who ever had the courage to stand up to him."

"I believe you." Tory was too intent on her career, on her life, to take someone else's. And now that I'd seen her art and her studio, I was even more certain.

Doc had been hassling her, but not enough to lead to deliberate poisoning. And the murder had to have been deliberate, planned in advance—there were no convenient poisons at Seattle Spice, the last place father and daughter had been before his death.

"Tory, tell me more about Doc. Your father. What was the conflict between you?"

A slow ragged breath escaped her. Her tongue flicked out over a dry spot on her lower lip, and she caught the lip in her teeth before the quivering became too obvious. "People think doctors only want to help them. They trust them. Sometimes they shouldn't."

"Do you know who killed him?"

She pursed her pale lips and said nothing.

I leaned forward, gripping the handset. "Look, I get that your father was controlling, and you wanted to live your life on your own terms, but I can't help you if you don't talk to me."

"It's no use," she repeated, her honey brown eyes hooded. "He always said he would do everything he could to stop me. I guess he finally did."

Fifteen

Seattle is to coffee as Alaska is to snow, New York to bagels, New Jersey to bad reality TV.

—Amy Rolph, *Seattle Post-Intelligencer*

AFTER LEAVING TORY AND THE JAIL, I CROSSED JAMES and drifted up Fifth, drinking in the cool air. The jail had reeked of despair, of fear mingled with innocence and guilt.

Inadvertently or not, Tory's last comment had revealed a killer motive.

But at twenty-eight, she was no kid. If the heart of the conflict was her art—my best guess—why care if her father approved or considered her a talent-free hack? She was doin'. No one gets rich working retail, and paints, brushes, and canvas are pricey. But while her building might have been hiding from the wrecking ball, she had clearly laid a good foundation.

At University, I veered under the marquee of the Fifth Avenue Theater. Its hand-painted carvings of dragons and lotus blossoms and the brass-knobbed red doors were as close to Beijing as I was likely to get. I stared at the posters for upcoming musicals, not quite seeing them. Why would

Doc follow his daughter, in disguise? Surely not just to criticize her career choice.

An artist, she was, to the core. Might as well ask her to change the color of her eyes—a color he shared. Did he not realize the depth of her commitment? Had he not seen her work?

A dead-end line of thinking. The better question: Who else might have killed Doc?

And that thought was equally disheartening. Because Sam was so obvious, and to those of us who knew him, so obviously incapable of such horror.

The midafternoon sun broke between buildings, reflected off the window of a men's clothing shop, and stabbed me in the eye. I blinked against the staggering light. Did I really know Sam any better than I'd known Tory?

At the corner, a weight as gray and heavy as the stone blocks of the buildings fell on me. But in Seattle, there's always a coffee shop nearby. Like many Seattleites, I have a love-hate relationship with Starbucks. Love how it's made coffee into community.

Love consistency, hate uniformity. Love that the original location, spitting distance from the Spice Shop, still beckons the hordes—they line up outside all day long. Love that it's made my city synonymous with great java. Hate that it swallows competitors whole instead of celebrating the entrepreneurial spirit that gave the company its start.

Love that serious coffee people nurture other business models besides the international chain. That there's room for unique roasteries and divine hole-in-the-wall coffeehouses where folks of all stripes debate blends and single-origin coffees, ethical sourcing, acidity and finish, drip versus French Press versus siphon pot extraction.

Sometimes you want an experience. Sometimes you just need a jolt.

I popped into the house of the green mermaid, ordered

a grande mocha latte, triple shot, and sank onto a high-backed stool in the window. The range of experience in the world—and our almost primal urge to compare and judge based on those experiences—has always intrigued me. Half the staff in this shop were twenty-somethings like Tory searching for their path.

At twenty-eight, my mother had been married with two kids. At that age, I was a new homeowner and a bride of one year. My parents hadn't considered Tag the best catch, but were smart enough to know voicing their opinions would only drive me away and wouldn't have kept me from the altar.

I'd been sure I'd found my path, before jumping off it and on to a completely different one at forty. And at sixty, my parents had taken another major turn, starting a new life in another hemisphere.

As a former supervisor of mine liked to say, it's a good thing it takes all kinds—because there are all kinds.

For the second time in two days, a sweep of black fabric caught my eye. *Oh, f-f-firetruck.*

"Pepper," the barista called in the nick of time. I grabbed my coffee, called "thanks" over my shoulder, and dashed out.

Where had he gone?

This time, the sight lines were wide open, and I spotted the tall, balding figure ambling down Union, Arf heeling beside him. No cops or cars in sight, so I dashed across Fifth against the light, mindful of the hot cup.

Where was Sam going? He set a brisk pace for a man well past sixty.

Hold on. Your dad is well past sixty, and he's in great shape.

But my dad hadn't spent decades on and off the streets, haunted by mental illness.

Sam crossed Union and headed up Fourth, me trailing.

We all have our own demons.

At Pike, Sam slowed for a white SUV.

"Hey, handsome. Going my way?"

He glanced down, startled, then grinned. "Hey, Miz Pepper. Take it easy. You outta breath."

"You've got longer legs than I do. Sit and keep me company while I drink my espresso."

"Nasty stuff. Puts hair on your chest."

"A chance I'll take." In Westlake Park, we settled on a bench near the granite arch and waterfall, Sam keeping a respectable distance between us. The ring and bell of steel drums on the far corner carried across the plaza.

"Haven't seen you around the last couple of days." I popped the lid off my latte and licked the coffee-tinged foam inside.

He tugged the lapels of his coat tight across his chest.

"Pretty upsetting about Doc," I continued. Lid back on, I took a sip, watching Sam from the corner of my eye. The milky caffeine hit my bloodstream like William Tell's arrow hit the apple. "Did you argue Thursday because he wouldn't let you have your spot, like we'd agreed? Or did something else happen?" Such frank talk was risky, but I figured I had to dive in and nab the truth fast. Sam would only sit in a public place so long.

"He showed up outta nowhere, acting like we should do what he said. Didn't bother earning respect." Sam's words echoed Jim's complaint about rules, and the resentment those who honor them harbor for those who violate them.

And they echoed Tory's veiled comments about her father's domineering nature.

"Those fool hobos," he continued. "Kowtowed to him. For no reason at all. He were like that."

If the online directories got it right, Damien Finch had been a cardiovascular surgeon. Not a profession for the weak-willed. My eyes narrowed. Who else, besides his daughter and the men of the street, had bristled at his unspoken expectations?

"You saw him Thursday morning, didn't you?" I hadn't

been the only one who'd recognized his beret. And I couldn't expect Misty to withhold her observation if asked. "Nice weather to go hatless."

He glowered but did not reply.

"Sam, they've arrested Doc's daughter. Tory."

Sam's eyes opened wide as the drawbridge over the Montlake Cut. "But she didn't do nothing, Miz Pepper. I swear—"

A movement across the park caught his eye. I turned to see what it was.

Two uniformed officers on foot patrol. Too far away to tell if they were watching us.

When I turned back, Sam had disappeared. Like a ghost, or a figment of my imagination.

But the terror on his face when I mentioned Tory's arrest had been all too real.

Sixteen

You can never get a cup of tea large enough or a book
long enough to suit me.

—C. S. Lewis

NO POINT SEARCHING. MAN AND DOG COULD HAVE
trotted down countless alleys or taken refuge in urban
alcoves known only to those in need.

Plus, if Sam didn't want to be found, he wouldn't want
to talk. And I'd invaded the privacy of people I cared about
enough for one day.

I sipped my coffee and watched the world go by, a virtual
parade of hipsters, youngsters, and oldsters. Couples, families, and gaggles of teenage girls. A few folks heads-down
on a timetable. Curious tourists. It was another one of those
magnificent Pacific Northwest days that make you forget
change is gonna come.

A trio of teenage boys on skateboards made a human
slalom course of the foot traffic. A young mother pushed a
stroller between me and the Arch, her toddler's chubby arms
reaching for the flowing water. "Fish, fish," the little voice
called.

And all of us dancing, in our own ways, to the Caribbean rhythms.

The patrol officers had vanished, too. I suspected they'd been too far away to recognize Sam, but just because you're paranoid doen't mean they aren't out to get you.

My stiff hips and shoulders needed a good wiggle. A stretch and the caffeine made me feel like a new woman, eager to get back to the shop before the effects wore off. I'd been racking my brain for a substance with both culinary and medicinal uses that could be disguised in a cup of tea, causing rapid death. Either there wasn't one, or I didn't know enough to spot it.

And Jane, my go-to source for all spice and herb arcana, had sworn that nothing in the shop could be used to kill. But in her distress, could I fully trust her?

When I reached First Ave, my feet took a detour.

To my surprise, Alex himself answered the restaurant's side door.

"Pepper," he said, booming. "My favorite spice girl."

"I was walking by and thought I'd pop in."

"Glad you did," he said, broad shoulders filling the partially open doorway. "We're in full prep mode . . ."

In other words, no time for interruptions. I understood—had expected as much—but felt a teeny sting of disappointment.

"About tomorrow," he continued. "Let me cook you dinner. Your place. Say, six."

"Six," I said. "Perfect."

Halfway down Virginia, I realized he hadn't even touched me.

EVEN for a Saturday afternoon, the shop was crowded. Sandra had a customer at her heels and a list in her hand, while Kristen conferred with a young woman poring over a stack of cookbooks. A short line had formed up front. I tossed my bag under the counter and helped Reed complete purchases and answer questions.

If Tory wasn't released soon, we might need to hire a replacement.

A tall, slender man with pale skin and neatly trimmed dark blond hair walked in, gawping as if he wasn't sure he'd found the right place.

"Welcome to the Spice Shop," I said. "How can we help you?"

"Uh, I just wanted to see . . ." His voice trailed off. Tag had told me about eager beavers who rush to the scene of gory crimes and car wrecks, seeking a vicarious thrill in other people's misfortune. This man made as unlikely a looky-loo as he did a serious cook.

His gaze lit on the tea cart. "Oh, this is where . . ."

I helped him out. "Seattle Spice has been here since the early 1970s, part of the Market's modern renaissance. This is our ever-popular signature tea." I poured a sample cup and handed it to him.

He took the cup reflexively, staring at it. The newspaper had said only that police were investigating a death on a Market sidewalk, with nary a mention of the shop, tea, or poison. But bad news spreads like Nutella on a hot crepe.

I picked up a box of twenty-four tea bags, hastily packaged less than twenty-four hours earlier. "For your wife? A souvenir from your trip to Seattle?"

"Uh, yeah. Sure. Perfect." Relief swept across his anxious face. I rang up the purchase. He lingered, examining the pepper grinders, running long fingers over stacks of books on salt.

"Whew. Thanks for the help," Reed said.

"'Bout time you showed up," Sandra said.

"It's been a madhouse." Kristen wiped up the oregano I'd spilled on the counter.

"Went to the jail." The building seemed to hold its breath for a millisecond, then let loose.

"How is she?" "What did she say?" "When will they let her out?" "You know that girl's innocent." The babble made it impossible to tell who said what.

"Whoa," I said, holding up my hands. The customer who'd bought the tea for his wife stared at me, wide-eyed, and headed for the door. *Parsley poop. I thought he'd already left.* With his long legs and dark pants, he looked like a colt that hadn't yet found its footing. "Thanks," I called out, hiding my embarrassment.

"She's fine—and not fine," I told my waiting staff once I was sure we were alone. "Safe, unharmed, terrified."

"Talking to you? Trusting you?" Kristen's questions held motherly concern.

I wiggled my fingers, speaking low. "Yes, and no. Sandra, do you remember a customer named Marianne? Friendly with Jane. Middle-aged, well-dressed, fancy highlights."

Sandra's brows dipped. "Yes, but now that you mention it, she hasn't come in for ages. What's she got to do with Tory?"

What to tell them? They genuinely wanted to help. "Not entirely sure."

"You're investigating, aren't you?" Kristen's and Reed's voices rose in harmony.

"Shushhhh."

Four or five thirty-ish women burst in, lugging heavy canvas shopping bags. A chunky blonde broke off from the huddle. "Is this where it happened?"

"Uh, outside," I said. A twitter of excitement chirped through the group. Kristen offered them tea.

Sandra rolled her eyes. "This has been going on all afternoon."

"Buyers or gawkers?"

"Buyers, thank goodness. Small items. Souvenirs. But not the spice tea. Actually, people aren't drinking the samples like they usually do, either."

Like my curious male customer, who'd left behind a full cup. I glanced at the newcomers.

"Okay, here's what we do." Taking a tip from how we helped our neighbors on cold-season mornings, we filled a tray with sample cups. "Be super schmoozy," I urged. Kristen winked, then circulated through the shop and out to the sidewalk.

With Zak out today, I took over reshelving the jars and tins. In some stores, herbs and spices are "serve yourself." We prepackage a few popular items, but years as a customer convinced me that Jane was right: The personal touch increases trust, and trust increases sales. And freshness counts.

My feet had just touched the floor, my hands on the ladder rails, when I heard a husky whisper. "They say poisoning's a woman's crime. Was it really poison?"

A short woman with a cap of blue-gray hair glared at me with glee. Or maybe that was distortion from her thick glasses. Oversized frames are back in style—I thought of Fabiola—but these had a genuine look of 1978.

"Yes," I whispered back. "We sell it by the ounce. How much would you like?"

A horrified expression chased across her frazzled features and she toddled away, muttering.

The steady flow of customers turned to a trickle by late afternoon, giving me a chance to snare Reed and explain what I needed.

He turned on my laptop. The annoying little network screen flashed on. "Cross your fingers that they haven't already disabled the network function." He punched buttons, sending the electronic mice inside the machine scurrying around, making connections. Minutes later, he'd installed a new version of Chrome and the familiar Bookmarks popped up across the top of the screen. "There you go. Your laptop is now synched with the office computer—bookmarks, history, and all."

I shook my head. He made it look so easy. "So can we trace the history?"

"Unless it's been wiped. But remember, we can only tell what sites were searched, not who searched them."

"That's okay," I said. "Just get me in."

"As soon as you start to follow the digital tracks, you change them. It's like quantum physics."

Right. The observer changes the object observed.

I was staring at the screen when Sandra stuck her head in the office. "All closed up, boss. Need anything before we go?"

"Any chance you could work Monday? I'll cover Sunday, but . . ." Tory usually ran the shop on Sundays, giving me a day off and Sandra two days.

She nodded grimly.

Reed called good night and the two of them left.

"I'll call you tomorrow," Kristen said. We hugged.

"Thank you. For everything. Eric, too."

I followed her out to the shop floor and locked the door behind her, then made myself a cup of hot tea. The origins of Jane's recipe remain a mystery, but the results are darned good.

Killer.

Back at the computer, I followed Reed's advice to take screen shots of each page that interested me and open it in a new window so I wouldn't mess up the history. What was I hunting for? I'd made most of the searches, to sites for distributors, growers, and competitors. And recipes.

Nothing out of place. No pages on "toxic properties of common herbs" or anything remotely similar.

I leaned back to think, the chair squeaking ominously. What about some kind of exotic bacteria? A year or two ago, several hundred people got sick after eating peppered salami. Experts theorized that birds or animals contaminated the pepper with salmonella during harvest or drying. The bacteria hibernated in the dried peppercorns, then reactivated when they came in contact with water, in the meat or in the diner's stomach.

Everything in our tea went through certified safe handling processes to eliminate risk. Besides, no one else had become ill, and bacteria wouldn't kill as quickly as Doc had died.

And if the autopsy had shown signs of such a thing, the Health Department would have closed us down faster than you could say "caraway."

If Doc died from drinking our tea, someone had to have added a toxic ingredient after the tea was brewed.

I banged my head on the back of the chair. *What was going on?*

The hot drink rejuvenated me, and for a split second, I wished I could smuggle some into the jail for Tory. I had absolute confidence in our tea, both before and after the tragedy on our doorstep. This tea had built the business and it would keep us going strong for years to come.

Take that, Detective Tracy.

Nothing on the computer indicated any research into poisons or toxic substances, but the police might find that evidence—or whatever they were looking for—on Tory's own laptop or phone. I had reached out a finger to power off when a web address caught my eye. The records page of the King County Superior Court website. I'd never had reason to search it, didn't know what was available online.

Another dead end. Turned out nonlawyers can search by case name or number and bring up a short summary of the file and docket, meaning a list of all papers filed and all orders entered. For pending cases, lay folk could check all scheduled court dates. But to see the records, you've got to fill out a request form online or at the courthouse.

So who had used the office computer and what records were they after? Judging from where this fell in the list of sites visited, and my admittedly vague recollection of what I'd looked at in the last few days, my guess was this search had been done Wednesday or Thursday.

Before Doc's death or after? And if Tory had run the search, what had she hoped to find?

The caffeine had worn off, and it was time to go home. Past time. I grabbed my bag and walked through the shop. Late-afternoon sun streamed in the clerestory windows, highlighting almost invisible particles in the air. "Incomplete thoughts," my late grandmother called dust motes. I made a mental note to get Zak up on the ladder; he was the only one tall enough to clean the cobwebs off the Indian silver chandelier.

I turned off the lights and let myself out, glad to have my key ring back.

And wondered, as I crossed Pike Place, weaving between farmers and daystallers loading up their trucks, who on my staff was hiding something from me. When I reached the Market stairs, I patted Rachel the bronze pig on the ham end and admitted I knew the answer.

But why? And how, how, how to get her to tell me.

Seventeen

Bees add flavor to honey naturally, through the nectars they forage. But you can spice up your honey with an infusion of lavender, mint, rose petals, or even a habañero.

TRACY HAD SAID HE WANTED TO TALK TO SAM. HAD HE figured out that had been the big man's beret wrapped up in the dead man's coat?

Of course, Sam hadn't written his name inside, like a kid going off to camp, and berets are hardly uncommon, even on bright sunny days in September. But Misty had recognized it, and no doubt others who'd gathered around the body Thursday morning had, too.

I paused, one hand on the iron stair rail, picturing the scene. Yvonne, the nurse, the orchard girls. The cheese maker. Who else?

Tag.

The Market had been his beat for years. He knew nearly every daystall grower and artisan, every shopkeeper, and every employee by name, and they knew him. And while Tag's charm and quick eyes might have doomed our marriage, they'd eased him into all manner of insights and confidences.

But the last thing I wanted to do was ask Tag Buhner for help.

To find Sam, I needed to get creative. Knocking on doors at each of the half-dozen low-income housing buildings in the Market would be time-consuming.

And anyone who knew where Sam lived would also know he wouldn't want to be found.

The Clinic would be closed, too, so no chance until Monday to find out about this medical referral the girls had mentioned, or fish for clues suggesting the nurse had twigged to Sam's presence at the corner when Doc died.

The only person who might know what help Tory had given Sam was Jim. Worth a chance. I retraced my steps and started up Pike Place toward the park.

Like many regular vendors, the orchard girls store their packaged products and displays in the Market's basement lockers but cart the empty fruit crates home to trade for full crates that relatives deliver from the family orchard east of the mountains. They were piling crates into their van, its engine idling, when I walked by.

"Angie, Sylvie, a quick question." They looked at me expectantly, eyes wide, faces sweet. "Thursday morning, did you see Doc—before he died, that is?"

One shook her head no; her sister nodded yes. "We'd already unloaded and you'd gone to park the van." She glanced at her sister, then back at me. "I picked up the last box and saw him coming down the hill. He was putting on that big coat of his, and he yanked that hat out of a pocket and jammed it on. Almost like he was putting on a disguise."

Exactly what he'd been doing.

"He got to your corner and peered in the front door." She paused.

"Then what?"

"Then a produce truck drove in and blocked my view. I

had to get my boxes into the stall and set up the displays. You know how it is."

Mornings in the Market, controlled chaos rules the cobbles.

"Did you see Sam?"

"No," she said.

"Yes," her sister said. "I'd totally forgotten. I was walking back from parking and I saw him headed for his corner. But I stopped to talk to Yvonne and the honey guy"—her cheeks flushed a lovely clover pink—"and like Angie said, there's all the trucks and commotion and stuff, so I don't know where he went or what happened. Ohmygosh, do you think . . . He didn't kill Doc, did he? I mean, he couldn't, but if it wasn't Tory—"

And that was the question.

Sylvie hadn't told the police she'd seen Sam, because she'd just remembered. But her sister . . . "Angie, did you tell the police you saw Doc looking in the window?"

"Uh-huh. The lights were on. I thought you'd come in early."

"Did you two ever notice Tory come in early? Or see her talking with Doc."

"No," Angie said as Sylvie added, "Not that I remember," one hand making a "who knows?" gesture.

A horn honked and we all jumped.

"Gotta go!" Angie waved at the impatient driver and the girls hopped in their rig and took off.

At the corner stood a logjam of the daystallers' rolling storage crates: one marked with a pair of dancing honeybees, another labeled HERB, and a third reading AYWA. Sounded like the name of an old ferryboat, or the abbreviation for some Washington town so dinky that I'd never heard of it.

I headed for the park. As usual, clusters of kids lounged on the grass and adults stood at the wrought iron rail, gazing at the wide world beyond. No sign of Sam or Arf. No surprise—no doubt gone to ground somewhere after their anxious flight this afternoon. No sign of Jim or his compatriots, either.

A couple left the rail, and I took their place. Raised my face to the last warm rays, the damp salt breeze moistening my cheeks.

What had I learned? That Sam had, in fact, been at my corner Thursday morning, and that he was terrified of something. And that Tory's arrest only added to his worries.

That Tory had not investigated poisons on my shop computer, but that she—I had little doubt it had been her—had tried to access court files.

Angie had spotted Doc peering into the shop, our lights already on. Had Doc gotten his daughter's attention? Had she talked to him?

Or, as Tracy believed, given him poisoned tea?

I needed to find out what court records Tory had requested. To ask her some good hard questions. And I had more questions about Doc and Sam, and what he'd seen.

All that had to wait. Business hours and weekends were cramping my investigation.

Bet that never stopped Brother Cadfael.

Eighteen

In ancient Greece, the word for cook, butcher, and priest was the same—magieros—and the word shares an etymological origin with "magic."

—Michael Pollan, *Cooked*

SUNDAY MORNINGS, LAUREL AND I MEET FOR BREAKFAST and a stroll. Sometimes Gabe joins us before dashing off to teenage boy world. This morning, we met at Louisa's on Eastlake, earlier than usual so I could walk off my Dungeness Crab Cakes Benedict before going to the shop.

"Where's Gabe?" I asked, leaning in for a quick hug.

"I took pity and let him sleep. He's studying for the SATs next weekend, and they played a double header yesterday."

"Win or lose?" The waitress set steaming white mugs in front of us, and Laurel reached for honey and cream. She's got doctoring her coffee down to a science.

"Two wins. He scored both goals in the first game, and the winning goal in the second. Fingers crossed for that soccer scholarship."

The high-backed burnished oak booths score big on charm, but they make my bottom ache, so I folded my fleece jacket into a cushion. We were seated, as usual, in a window booth, the clerestories tilted open to let in the morning air. Church bells rang for nine o'clock services. But this was my church: the communion of sinners and seekers over coffee, eggs, and the best Challah French Toast on the planet. Laurel was just perverse—or ecumenical—enough to order it with a side of bacon.

She slid the *Seattle Times* across the smooth, dark table, open to the death notices. " 'Damien Finch, MD, 64,' " I read. "Longtime Seattle cardiologist and surgeon; died Thursday, September 11, of undetermined causes. Services pending." The name of a prominent funeral home followed the notice.

"Sixty-four used to sound old," she said, cradling her mug. Her wild, graying curls flew free today, and she'd draped a soft purple paisley scarf over a loose white blouse.

Despite my makeshift seat cushion, I squirmed. "Pending. That must mean the body hasn't been released. They may not be certain about the cause of death yet."

"But they know the manner of death—at least, they think they do, or they couldn't charge Tory with murder." We called on the random smattering of legal and forensic terms gleaned from our marriages.

I pulled out my phone. The joint catered to a younger, more casual crowd than Maximilien, with less persnickety waitstaff. A toddler at the next table sang her ABCs over and over, stopping each time at P. I found the funeral home's website.

"Ah, here's the listing. No further details yet."

"But you already know who his family is. You talked to her, right?"

Last night, I'd followed up on the snooping that had given me Damien Finch's profession and his clinic address, and dug around in the state's online property tax records. No property listed in Damien's name, but Marianne Finch owned a house in Seattle's tony North Beach neighborhood. The area overlooks Puget Sound north of Golden Gardens, an urban refuge at what had been the end of the streetcar line a century ago. It boasts sunset views and classic older homes, many waterfront, and priced to match. Off my turf, but I suspected I'd be getting to know the neighborhood a lot better real soon.

"Yes, but—" The waitress refilled our mugs, and I waited until she'd gone, speaking in a hushed voice. "She says she didn't kill him, and I believe her. But she's convinced no one else will, and it's taken the fight out of her."

"You have to persuade her. Justice will prevail."

"She doesn't believe that." But why? A woman who spontaneously gave old men hot drinks, who helped them find medical care—what left her convinced that justice was outside her grasp?

Mentally, I replayed our conversation. Tory had said her father always got what he wanted. But he hadn't: He'd wanted to talk, and she had refused.

No, that wasn't quite what she'd said: "He always said he would stop me." And what had Jim said of Doc? "Interfering after he's dead."

What did Tory think her father was after? What was so awful between them that she refused to listen?

Legally, all she had to prove was a reasonable doubt about her guilt. But to stop this train wreck sooner rather than later, I needed to give Detectives Tracy and Spencer another suspect.

Who?

What one detail explained her doubt? And what details would prove her innocence?

"I'm seeing Alex tonight," I said as the waitress slid hot plates in front of us. "He's making me dinner, at the loft."

"Now you're cooking with fire, girlfriend."

I grinned and picked up my fork.

AFTER breakfast, we headed for Gasworks Park, built on a point of land at the north edge of Lake Union. The old gasification plant, abandoned decades ago, offers water, space, vistas, curious structures, and cool public art. Plus the gasworks, all rusty obsolescence. The boiler house had been turned into a covered picnic shelter, and the compressor thingy a children's play barn, the original equipment cleaned up and brightly painted.

My dad used to bring us here to fly kites on the hill. I still love standing in the middle of the Sun Dial—a marvel of bronze, concrete, water, and inlaid shells near the lakeshore—and seeing where my shadow falls. Today, though, a woman in a ministerial purple robe stood in the center in front of a young couple—he in a dark suit, she in a short, lacy white dress. Wedding guests ringed them.

We paused, smiling. Who doesn't smile at a wedding?

"Keep the pressure on," Laurel said when we got back to my car. "Keep asking questions. Keep seeking the truth. And call me if I can help."

I dashed home, parked the Mustang, and trotted up the steps from Western to First. Hurried past the shops. Waved to my buddies at the newsstand and the corner florist and hustled to our front door.

Head bent over his phone, Reed lounged against the wall by the door. Where the CSI detectives had taken prints and I'd scrubbed black print powder out of pink stucco.

When would this horror end so we could get back to normal? With a full staff, no suspicious glances, and no rumors or gossip? Justice would prevail, but sometimes it needs a kick in the rear end.

I switched on the lights and got the cash drawer ready while Reed started the tea. It had been ages since I'd worked a Sunday. Busy in summer, slowing as the weather turns, Sunday sales trend toward gifts and prepackaged items. Thank goodness Sandra had been able to create enough replacement tea to keep us going for a while.

Did Tracy have any idea what havoc he'd wreaked?

Wrought, wrocked—whatever. He wouldn't care. Did our insurance policy cover the cost of replacing product and equipment seized as part of a criminal investigation? I made a note to check.

An hour after opening, we had the place to ourselves for a few minutes.

"Reed, what do you know about Tory outside of work?"

He wiped up a spill on the tea tray, avoiding my gaze. "Not much. You know how she is."

"And I know how you are. Mr. Social Butterfly."

A smile teased his lips. "I run into her sometimes. At clubs, or on the Hill."

"With Zak?"

His expression brightened but quickly became guarded. "Yeah. They're great together. But she thought you might make one of them quit, so she wanted to keep it quiet. To prove it wouldn't interfere at work."

What contradictions we all are. Tory projected such self-confidence, but didn't show her artwork, and feared letting her boss know she'd fallen for a coworker.

I consider myself open of mind and heart. Had I known, would I have been as understanding as I hoped?

Dating. That conjured up an image of Alex. I smiled and tucked it away for later.

"She ever talk about her family? About Doc?"

Reed swept his bangs off his face. They promptly fell back down. "He came in once. You weren't here—might have been a Sunday. She listened, then told him to leave."

"How was he dressed?"

He tilted his head. "Normal, now that you mention it. Without that funny coat and hat."

Puzzle pieces shifted in my mind. He knew where his daughter worked—possibly from Marianne. But when he had something to say to her, he came here—suggesting he didn't know her phone number or where she lived.

But she didn't want to talk to him. So had he started watching her? Following her. Stalking her, in hopes she'd give him another chance to plead his case.

What could be so important?

"Do you remember when?"

He thought a moment. "Mid-August. Right after summer school ended."

A month ago. That fit—we'd started seeing Doc just before Labor Day. He had to know Tory would see through the disguise. Still, it gave him an opportunity to watch. To keep an eye on her.

The front door opened and a pair of women—sisters, I guessed—sauntered in. They'd come from the Sunday chef's demo—a local chef showing how to make a meal from the day's tastiest offerings—and wanted seasonings to help them re-create the magic.

Moments later, the door burst open and in strode Zak, all six-two and two hundred pounds. The sleeves of his black T-shirt rode up on his bulging upper arms, showing off enough ink to have kept Madame Lasorda, the Market's tattoo queen, busy for weeks.

His eyes looked wild and a bit frantic.

"Zak. Stop." I put my hand on his chest. "Breathe."

I left the customers to Reed and headed to the back room, Zak on my heels. I shut the door, then leaned against the small sink that stood between the office and the restroom, clearing the way for Zak to pace. From toilet to desk, two and a half strides.

"She won't talk to me. I understood when she sent me away yesterday, but two days in a row? We're supposed to be a couple. Why is she shutting me out?"

"Zak, Tory's a complicated woman. This is all really complicated."

The pain on his face spoke volumes about complication. His pacing slowed. "I've got to help her."

"Sit." I pointed to my desk chair. "Tell me everything you know about her family."

"It feels wrong to tell. She's so . . ."

"Private," I said. "It feels like betrayal. It's not. It's love." His eyes told me I was right.

He sat, big bald head in his hands. "She grew up in the north end. Only child. Her mother died when she was a kid."

"Sounds tough. Her father remarried, though, right?" Had Doc worn a wedding ring? I pictured his hand, lying open on the sidewalk, but my memory homed in on the Spice Shop cup rolling out of his fingers. Besides, lots of married men don't wear rings. Tag never had.

"Yeah. Two older stepbrothers she barely knows. She never said much about her stepmother, but I got the impression she understood Tory's problems with her father."

"And what were they? Time to come clean."

He stared at the floor, shaking his head, and I realized I had two employees in crisis, not one. I tried to think like a father. Like a widowed doctor with one precious child.

At last, he raised his eyes. "I can't understand why a parent would stand between his child and her dreams. My folks hauled me to piano lessons and band camp. Bought me my first guitar. My dad took me to concerts of bands he hated because I loved them. Though he ended up kinda liking them, too."

"Because," I said in Universal Mother Mode, "parents fear the things they think will hurt their children. Like bad marriages or dropping out of college. Or coming out of the closet." Although Reed's parents seemed cool about that. "And choosing careers in the arts, where only the very lucky reach the level society values."

"I know. But I don't *get* it, you know?"

I probed, but he knew nothing more about Doc and Tory. "The Martinez girls said Tory helped Sam when he needed some medical attention. Did she take him to the Market clinic?"

A spark lit up Zak's eyes. "Was it Sam?" he said. "I never knew. No, not the clinic here. She took him to her father's office."

WHEN one of the city's premier chefs promises to make you dinner, what do you do? Prepare for magic. Stick white in the ice bucket and open red. Set the table with your favorites: Fiestaware, white linen napkins scored way on sale at Sur la Table, and my grandmother's sterling, Carillon by Lunt. And French wine tumblers. My style is nothing if not eclectic.

Step back and admire it all. Adjust that one stray spoon.

And slip into your favorite dress. I chose sleeveless with a deep V-neck and a long, swirling, angled hemline, in shades of blue shot through with silver. It went well with my dark hair, scrunched into loose curls rather than my usual spikes, and brought out the specks of blue in my hazel eyes. I added a sweeping line of ultramarine above my black eyeliner, and donned silver loop earrings and bracelets from the import shop.

What music? I had no idea what Alex liked. My iPod playlist—meant for walking—might be a tad raucous for a romantic evening at home. So I loaded a few mellower faves into the CD player: Chris Botti's trumpet genius, Cold Play, classic Pearl Jam. And for the quiet side, Gloria Estefan's *Standards.*

Some people are more "ish" than others when it comes to time, so when my eyes kept flicking to the schoolhouse clock on the wall, watching the hands tick tick tick past six, I told myself to chill. Poured another glass of water and picked up the Brother Cadfael mystery I'd started Saturday night.

Put it down and rearranged the display on the coffee table. My heart, the clock, and the music all beat in different rhythms.

At six twenty, I decided something must have happened at one of the restaurants, or to his car, and double-checked my phone for a message or a text. Nothing. "Still on?" I typed.

Then just to be sure, I left a voice mail.

At six thirty, I opened the white, a lovely Italian Verdicchio. A shame to drink it alone, but more of a shame to let it sit on ice, cold and lonely. At six forty-five, I was convinced he'd been in an accident, and at six fifty-five, I broke open a box of Italian flatbread crackers and sliced up prosciutto. Turned the knife to yesterday's leftover melon and it slipped.

"Yow." They say dull knives hurt worse than sharp knives, and they're probably right, but that's no consolation when you see the skin on your forefinger split open, a thin red stream leaking out. I stuck my finger in my mouth, then made a soft fist and shook it in pain.

Was Alex hurt? I wondered, rummaging in the bathroom for a Band-Aid.

I wiped blood off the butcher block and refilled my wine. Worry mingled with anger and embarrassment in an uneasy stew. I felt guilty feeling mad—what if he wasn't okay?

Odds were Alex was just fine. He's the kind of man who is always fine.

The more time that passed without a word, the worse I felt, getting stood up in my own house.

At seven thirty, I pronounced myself ditched. I tossed my sparkly blue dress into the wicker laundry basket and pulled on black yoga pants and an oversized white I ♥ COSTA RICA T-shirt.

Saturday after work, I'd plunged into the adventures of Brother Cadfael, falling asleep moments after finishing *A Morbid Taste for Bones*. Now I fished in my mother's box for the next—*Monk's Hood*? No—that came later. *One Corpse Too Many*.

I sighed. How many are too many? Depends whether

you're a shopkeeper or a medical examiner, I guess. Or a detective. Hadn't Cadfael, in his callow youth, left a woman behind, gone off to battle in the Holy Land, and forgotten to return for a decade or two?

Alex Howard, I thought as I speared the last chunk of cantaloupe with a sterling silver fork, my cut finger throbbing, had better have an excuse so good.

Nineteen

With all the coffee shops in Seattle, you'd think the people would walk faster.

—Paul Levine

"LOOK WHAT THE DOG DRAGGED IN," MY FRIENDLY espresso maker said, in her singsongy Ethiopian accent. Her dark eyes laughed.

Not with me. At me.

"Better make it a triple." I'd need that much caffeine to climb my way up the Market steps. Today might be an elevator day.

I wasn't hungover on alcohol—although I had drunk my share of the Verdicchio before switching to decaf spice tea. Call it the aftereffects of too much emotion and too many late nights for a woman with an early bell. Alex's no-show had triggered a surge of negativity, a virtual replay of every time I'd ever been stood up, let down, or otherwise tossed around. At least I'd been home, where I could climb into my jammies, rant, rave, stalk, stomp, and cry without anyone knowing. Anyone except for my sweet neighbor who came over once to check on me, using his own white linen handkerchief to dab at my eyes and telling me any man who missed a chance with me was a fool not worth crying over. "Present company excepted," he'd said with a wink.

Alex had sent a text at half past twelve. I'd glanced at the phone on my nightstand, read the message—*So sorry. Friend showed up unexpectedly for the wine show. I'll make it up to you*—and returned to the cold comforts of Brother Cadfael's Benedictine Abbey.

Clutching the sacred caffeine, eyes scraped raw, cut finger throbbing, stomach sour with that hollow feeling left by tears of disproportionate anger and hurt, I stepped out of the elevator and lumbered through the Main Arcade to Pike Place. To the hustle and bustle of Monday morning, the clatter of wheels on cobble, the stuttery clang of metal doors creaking up their rollers and latching loudly into place. Waved to the butcher, the baker, the candlestick maker.

And stopped dead in my tracks.

What in blue blazes was my Mustang doing in the middle of the intersection? Off-kilter, its right front wheel perched on the curb next to the Spice Shop, blocking traffic and forcing peds to detour.

I broke into a trot. Not so easy with a tote on one shoulder, coffee in hand, and cobbles underfoot, but—my car . . .

Next thought: My father will kill me.

Third thought: But I'd parked it yesterday, in the secure, covered lot at my own building. How . . .

Fourth: Why does the bad stuff always happen on Tag's shift?

On foot, his wheels leaning against the side of my shop, Mr. Bicycle Cop surveyed the shiny dark blue Mustang. My father had pampered it for more than forty years, since he came back from Vietnam, bought it from his commanding officer's widow, and drove it from San Diego to St. Louis to Seattle, where it had lived a safe and happy life ever since.

"It's not as bad as it looks. And it's not your car."

"Well, yeah. It's my dad's." Tag knew that. Up the hill, Olerud got off his bike and crouched, studying the ground.

"No, it's not." Tag pointed at the plates. "And they didn't pull a switcheroo. See the venting behind the door? Slightly different model."

Sure enough. Tag might prefer two wheels, but he has an eye for automotive details.

"So whose is it? And how did it get here?" The heat of the cup stung my cut finger. I switched hands.

"Dunno yet. Glove box is locked. Waiting for dispatch on the registration." Tag went on. "Eyewitnesses saw it parked up the street, right below First. Just lucky it hit the curb where it did."

But for the curb, it would have rolled into Pike Place, plowed through the street filled with farm stands and foot traffic, then smashed into the daystalls on the opposite side. I shuddered and glanced back up Pine.

"The hill doesn't look that steep."

"Pepper! You're okay! We wondered what happened when we saw your car."

Angie, with Sylvie right behind her.

"It's not mine," I began, catching sight over their shoulder of Yvonne's worried face. "I'm okay," I called to her. "Nobody's hurt."

The girls looked relieved. Yvonne nodded curtly and turned back to her sunflowers.

"Towing unit's on the way," Tag said. "They'll check it out." Olerud beckoned and Tag trotted up the hill.

"Poor, sweet car," I uttered, giving the Mustang a consoling pat on the hood. The mere sight of that front bumper scraped and bent hurt. Whoever owned it was in for a nasty shock.

The tow truck came and went before we opened, leaving no sign of a problem except a gouge in the concrete. Zak arrived, less bedraggled than yesterday, but no less unhappy. I rubbed his arm in a sisterly way. "I'll talk to her."

And we got down to the business of selling spice.

Half past ten, the cavalry arrived.

"Heard you had a little trouble this morning," Detective Tracy said, a button on his camel-hair jacket hanging loose.

"No. Oh, you mean the car. Well, Officer Buhner knew right away that it wasn't mine, and it didn't hit the building, thank goodness. But what's a runaway car got to do with you?"

"Maybe nothing." He scanned the upper shelves as if he expected prehistoric creatures to emerge. "But anything out of the ordinary that happens near the scene of a homicide catches my attention."

Made sense, but I didn't have to like it.

"It's odd," Tracy said, "that a car nearly identical to yours would plunge down the street and crash to a stop at your front door. And a vintage car at that—not your average Toyota Corolla."

"Have you found the owner yet? He must live nearby, if he parked here overnight. But I've never noticed another car like mine in the neighborhood."

"Belongs to a winemaker from Walla Walla staying with a friend nearby. Came in for a wine show or whatever they're called, and parked on the street. Not the brightest grape in the bunch."

That car, overnight on a downtown street? I had to agree. "Good story to take home and tell at tasting parties," I said. "But it obviously has nothing to do with Doc or Tory."

He gave me that enigmatic smile that makes me want to strangle him. "Nothing's obvious, when it comes to Ms. Finch."

True enough. "Doesn't she have to be arraigned soon?"

"Within fourteen days of filing charges," Tracy said.

"Meanwhile she sits in jail?"

"The smart ones start working on their defense. If they have a defense."

If blood could boil.

A few minutes later, I stepped outside to gauge the foot traffic. A typically slow Monday. Spencer, looking like she'd just stepped out of Nordy's, emerged from Upper Post Alley and stopped on the sidewalk, studying her notebook. A moment later, Tracy joined her. They spoke briefly before crossing the street.

More witness interviews, I guessed. Looking for more evidence implicating Tory.

Leaving me to find the real killer.

IN its early days, no doubt the King County Courthouse conveyed authority and dignity, and a heavy dose of civic pride. Built of pale gray granite quarried north of the city, with the decorative frills typical of the early twentieth century, it had suffered mightily from its 1960s modernization, the early grandeur not yet completely restored.

My last trip inside the courthouse had been to finalize my divorce. The present errand was only slightly less unnerving.

"I'm here to pick up some records," I told the woman behind the counter in the Clerk's Office. "Online request. For Tory Finch." Fingers crossed that no one asked for ID or cross-checked the jail roster.

I waited on a long high-backed bench, phone in hand. A voice mail from Laurel, reminding me of Flick Chicks tomorrow night. A text from Tag telling me he shouldn't tell me but they'd located the owner of the other Mustang and all was well. Sweet of him, though Tracy had already spilled the beans.

And one from Alex, saying he'd swing by the next chance he got.

"Ms. Finch?" The clerk had returned to the window, but held no documents. "Sorry, but your records haven't been copied yet. We're shorthanded—one out sick, one on maternity leave. Thursday's my best guess."

"Thursday?" What if they figured out by then that I wasn't Tory? She was in enough trouble already. But begging would get me nowhere.

"Or maybe Friday. We'll call you."

A block away at the jail, an eery quiet filled the waiting room. Slow day. The guard sang out my name a few minutes after I cleared security.

Tory fidgeted in the orange plastic chair, her expression a mixture of fear and relief.

"I thought hard about what you said. I'm meeting my public defender this afternoon." She gripped the handset like the pull cord on a parachute. "I didn't do it, Pepper. Say you believe me."

"I believe you." We locked eyes. "Zak's beside himself. Why don't you want to see him?"

She bowed her head, resting her forehead on the heel of her free hand. "It's complicated," she said, echoing my words to him.

"You do love him, don't you?" The picture in her bedroom said yes.

"Of course." Her head snapped up. "But he's . . . he's ready to settle down. Get married. Start a family." The flush in her cheeks reminded me of the dried rose petals we buy from an herbalist in Carnation. "And I want that, too. But I've got things I need to do first."

That bite in my jaw again. *She's not you, Pepper, waiting for Tag. Waiting too long. She's still young.*

"Like proving yourself as an artist. Like proving your father wrong."

Her body tensed. My hand rose and reached toward hers, toward the Plexiglas separating us, willing but unable to breach the divide. Her golden brown eyes, so like her father's, welled but she held back the tears.

"He wanted me to be an X-ray tech. Called art a dead end. But it's all I've ever wanted to do."

"He was trying to protect you."

"No. He never believed in me."

No point offering false reassurance. "Tory, who could have killed him? Who wanted him dead?"

Her shoulders sank. "I keep asking myself. My

stepmother? After all these years? He was good to her, far as I could tell." She tilted her head, brow furrowed. "When he was trying to talk to me, he said something about the clinic arrangements, making things right. But I can't remember everything he said—I was too upset."

"Who else could have been that angry with him? Someone burned in a business deal?"

"He always seemed to be at odds with someone. Doctors always think they're right, you know? But who? You gotta be pretty pissed off to plan murder. Especially—I mean, you know, what would be the point?"

Before I could ask what the heck she meant, she went on, knuckles white against the black handset. "Pepper, what do I do?"

"First, prove you didn't kill him. Then live a full life. Marry Zak and have funny little bald babies who can sing and rock, and draw and paint. Make art. Make love. Make dinner. Make your life all the proof you need."

Silence fell, as if everyone in the visiting room had heard us. Then the chatter resumed.

She'd already hung up her handset when I remembered my other question. "Tory, did you take Sam to see your father?" Had something gone wrong, explaining the animosity between the two men?

The guard gripped Tory's upper arm firmly, leading her away. "What?" I thought she said. I repeated myself. She said something I couldn't hear. I tried to read her lips as she said it again.

But it made no sense. When shop talk turned to sports, Tory turned a blind eye and a deaf ear.

So why tell me to go see Ken Griffey, the Mariners' long-retired All-Star centerfielder?

Twenty

In the first century AD, Pliny the Elder reported that Arabs fooled their Mediterranean neighbors into believing that cassia, cinnamon, and other spices came from deep in Africa, to keep the trade to themselves—and keep prices high.

—Ian Hemphill, *The Spice and Herb Bible*

FIRST STOP AFTER JAIL: A LATE LUNCH. I DROPPED INTO the Thai place near the courthouse, half expecting to see the Dynamic Duo, but no such luck.

Plenty of other cops, in uniform and out. Several smiled blandly, as if unsure whether they knew me.

At the next table, a young woman wearing a leopard print tunic over black tights, gray leg warmers, and fuzzy boots pulled a pen out of her felted wool bag. A little early in the year for such a warm outfit, given the clear skies and temps in the high seventies, but better than the UGGs and sundress combo I'd spotted over the weekend. Her companion, a dark-haired man of about twenty-five, favored green camo, a red bandanna tied around his head Jimi Hendrix style. No eavesdropping, I swear, but their voices tingled with excitement as they filled out the application for a marriage license.

Making me all the more determined to get Tory out of jail.

Outside, I called the Public Defender's Office. Tory's attorney was with a client, so I left a voice mail. A supportive employer wanting to help had to be a good sign.

Next on my list: Scout out Damien Finch's office.

Like Rome and San Francisco, Seattle is a city of hills—although our forebears tore one down in a series of cuts and scrapes known as the Denny Regrade, and leveled a few other high points. In my skirt-and-heels days, I'd joined the ranks of office rats who scurried uphill from First to Sixth by escalator. My own office building could be entered on Third and exited on Fourth, no sweat.

But the escalator route still leaves a trek to cross I-5 and scale First Hill, Seattle's first "good" neighborhood, once nicknamed Profanity Hill but now known as Pill Hill. Medical offices had long replaced the railroad tycoons' mansions, orbiting the hospitals like moons circling Jupiter.

Despite last night's self-induced trauma and this morning's Mustang shock, my conversation with Tory left me hopeful.

And the green curry with eggplant left me fortified.

As usual, the sight of the Cathedral and its twin towers struck a deep chord, and medieval harmonies sounded in my mind's ear. (Not a phenomenon I confess to just anyone, not wanting to spend the rest of my days locked in a tiny room in the psych ward.) The trees had begun changing color, scattering rubies, amber, and gold nuggets on the sidewalks and narrow, car-lined streets.

The crew was already at work at Jimmy's Pantry in the Cathedral basement. More volunteers would arrive later. Between four and five o'clock, they'd serve a hot meal and distribute bags of food. I breathed in the homey scent of a vat of simmering chicken stock. Just like a soup kitchen ought to smell.

I handed the director my monthly offering—a bag of herbs and spices, outdated but perfectly usable. She thanked me with a radiant smile.

"A quick question," I said. "Do you know a man named Sam? Tall, black, sixty or a little older. Usually has a dog with him. One of those black-and-tan terriers." I'd never had a dog, didn't know much about the different breeds.

"Arf. He's a mix, mostly Airedale, I think. Sam comes in quite often, usually with Jim, the man with the burns." She tilted her head, trying to recall. "Now that you mention it, I'm not sure I've seen Sam in a few days. Jim might have come in alone yesterday."

"Any idea where Sam lives?"

She shook her head. "Some of our clients don't like to stay put. Thanks for the spices." She picked up the bag and headed back to work.

I'd pushed my luck and been dismissed.

THE address Google had given me belonged to a glass-front building near Swedish Hospital. I held the door for a gaunt man rolling a walker and he flashed me a toothy smile. Inside, a signboard listed the building's occupants. Before I could read it, a glass door opened and a man in a white coat, stethoscope around his neck, held it for a slim, sixty-ish woman in a cherry red suit. His sandy hair tinged with gray, rosy cheeks, and round glasses gave him the look of Bill Gates crossed with Sunny Jim, the peanut butter poster child who'd smiled at freeway traffic from atop the factory for decades, until a fire destroyed the empty building a few years ago.

The cut of her pencil skirt and collarless jacket, along with her tastefully clunky gold bracelet and necklace, spoke of a woman accustomed to dressing for the evening, not the office.

The door opened again and a tall, thin man emerged.

Vaguely familiar, but I couldn't place him. He kissed the woman on the cheek, nodded curtly to the doctor, and hustled out the door.

The woman laid her long, red-tipped fingers on the doctor's sleeve, saying something too low for me to hear. He flushed uncomfortably. And I knew beyond a reasonable doubt as the highlighted blonde in the spiky red heels swept past me without a glance that this was Marianne Finch in action.

She who hesitates loses her mark. I gave her a moment, then followed, brain racing.

I had given her a moment too long. She slid gracefully into a yellow taxi idling in the covered drop-off zone.

As she did, her eyes met mine.

Back inside the lobby, I read the names stenciled on the door Marianne and the doctor had exited. I covered my mouth to stifle a laugh.

"Pepper Reece. Any chance for a minute with Dr. Griffey?" I asked the receptionist. "Personal, not medical."

She opened her mouth, presumably to say something like "Make an appointment, he's booked three weeks out, and I'll need a copy of your insurance card," when the man himself stepped from behind a rolling rack of files.

"Do I know you?" He cocked his head and squinted.

"It's about Tory Finch."

"Ah. Stephanie, hold my calls," he told the receptionist. She hit a buzzer and the lock on the door between the clinic offices and the waiting room clicked open. I followed the white-coated doctor down the hall to a starkly unadorned room. The only spots of color besides his cheeks were his maroon-and-white-striped tie and a fake ficus in the corner.

"Ken Griffey. Not *that* Ken Griffey," he said, enjoying the familiar joke. His pleasure faded quickly as we shook hands. "Terrible business. I would never have thought she could—"

"She didn't," I said. "She swears it, and I believe her."

"None of us wants to think someone we like capable of hurting us. Defeats our belief in our own good judgment. But from what I hear, the evidence is conclusive." He leaned back in his black leather chair, steepling his fingers. "Not sure what I can do for you, Ms. Reece."

"I saw you with Mrs. Finch when I came in."

Griffey spoke as if delivering bad news to a patient. "Marianne is devastated. We expected it at some point, of course, but not like this. And the impact on the clinic . . ."

"Surgeons start work early, right? So why was your partner slumming in the Market every morning, disguised as a homeless man?"

His eyes narrowed. "A homeless man? You must have him confused with one of Tory's projects."

"Ah, the patients. Why bring them to you and not her father?"

A less-than-sunny look crossed his face. "My partner . . ." he began, "was a complicated man."

Family trait.

"Dr. Finch," he continued, touching his forefingers to his lower lip and glancing down, "was on leave from his practice."

Oh. "That must have been hard on you. Doubling your workload."

"Temporarily, yes. But that's what partners do."

Dump on each other, or help each other out? Again, Griffey spoke in a tone of controlled sympathy. Perfectly appropriate. So why did I suspect the good doctor of using bedside manner as a cover-up?

"Why take a leave?" I asked. "And why hang out in the Market, tailing his daughter?"

"Ms. Reece." Dr. Griffey sat up, hands flat on his gleaming desktop. "I get the distinct impression that you're fishing for dirt on Dr. Finch. You'll have to do it elsewhere."

One more try. "What will happen to the practice now that he's gone? Now that it's all your responsibility?"

The rosy spots that gave him his boyish appearance darkened into ragged red splotches, and he stood. His pale hands trembled. "That's none of your business. Now, if you'll excuse me."

In other words, my HR brain said as I made my way back to the waiting room, Dr. Griffey was mightily peeved—and not just because I had dared to question whether his partner had been murdered by his own daughter.

". . . if you hear of anything. 'Cause I'm afraid I'm going to be looking real soon." The receptionist spotted me and reached for her ear to click off her headset. "Gotta go. Bye."

"Thanks, Stephanie," I said, crossing the empty room and heading out. So much for the double workload. One doctor dead, the other anxious. No patients in sight and the receptionist job hunting.

"So old Doc Finch croaked, leaving Griffey on his own."

I glanced around the lobby to see who'd spoken. To my surprise, it was the elderly man I'd met on my way in.

"You're too healthy to need either of 'em," he said, patting the space beside him on the padded bench.

I sat. "You're back. Were you Dr. Finch's patient? Sad news."

"They sent me across the street for lab work. These doctors. They all want tests, tests, tests. Line their pockets with tests. Griffey had me come in at the crack of dawn last week, Wednesday, if I recollect, and he wasn't even here. Breezed in midmorning. I ought to send him a bill."

Last Wednesday? Had Dr. Griffey perhaps detoured to the Market before work? Tailing his own partner, for reasons nefarious or otherwise?

The old man waved a gnarled hand at the cardiologists' door. "Finch was even worse. Never imagined I'd outlive the SOB."

"I never met him." Not as a doctor anyway.

He snorted. "Lucky for you. Wonder if the new guy will be any good."

So many threads to follow. I felt like a spider with flies in every corner of the web. "They've found a new doctor so soon? Dr. Finch just passed away last week."

"Word is, he'd already decided to retire and brought in his own replacement. Caused quite a stir in there, I heard." He clucked. "I saw him walking around with Finch. Tall, thin guy. Young—well, he wouldn't look young to you."

I frowned. The man I'd seen earlier, the one who kissed Marianne's cheek?

"Finch liked riling folks up. Bet I wouldn't have any heart trouble if he hadn't been my heart doctor." His laugh caught in his throat and turned to a cough.

"Are you okay? I'll get Dr. Grif—" I started to rise, but he yanked me back down, his grip surprisingly strong.

"It only hurts when I laugh," he said, eyes dancing at the punch line to the old joke. "Finch burned through partners and staff like Congress burns through the billions. I thought Griffey could handle him. Don't be fooled by the Boy Scout look—he's a sly one, Griffey is. Not as wily as Finch, though, I'll venture."

"Mr. Franklin?" The receptionist stood in the doorway. "The lab called in your results. Dr. Griffey will see you now."

"You take care, young lady," Mr. Franklin said as I stood, unsure how to help. He wrapped his fingers around the handles of his walker, gave a mighty shove, and creaked to his feet, then used a toe to unlatch the wheel lock. "Don't fool around with your heart."

Twenty-one

Unsure about an old spice? Don't make up for age by doubling up. The lighter volatile oils in a spice deteriorate faster than the darker or lower notes, throwing off the balance and creating sharp, potentially bitter flavors. Replace it instead.

"SHE WAS SUPPOSED TO MEET ME OUTSIDE THE CLINIC," I told the cabbie. "But I can't find her anywhere. Did you run her home already?"

"Where to, miss?" The driver's lilting tones spoke of Jamaica, and I wondered whether he'd braved these hills in a Pacific Northwest winter yet.

I gave an exaggerated sigh and lounged against the cracked vinyl upholstery. "She went home, right? To North Beach? The woman in the red suit. My aunt. She seems fine, but she'd forget her head if it wasn't screwed on." I knew the address, but couldn't be sure that's where Marianne had gone. "Not screwed on too tight, if you know what I mean."

He grinned at me in the rearview mirror and pulled away from the curb. "She all right, Miz Finch is."

Uh-oh. He knew her. Tred carefully. "Well, with Uncle

Damien gone, we're all pretty worried. And now my cousin's been charged with killing him. It's such a mess."

He merged slickly into the northbound traffic on I-5, no mean feat. We squeezed through the downtown congestion and picked up speed.

I sighed again. "Uncle Damien wasn't easy to get along with. He hasn't—hadn't—spoken to my dad in years." True enough. They weren't related. Not even acquainted, far as I knew.

"Families," he said. "They kill you with love sometimes." He flashed bright teeth in the mirror, a joyless smile.

We exited the freeway at Eighty-fifth and headed west toward the Sound. What was I doing, taking a cab all the way up here to confront Marianne Finch? At best, a woman wracked with anger and grief. At worst, a killer.

On the dashboard, next to a placard reading ROBBIE, the electronic meter's green lights ticked away. Heading into danger, not to mention blowing every penny in my pocket.

I breathed in deeply, slowly, channeling the yoga teachers from my childhood home: *Inhale strength, exhale flexibility.*

"Good clinic. Good doctors, nice patients. Your cousin, I see her sometimes when I wait." He watched me watch him. "She not come for a while. Not since." He slowed and turned right.

"Not since what?"

"Big yelling. Her and Doctor, before I took him home. He didn't like to drive, not since months." He flicked another glance at me, and appeared to make a decision. "Young doctor—Griffey. He pull Dr. Finch away, inside. Your cousin, she sit on the curb, so sad. I give her a lozenge." He dipped long fingers into a cup holder stuffed with individually wrapped throat lozenges and held one out to me. Lemon and eucalyptus. "She say thanks, but she never cry."

We turned left, then right again, each street narrower than the last, then left into a dead end. My head spun, all sense of direction gone. Robbie looped to a stop in front of a sloping lawn leading to a Tudor faced in red brick and fieldstone, the front door and window trim painted a bright, cheery red. A magical woodland surrounded the house.

"She a tough one, that girl," he said.

But I didn't reply. I had seen this place before. In Tory's painting.

"YOU'D better come in and explain yourself," Marianne Finch said, her suit and heels the same shade as the door. Striking features, but makeup couldn't hide the puffiness around her eyes.

"I'm Pepper Reece, owner of Seattle Spice, in the Market. Where your daughter works."

"I know who you are," she said. "And Tory's my step-daughter. But I raised her from age thirteen."

Her heels clicked on the stone entry, making a hollow sound when she crossed the dining room floor, oak inlaid with mahogany. I followed slowly, each step confirming my impression of a storybook house. Plaster walls, coved ceilings, iron stair rails and sconces that looked hand-forged. In the kitchen, a showpiece of cherry cabinets and hand-painted tile, Marianne gathered cups and began making tea.

I gazed out the mullioned French doors on a backyard straight from the pages of *Fine Gardening*.

"We'll sit outside," Marianne said, toeing off her heels and stepping into a pair of blue garden clogs waiting by the door. She picked up the tray and I followed her out to the patio, paved with the same stone as the entry.

The deep border of flowering shrubs and perennials winding along the edge of the woods instantly captivated me. Hydrangeas, hostas, and flowers I couldn't name but had seen in the Market bloomed bright against a backdrop of native trees—evergreens strung with red vine maple and dotted with golden birch. In the far corner, a grapevine thick with dark purple fruit climbed a cedar trellis.

I turned a few degrees and the horizon fell away, leaving only water and mountains, the sky, the sun, the Sound.

"I suppose I shouldn't talk to you," Marianne said. "Or at least not turn my back on my teacup."

"I'm sorry for your loss. It must have been quite a shock." I took the wrought iron chair across from her and accepted a white porcelain cup, the style a perennial favorite at Sur la Table.

Her gaze dropped and her mouth tightened. Her left cheek twitched.

The familiar aroma of spice tea filled my nostrils. "You haven't been in the shop in months. How did you get our tea?"

She pinched her lips together. "My husband forbade me from going to the Spice Shop, or to his daughter's apartment. So we met for lunch. She brought me spices, in unmarked bags, and tea."

"He didn't recognize the smell?"

"Oh, I never drank it around him. He'd have thrown it out on the spot."

"I understand," I said, though I didn't. "I had a strong-willed husband myself. Your husband's first wife died when Tory was a child?"

A shadow crossed her face. "Pancreatic cancer. A dreadful way to go."

"You knew her?" A surprise.

"Carolyn was my best friend. We lived two doors apart. Not on this street. Damien and I wanted a home of our own."

"You've got the touch. This garden is paradise."

She shook her head. "All Damien's doing. He hired out the hard jobs—surgeons need to protect their hands. But he designed it, and chose all the plants himself. He could spend hours prowling through nurseries." She stuck out a foot in the too-big garden clog. His.

So Tory's creative talents came from her father.

"Big house," I said. "Did you raise your children here, too?"

"My boys were grown by then. One's an architect, one's

a doctor. They were glad to see me happy, and not alone. It was hard on Tory, though. I think . . ." Her tone softened and her gaze seemed to fall inward. "We married five months after Carolyn died. We'd been friends for so long that it felt natural to us. But Tory couldn't see that. In a strange way, a child's way, I think she saw our quick marriage as a reason to blame her father and me for her mother's death. I've often wondered whether we should have anticipated that, and waited a little longer."

"So she resented you for taking her mother's place."

She cradled her cup, not drinking, and nodded. "They were very close. Carolyn had the biggest heart. She taught Tory generosity—they worked on school food drives, volunteered with Toys for Tots, you name it. I tried to continue that. And now, she's accused of murder. I don't know what to think . . ." Her voice trailed off.

"Tory is passionate about painting. Why did your husband oppose her plan to become an artist?"

She sighed. "You must understand. He adored her. She was all he had. He only wanted what was best for her."

We sometimes break our own rules to help other people. The way I'd interjected myself into Tory's personal life while resisting Tag's protectiveness. At least now that she'd consented to my involvement, I could acquit myself of meddling. "Isn't that her decision?"

"Do you have children? No? Then you don't have a clue, and you don't have the right to question me."

"Maybe not, but isn't the point to raise independent beings who make their own decisions?" To stand back and get out of the way.

"It's complicated," she said.

Why did everyone in this family keep telling me that?

Her gaze drifted off, unseeing. A squirrel dashed across the patio, a pinecone in his mouth. Somewhere in the neighborhood, a lawn mower roared. I drank in the afternoon glow, one eye on Marianne.

"I don't know what Ken Griffey told you." She raised the cup to her lips, then set it down without drinking. "But my husband was trying to make everything right while he still had time."

While he still had time . . . Old Mr. Franklin's comment about Finch retiring had nagged at me. Finch didn't seem like the kind of man to retire voluntarily at sixty-four. A hard-driving man could only putter so long, even in a garden like this.

I hazarded a giant leap. "Your husband was ill, wasn't he?"

She stood and stretched a manicured hand toward a tall, green-glazed planter. Touched a geranium the same shade as her nails and suit, long fingers caressing the petals. "Damien did not believe he was wrong in how he had treated his family." Her full red lips twitched wryly. "Damien never believed he was wrong. But he did not want to die unreconciled."

"How much time did he have?"

"Not long. Pancreatic cancer. By a sad twist of fate, the same disease that killed Carolyn." Her eyes moistened.

"Tory knew, didn't she?" That's what she'd meant, by asking what would be the point of killing him. Everyone knew but me. And Spencer and Tracy?

"He came up with that crazy disguise—to watch her, gauge the right time to talk to her. I thought it was silly, but he was as stubborn as she was. He should have told her when he was diagnosed, early this summer. Withholding the news made things worse. He was still treating her like a child."

"She brought street people to the clinic," I said. "Did he treat them, at her request? Or refuse?" He didn't seem like a pro bono kind of guy.

"I don't know about that." Marianne focused on her own tangled grief. "I encouraged him to talk with her, for both their sakes. Now I wonder what I've done. Did I send him to his death? I thought I knew the girl, but now . . ."

"Mrs. Finch—Marianne. I've been to the jail. Twice. Tory didn't kill him."

"You can't be sure." Her voice cut the air.

"Think about it." I set my cup on the table and leaned forward, elbows on my thighs. "Poison is either a complete accident—using peanut oil in a stir-fry, not knowing the other person's allergic—"

"He'd done so much for her. Paints, brushes, canvas. Private lessons. But he wanted her to be practical, to be able to support herself."

"—or it's deliberate. The killer plans the crime. Unearths a toxic substance, finds something to put it in, makes sure the target gets it. That's what happened here. Your husband was the victim of a deliberate crime. Tory, the girl you raised. Carolyn's daughter. The girl with the big heart and an artist's soul. Do you honestly believe she could do such a terrible thing?"

Marianne Finch sank slowly into her chair, gripping its arms.

"Whoever killed him didn't know he was dying," I said. The same logic applied to the widow. Unless there was some other reason, something else she gained. Freedom from his demands? Money? What if his legacy to Tory was large, and Marianne framed Tory to deprive her? The thought made my brain hurt. "Marianne, your husband loved this house. Why is only your name on the title?"

She looked surprised. "Nearly everything is in my name, for liability reasons. It's a common practice for doctors. People file lawsuits over anything these days. You've got to protect yourself from your own business."

"Did your husband have disputes with business partners?"

"That was all resolved," she said, glancing away quickly. Too quickly?

"Had your husband already found someone to replace him?"

"It wasn't final, but yes. And it was the right thing to do.

That's what I was discussing with Ken this afternoon." She exhaled. "Pepper, my husband was stubborn, but he loved his daughter. He grew up in poverty. He watched the struggle kill his mother. Everything he ever did was to save his only child from that fate."

Even the dead have motives the living can't guess.

"Did he provide for her in his will?"

"No. What little he officially owned went to me, except a life insurance policy that benefitted her. She didn't know about it. He'd made very clear that if she didn't follow his wishes, she would get nothing, but in the end, he provided for her. He was demanding, but not heartless." Recognition crept across her sad, pretty face. "The detectives may theorize that she killed him for the money, but she didn't think she was getting any. Even if she'd wanted it, which I don't believe. And she wouldn't kill for revenge—not if she knew he was dying. So if you're right about the poison . . ."

Time for me to leave. Past time, if the deepening lines in Marianne Finch's face were any indication.

I stood. "Please visit Tory. She needs to understand she's not in this alone."

Leaving Marianne Finch to puzzle out her grief and confusion, I circled through the side yard. Flat turtle-shaped pavers led past a row of dogwoods, a few pale yellow blooms clinging to their branches. A six-foot-high wrought iron gate with a moonlike disk of cast glass in its center opened to the front yard. One hand on the latch, I paused to gaze out at the sparkling waters of Puget Sound. Deep, cold, treacherous, and soothing, all at once.

Damien Finch had mastered the art of gardening. But the art of dying?

A whole 'nuther story.

I headed down the street, aiming for the nearest arterial and a bus route, replaying my theories.

Tag always says in investigating, focus on the simplest explanation. That meant cross the widow off the list. Unless I found some reason Marianne would kill a dying man that didn't also apply to her stepdaughter. In short, the price of eliminating Tory was to eliminate her not-evil step-mother.

I needed to confirm that Tory knew her father was ill. Marianne was certain Damien had told her, and it made sense. But why refuse to talk to a dying parent?

More puzzles.

That brought me back to Sam. I doubted he had the ability to plan so complicated a crime, even if he'd had the desire. Clearly he had not known who Doc was, or that the man was dying.

My own theories left me out of suspects. But what of Dr. Griffey? And those mysterious past business partners, from the clinic or other ventures.

A block from the Finch house, a yellow cab stood by the curb. A tall, dark man in black pants and a short black jacket leaned against the driver's door.

"You waited?"

"You need a ride, yes, miss?"

How could I pass up such a sweet offer, even if it did cost me half an arm or part of a leg?

"Robbie," I said, "Tory, Dr. Finch's daughter?"

He nodded.

"She's not my cousin. She works for me."

He nodded again and we got in the cab. "You smell of spice, like she does."

"You told me you saw her arguing with her father. Do you know what about?" I sucked on the lozenge he'd given me earlier and watched as he merged into traffic effortlessly. "And did you ever see her bring one of the street people to the clinic?"

"Oh, yes." He flashed his big grin at the mirror. "She have a kind heart. She bring those men up, after hours. But then, they yelled, like I tell you, and she not come back. To the Market, to your shop?"

"Yes, please. Was one of those patients a black man who lives downtown, a man Tory knew from the Market?"

He exited the freeway at Olive and drove down the hill. "Oh, yes, indeed. I take him home for her once."

Sam. I gripped the back of the front seat. "Where, Robbie? Do you remember? I need to find him. He might be in trouble."

Robbie switched lanes. "To the Market. He say it's his home. That's all I know."

He pulled up to the curb by the newsstand, and waved off my attempt to pay him. "You be kind and help find who killed the doctor. That be payment enough."

Kindness, the fuel that makes the world go round. I watched him drive away. I had more questions for Tory, but visiting hours were over. Plus I really did have a shop to run.

And kindness doesn't pay the bills.

Twenty-two

Now recognized as the fifth taste—along with sweet, salty, bitter, and sour—umami is a savory, brothy taste high in glutamates, like mushrooms, cured meats, or Parmesan on tomato sauce.

A YEASTY NOTE HIT MY NASAL PASSAGES WHEN I OPENED the shop's front door. Either we were hosting a bakers' convention, or Sandra was getting a jump on popcorn seasonings for winter and fooling around with brewer's yeast.

No customers. No surprise, late on a Monday afternoon. Reed refilled tea canisters, while Sandra sat in the mixing nook, measuring and muttering.

Jars of yeast, cumin, and chili seasoning covered the table. "So are we going *Back to the Future*? Is it 1970 again? What is this?" I picked up a commercial jar of powdered buttermilk.

"I'm experimenting with a ranch dressing mix for popcorn. Retro, the way to your heart."

"Touché. Make it the 1950s and I'll love you forever. Where's Zak?"

"Ha. I've heard that one before. I let our boy take off

early, to visit Tory and meet with her lawyer. Figured you'd approve."

I nodded.

"Boss." She studied me over her pink-and-purple-striped cheaters, her playful brown peepers momentarily serious. "Hate to bring this up, but we don't know when Tory will be back. And it's not high summer, but we're still busy."

I stifled a groan. Our staffing shortage wasn't going to resolve itself. Kristen had the day off, as a payback for Saturday. She was working more hours than she wanted, and Reed had classes most mornings. That left three of us full-time. "We've gotten a few inquiries lately. I'll take a peek, see if the right person's already in the file."

"Thanks, boss." Sandra pushed a group of jars aside and reached for the buttermilk, black pepper, and dill. "I put my picks for recipes using the blends on your desk."

I poured a cup of spice tea and headed for the office. Gone the days of dropping off résumés and hoping for a call back. Most applications come through e-mail, not the front door, with paper apps used mainly for reference checks and to document the file after hiring. Both Sandra and Reed had filled out new apps this morning, and the personnel files were now complete and up-to-date.

Except, of course, for Tory's.

I pushed the "on" button and waited for my laptop to spring to life. Crossed my fingers that all the backup files had downloaded properly.

Best shot might be to call the cooking schools and ask for a student in need of a part-time gig. Maybe a recent grad wanting daytime hours or a food job without the stresses of restaurant work. And I could put in a word with our suppliers and restaurant customers.

You'd think supertasters would dominate the food biz, but not so. Folks with extraordinary senses of taste and smell tend to be too sensitive to bitter and sweet, and to crave salt, possibly to tone down the other tastes. Better to hire a foodie with a high-average sense of taste and smell, like Sandra.

Or me. I've got a decent nose and a good palate. But I lack experience. Probably because I spend too little time with the spices and too much time handling inventory and invoices.

And investigating murder.

I clicked on the Job Openings folder. "Yay!" I cheered out loud when it opened, intact. One good candidate, the e-mail dated two weeks ago. I got out my phone and reached for a pen to take notes of the interview. No luck. I shuffled the papers—it's much harder to keep a small space neat and tidy than the larger office I'd had at the law firm—and spotted not a pen but the warrant and inventory Tracy had left. I'd given them a cursory glance, simultaneously irked that a key employee was under arrest and my business subject to search, and grateful that they hadn't closed me down.

Certainly I'd realized that their focus on the tea and service items meant they thought the threat originated inside the shop. Logical enough. But they'd stopped there, convinced they had their killer.

Now that I knew more about the case, and Tory's relationship with her father, the inventory warranted a second look. If I understood better what they were thinking, maybe I could point them to someone else.

But who?

I tucked the inventory and recipes in my bag. Found a pen underneath yesterday's mail. Called the applicant. No answer. I left a message.

My Thai lunch had long worn off. Time to get a move on, snare some of those darling fingerling potatoes I'd seen earlier at the farm stall. And tender stalks of broccolini. Its subtle sweetness and peppery kick give it a more interesting flavor than traditional broccoli or even broccoli rabe, and it pairs well with potatoes.

Ooh, a frittata. I nearly rubbed my hands in anticipation. Laurel had suggested one to showcase the savory blend, and this might be spot on.

Not quite on the same comfort food level as mac and cheese, but darned close. Especially with a hefty dose of grated Parmesan inside and more broiled on top to a perfect salty-gold crunch.

The larger produce stands in the Market buy from the growers for resale. Some farmers or growers—the orchard girls, the flower sellers, Herb the Herb Man—are regulars in the daystalls. A few years ago, the Market started "Express Markets" scattered around downtown, where growers sell their own produce, flowers, honey, and other items. Downtown residents love it, and it's a boon for workers who can't get to the Market on their lunch breaks.

And several days a week, farmers set up tents on Pike Place, in the block across from the Spice Shop, to sell directly to the customer. Most run specialized operations, like the father and daughter who grow the tastiest tomatoes in the world, or the fruit seller with the juicer and smoothie machine.

My favorite, a lanky kid from the Skagit Valley, grows organic greens and a few other choice veggies. His father, a Superior Court judge who practiced in my firm before it went kaput, couldn't have been more supportive of his son's choice of a radically different path. Too bad Damien Finch hadn't had his counsel.

"A pound each of the broccolini and the fingerlings. And a couple of small red onions."

"Get an extra pound or two of taters," he suggested. "Make a big old potato salad, sprinkle in some caraway and fresh dill."

"If I bought that many potatoes, I'd eat them. And my hips would explode and I'd have to come work the fields with you."

He grinned. "You'd be welcome, anytime."

Up to the Creamery for eggs. I nestled the half carton safely into my bag and turned to leave.

"Pepper." It was Angie Martinez, a bottle of kefir open in her hand. "How's Tory? Zak said you saw her."

"Hanging in there. I'll tell her you asked." Eureka moment. "Angie, if you know anyone who needs a part-time job, temporary, maybe longer . . ."

She thought a moment. "A friend at the deli is looking for more hours."

"Send her in. One more thing. You're outside all day. You see more than I do. Ever see Doc talking, arguing with anyone? Anywhere?" I'd already asked her questions about Doc and Tory, but people don't always remember things the first time, or make the leap from one question to something else that might be more important.

But the answer was still no, darn it. I asked the Creamery staff the same question; got the same answer. Asked the beekeeper, the flower sellers, and Herb; more noes. Asked my farmer friend and his neighbors, all busy breaking down their tents for the day. All said no.

I paused to check my phone, then dropped it back into my tote. Back to the task of finding out who hated Doc. I scoured Post Alley, quizzing everyone who had a moment to talk before closing if they'd seen anything unusual.

No, no, no.

Jane always says a retailer's job is to "get to yes." I itched for "yes."

The door to Vinny's wine shop and tasting room opened and out stepped Alex Howard, his arm draped across the shoulder of a willowy blonde in a short skirt and high heels. She laughed and slipped her arm around his waist. They strolled away, eyes drinking in each other.

I leaned against a pillar, out of sight. Caught my breath. Alex had said his "friend"—I drew air quotes in my mind—was here for the wine show. Wine shows give winemakers opportunities to pitch their wares to restaurateurs, distributors, and shop owners. Organizers often invite specialty food producers and retailers—like the Spice Shop.

Until Alex's late-night text, I hadn't heard boo about a wine show.

Tracy had said the Mustang that wasn't mine belonged to a winemaker.

Was it too strange, too much of a coincidence, to think that this had been a very small show, for one winemaker and one restaurateur?

And what were the odds that Alex would date two women who drive dark blue, late-sixties Mustangs? If we were dating. If he and this woman were dating.

Whoa, Pepper. Their sashay up the Alley might be suspicious, but don't jump to conclusions.

Jumping to conclusions isn't nearly as much exercise as running in circles.

I popped into Vinny's. Asked if he'd seen Doc around the Market. Another no.

"I heard there's some kind of winemakers' deal going on in town. You involved?"

"Huh? No." He shook his head. "Winemaker from Walla Walla was just here, but she's dropping in on a few key customers. No trade show."

Had she lied to Alex, or had he lied to me?

I breathed in calmness—for a yoga dropout, the aphorisms were coming in handy today. When Vinny asked what I'd picked up for dinner and suggested a nice Italian white from the Piedmont, I said yes.

Nice to finally hear the word.

I'M all for fun food adventures—the memory of Friday night's flavor fiesta lingered on my taste buds—but we crave comfort food for good reason. After running around all day playing detective and fretting about my staff, my shop, and my car, comfort called.

I scrubbed the potatoes—no peeling; that's where the vitamins are—and dropped them into an inch or two of broth in my mother's cast-off cast iron skillet. Her Earth Mother pan. So glad healthy eating has evolved since those days of brown bread bricks speckled with wheat germ and toasted sunflower seeds. An era when cinnamon was the only spice in sight, although in Zen-hippy-activist households like ours, the occasional curry added an exotic touch. Back then, strict wholesome cooks banished salt to the pickle barrel and considered pepper completely unnecessary. I tried not to take it personally.

While the potatoes simmered, I sliced the onion and chopped the broccolini, careful to keep my injured finger out of the way. By the time I'd uncorked the wine, the potatoes had absorbed the broth and I added olive oil and the other vegetables. Poured a taste of wine and took a sip.

"Yes, Vinny," I told the glass.

I adore my kitchen. Not just because I chose everything in it. When I cook here, I become one with the process. Nothing intrudes. Just me, my ingredients, and the elements—earth, air, fire, and water.

So when thoughts of The Case floated through my brain, I sent them packing. Beat eggs, added Parmesan, salt and pepper, and the Spice Shop's special new Herbes de Provence, and poured the mixture into the skillet. Sprinkled on the last of the cheese and cooked the frittata until the eggs were set—about how long it took to drink half a glass of wine.

Heat releases the fragrance of herbs—more precisely, it breaks down the volatile oils, releasing their aromatic particles—and I sniffed the air, seeing how many I could detect. Not a fair test, since I knew what was in the blend, but I gave myself a passing grade, and slid the skillet under the broiler.

That gave me time to change my work clothes and refill my wineglass.

I set the inventory aside for later. It's not comfort food if you distress yourself while eating.

Instead, I got lost in Brother Cadfael's world, a foot tucked under my bottom, book in one hand, fork in the other. No sooner had King Stephen's siege of Shrewsbury ended than a new widow asked Cadfael to investigate her husband's murder. The twist? She was the woman he left behind decades ago when he marched off to save Jerusalem from the infidels.

I'd nearly finished my generous wedge, the eggs perfectly set, the cheese on top perfectly crisped, and was contemplating a perfect second when my phone rang.

Scaring the paprika out of me. Why was a phone ringing in the middle of Vespers?

For the umpteenth time today, I did something I hardly ever do. I answered without checking the caller.

"Pepper, you're there." Alex's rich voice mingled notes of relief, irritation, and exasperation. (My sensory detection skills had been honed on the phone and in the office, after all. They aren't limited to evaluating spices.)

Not exactly the last person I wanted to talk to, but well down the list. I'd been a lot more concerned about his safety, and open to his explanation, before I saw him escorting the winemaker so, shall we say, attentively.

"You didn't text me back," he said.

"Sorry. I figured you were busy." As I'd witnessed this afternoon. I knew I was overreacting, which only made me more irritated. I had no rights to him.

A long pause. "About last night. I won't lie to you. An old friend showed up unexpectedly, and we got talking, and grabbed a bite, and before I knew it . . ."

She wasn't old, and she'd looked like more than a friend.

"Then she had some trouble this morning and I had to give her a hand."

Ah. Car trouble? Blue Mustang trouble?

"But I should have called you earlier last night," he finished.

"You should have called me, period. You texted, more than six hours late. When you're blowing someone off, you should at least call." My own personal rule, made up on the spot.

"I'll keep that in mind." His tone cooled, but I didn't care. I hadn't done anything wrong. And yet I was the one who'd apologized.

The spasm in my jaw told me that wasn't right.

But I've always been a one-man woman, and if a guy isn't a one-woman man, then he isn't the guy for me. Better to find that out sooner than later. To know what the deal-breakers are before they become heart-breakers.

And when someone says they won't lie to you, they're probably lying.

"Good night, Alex." I tossed the phone into a wicker basket on the coffee crate.

Medieval mood broken, I brewed a cup of spice tea and settled on the couch to reread the warrant and inventory.

"Evidence of premeditated murder," the warrant said. That meant planning and intent. No "crime of passion." It meant they suspected Tory had purchased a poison, brought it to work, put it in a cup of our tea, and given it to her father.

Witnesses put Sam on the scene, and Tory inside. But while no one I'd talked to had seen her open the door for Doc, let him in, or give him tea, nothing I'd learned ruled that out.

They'd found no poison in the shop. Dozens of people, including every employee, had drunk that tea on Thursday, after Doc's death, and no one had reported even the slightest problem. Nothing the police had taken from the shop could have implicated Tory.

Unless they'd found something in her purse. Or her apartment.

Tracy had said they had two weeks to arraign her,

meaning haul her into court and formally charge her. Maybe they didn't think they had enough evidence yet. Maybe they were still searching for the smoking gun—or the smoking tea bag.

Could we keep that train in the station, to mix my metaphors?

I scrolled down the inventory of items seized:

—Tea, loose, in cellophane bags and one large bulk canister. Location: behind the front counter. *The tea we use for brewing samples.* Tea, in individual bags, boxed. Location: various.
—Large electric brewing device.
—Large orange insulated drink dispenser.
—Paper cups.
—Straws. Garbage cans, two. Recycling bins. Rubber stamps.

The cups again. My first question, almost the moment I found Doc on the sidewalk, was how he'd gotten the cup. The cops had concluded, logically enough, that Tory had given it to him that morning.

Except for our name and logo, that cup could have come from half a dozen places a stone's throw from the shop. I closed my eyes and pictured it lying on the street, inches from Doc's outstretched fingers.

And clearly saw our logo on it.

I put aside the simple explanation—sometimes it's simply wrong. Had the killer filched one of our stamps and used it to frame Tory? To frame us?

Unlikely. We had two stamps. Tory and Reed had used them Wednesday morning. Then, if they followed their usual practice, put them away in a tin box on the bottom shelf of the tea cart.

Where nearly anyone could have gotten to them.

But had I seen the stamps between then and Friday

morning, when Tracy and crew had bagged them up and listed them on the inventory? No way to tell.

And the last item: Computer files seized from office.

I set the papers on my coffee crate and visualized the scene outside, start to finish. From the moment I spotted Doc until the EMTs had loaded his body into the ambulance.

My mental film froze on the image of Sam's beret falling out of Doc's coat. Sam had been there. I just didn't know why. Or how Doc had gotten the beret.

What would Cadfael do?

First, he'd putter in his workshop, checking his tinctures and oils, the bubbling brews, the racks of drying herbs. My equivalent: Make another cup of tea. I opened the infuser and dropped the wet leaves into my kitchen counter composter. (My neighbors turn it into rich, dark compost, giving me a generous share for my herbs and tomatoes.) Refilled it, dropped it in my mug.

The only way to make a single cup of tea in the shop is to microwave hot water and add a tea bag, or nuke a cup of leftover tea. Then add poison. But we'd emptied out both pots the night before, and I'd seen no bag in the cup near Doc's hand.

I pushed the lever on my kitchen sink for instant hot water, a feature I highly recommend.

So I didn't know how Doc had gotten the tea, or how it had been poisoned. Whatever the substance, it must not have had a taste that would instantly warn anyone off.

I carried my tea back to the couch. Cadfael was trusted, but sly. He saw what wasn't there, but should have been.

What did that mean here, in *The Case of the Poisoned Imposter*?

Evidence of someone present at his death with a motive to kill him.

Dang it. No one anywhere near the scene had any motive except Tory. And Sam. No one else in the vicinity even knew Doc.

I sank onto the couch, the lights on the Viaduct whizzing by. Was that true? Had any of his colleagues, his business rivals, followed him to the Market? Anyone who might have been angry with him, but hadn't known he was dying.

And how had Doc gotten to the Market? Robbie said Doc didn't drive anymore, presumably due to his illness.

The idea of a doctor calling a cab to take him to the Market so he could disguise himself as a street man and spy on his daughter was almost ludicrous. The idea of the tenderhearted, sharp-eyed cabbie poisoning the man—a reliable fare—was even more ridiculous.

The idea that said cabbie might have noticed something relevant—now that might have some merit. Though I thought he'd have told me already.

What about the widow? I'd all but ruled Marianne out, but maybe I shouldn't have. She had our tea—she'd served it to me.

No. She hadn't sent him off for the day with a warming-but-deadly cup. The moment he smelled it, he'd have dumped it out, furious that she'd defied his orders to shun Tory. I reached for my phone and made a note to ask both Marianne and Robbie how Damien Finch had gotten to the Market that fateful morning.

Once again, I circled back to the cup of tea. Where had it come from, if not from someone inside the shop? From Tory?

When stymied, Cadfael often sat in the Chapel, letting the angelic hosts gathered there wash over him, until insight struck.

I loaded the CD player. The sepulchral tones of the Tallis Scholars and Anonymous 4 rose to the rafters and echoed off the old bricks and pipes. I love my loft the most when I feel the history in the place, when it evokes my connection to the things, the people, the places I cherish. Tory had loved the Market. I pictured Doc and her mother taking her there as a small child, as my parents had.

I sipped my tea, savoring the cloves and citrus. Jane had created the perfectly balanced recipe.

Who would know about poisons besides, hypothetically, the Spice Shop staff?

A doctor.

Everything I'd learned about Damien Finch said he was a proud, arrogant man. Did that make him more, or less, likely to kill himself to avoid the ravages of illness?

But I could not imagine him taking such a drastic step until he'd reconciled with his daughter. And if he had intended the life insurance policy his widow mentioned to provide for Tory, surely he would have realized that suicide invalidates most policies.

Had someone who knew he was dying wanted to keep Tory from getting that money? But why?

I had to believe Detective Tracy knew of Doc's illness, from the widow or the autopsy, and was asking these same questions.

Thinking of Brother Cadfael and his jars and tonics reminded me that I had recipes to ponder, and labels to choose. But now I knew what to do. I zipped around the loft gathering a few of my favorite things from windowsills, the kitchen shelves, the vintage leather suitcases stacked beside my bed. I packed and padded them carefully into my grandmother's 1940s train case, a warm contentment settling over me.

One more task before curling up with my favorite monk. I checked the funeral home website. Services had now been scheduled for Wednesday afternoon at St. Mark's Episcopal Cathedral. I would be there. Like Brother Cadfael, I would make myself as unobtrusive as possible.

Watch, mingle, and listen.

And pray for the answers.

Twenty-three

Although some say that the term "nose to the grindstone" originated with millers, who judged quality by the aroma freshly milled grains released, linguists trace its roots to knifemakers. First used in print in 1530 to mean treating someone harshly, it's evolved over the last two centuries to refer to discipline and hard work.

TUESDAY MORNING, I WOKE UP DETERMINED TO PUT my nose to the grindstone, to figure out who had wanted Damien Finch dead. Anyone who knew he was already dying could be eliminated, unless they killed him to frame someone else. So I also had to ask who hated both father and daughter.

I bounded up the steps and wove my way through the maze that is morning in the Market. Held my breath as I neared the shop, but all looked right today. I breathed a sigh of relief.

The vigil for Doc on my doorstep long over, none of the men who spent their days on the streets were around.

"Boss, if we're gonna get those blends out, we need labels. It's time to decide," Sandra said.

"Don't you fret, don't you frown." Finally, I knew how to put my mark on the shop.

As we readied the shop for the day, my thoughts turned once again to Tory and the strained family relationships. Despite Marianne's explanation, I couldn't imagine cutting your daughter out of your life. Or a wife and stepmother going along with such an unreasonable demand. But Marianne had done the best she could, helping Tory get a decent job and checking on her occasionally.

But though Marianne looked more like a woman trying to navigate troubled waters than a suspect, I worried that I was crossing the widow off the list too soon. Last night, I'd thought a lot about the challenges of loving a difficult man. Tag was flawed, especially in the honesty and fidelity department, but he wasn't truly difficult. More like I imagined a young Cadfael—headstrong. Not like Damien Finch and, I suspected, Alex Howard: unconcerned about others' feelings, men who view compromise as giving in when they're right.

If the old man in the waiting room was to be believed, Finch ran through partners like race horses through the finish line. How could I figure out who he'd practiced with? Neither Marianne nor Dr. Griffey was likely to tell me. Tory hadn't known—she'd left home and her father's good graces ten years ago.

Zak arrived for the day. I plugged in the makeshift tea service. The red light on the pot flashed on and a lightbulb went off in my brain.

"You two okay here?" I asked Sandra. "I've got errands to run. And a clue to chase."

"Piece of cake." She gave me a mock salute, and I hitched my tote over my shoulder, energized by its contents and the pink shoes on my feet.

On my way out of the Market, I kept an eye peeled for Sam, and asked everyone I met—in a casual, offhand manner—whether they'd seen him.

The word "no" is no fun at all.

At Third and Madison, I popped into my old building and rode the escalators up to the Fourth Avenue lobby, then crossed the plaza to Ripe Café and Deli.

"Apricot crumb cake." Laurel set plates and forks on a small corner table, next to our coffees. "My new baker is a prize."

"Speaking of new employees, I need somebody part-time. Get any applicants you can't use, send 'em my way."

Her fork stopped halfway to her mouth. "You can't give up on Tory."

"I'm not. But who knows how long it will take to get everything straightened out."

"What have you learned?"

I filled her in. "So I'm headed upstairs."

She smiled. "Your grandpa should have called you Tiger."

"His second choice."

"UPSTAIRS" meant "up elevators," to the forty-second floor.

"I can't thank you enough," Callie Carter said. "My mother brought a bushel basket of apples from her trees and insisted on baking pies. She has no idea she wasn't using her own mother's nutmeg grinder."

"Thank me with research assistance." I explained what I needed.

She walked me down a hallway, past the offices of two dozen lawyers who'd lost their jobs along with us and formed their own firm, representing start-up businesses and small corporations. Callie worked part-time, researching public records and private databases, contributing to the firm's blog and newsletter, and training new lawyers and legal assistants in research. "Law libraries are changing faster than Lady Gaga between songs."

Gone the long stretches of floor-to-ceiling bookshelves full of musty, leather-bound volumes of court decisions dating back to territorial days. All that was digital now. Smaller bookcases held specialized treatises and references, while each lawyer had her own personal collection.

"But we still have microfiche." She gestured at the giant reader. "And I can call up old corporate and partnership filings on the state database, even if they're dissolved or inactive. Information never goes away."

I gave Callie my short list of names—Damien Finch, Marianne, Tory, Ken Griffey—and crossed my fingers that she was right.

"CHICA!" Today, the fabulous Fabiola was decked out in skinny gold pants and a jacket of giant silver sequins. On her head perched one of those jaunty blue caps flight attendants wore in the 1950s, feathers pinned to one side with a copper star. She was barefoot, a pair of high-heeled vintage Spectators on the floor beside her chair.

I air-kissed her cheeks. "You go shopping in a bank vault?"

She flashed me a shiny grin. "So you're ready to decide. What will it be?" Sparkly gold polish glinted on her nails.

I opened the case and withdrew my stash, item by item. At each piece, her eyes grew wider and brighter.

"Where did you find all this? It's a treasure trove."

"It's all mine. Midcentury American, mostly, but this label is on the back of that old Chinese apothecary in the shop." I pointed to a photograph I'd taken this morning, leaving the original antique label in place. "And this pill bottle is late nineteenth century."

"I know just the right font." She tapped keys on her computer, scrolled, tapped again, waited for my response.

"Yes. Yes, yes, yes."

"Huzzah!" she shouted, punching a fist into the air. "Now that I know what you love"—she gestured to the shakers, tins, bottles, jars, postcards, and other ephemera—"I know exactly what to do for you."

What you love—the secret to a happy life. And a happy shop.

IN the summer of 1889, a cabinetmaker's glue pot caught fire. The blaze spread quickly, leveling much of downtown, including the lumber mills and shacks of Skid Road. New city codes required all reconstruction to be brick or stone, not wood. Fabiola's building proved the city fathers right.

I dashed across Cherry to another sturdy relic, and ducked into the Mystery Bookshop.

"Hey, Jen. Twice in one week. How you doing?"

Jennifer the ex-paralegal came around the counter to hug me, her dark hair piled loosely on top of her head. "Great. Selling books is a lot more fun that drafting answers to interrogatories and summarizing medical records."

"I believe you." We shook our heads at the shared memory of watching our trusted employer implode. "I need a book."

She gestured at the floor-to-ceiling shelves, and the tables stacked high with hardcovers and paperbacks. "We got 'em."

"This one." I showed her the printout from a website called "Stop, You're Killing Me," which catalogs every mystery ever published, by author and lead character. "I'm reading Brother Cadfael, in order, and I'm missing one."

Her eyebrows rose. "That's quite a project." My list in hand, she headed for the historical mysteries. Her fingers danced expertly across the spines until she found her target. She handed it to me, then marched to the back of the shop. "Let me see if I can find . . ."

I followed slowly, perusing the back jacket copy.

"Thought we might have a copy of *The Cadfael Companion*. Came out when the BBC did the TV show. But how about this?" She handed me a gently used hardcover titled

Brother Cadfael's Herb Garden. "Good reference for a spice shop owner."

Yes, indeed.

NEXT stop, a spice delivery to the Grand Central Bakery, a block south.

I dropped off the order and walked out the back of the building, another grand post-fire edifice. As always, I stared in awe at the incredible wall of ivy extending to the roof line, leaving the windows and a few patches of red brick peeking out.

Occidental Park has an old world feel—if the old world boasted hand-carved cedar totem poles along with its cobbles and wrought iron lampposts. No Pioneer Square Farmers' Market today, and no Out to Lunch concert. But near the band shell, a sax player blew his horn for the pigeons and passersby, and office workers eating bakery lunches.

And if I'd guessed right, one scared man who loves street jazz.

On the far side of the Square, Sam huddled behind the granite blocks of the firefighters' memorial, wearing a too-small Mariners cap. As the former wife of a cop, I have a tender spot in my heart for this monument, erected after four firefighters were killed battling an arson fire in a frozen Chinese food factory in the International District. I still remember Tag working double shifts, coming home reeking of smoke, eyes red-rimmed from strain and emotion.

Arf scrabbled to his feet at my approach, but didn't bark or growl.

"Care for company?" I said, sinking to the cobbles.

Surprise flowed through Sam's gentle features, though it didn't erase the sadness that clung to him. Arf sat, and I scratched the magic spot behind one ear.

"How'd you know where to find me, Miz Pepper?"

"Followed the music." Arf settled his big head on my leg, and we listened to the sweet, tangy melody.

"Why'd you leave the Market, Sam?" I said when the sax fell silent. "Place doesn't feel right without you."

Sam's breathing got louder and louder, as if his lungs wanted him to speak but his brain didn't. Finally, he spoke, his voice so deep and quiet I had to lean in to hear.

"I were there, Miz Pepper. When Doc died. It were awful."

My fingers caught in Arf's wiry coat.

"I don't want to remember, but I can't forget." He tugged the faded blue ball cap down lower. "It were my turn for that corner, and he wanted it two days in a row. I gave him grief, and he—he . . ."

"Talk to me, Sam." I kept my voice calm, conversational. I had to get the story without upsetting him. Without sending him to ground.

"He grabbed my coat." Sam grabbed his own lapels, demonstrating. "I thought he was shoving me, and I yelled at him, but he weren't. It was weird—one side of his face went all red, the other ghostlike. Like Jim and his scars."

I nodded and he went on. "It were like he got dizzy, or were having a heart attack, grabbing me so he didn't fall down and crack his head." His big hands reached out, replaying the interaction. "I held him, gentled him to the ground, wrapped his coat around him."

And that's when he lost his beret.

"He were clutching, moaning like it hurt something bad. Like this." Sam placed his big hands under his jaw, heels shoving up, neck strained, dark eyes open wide.

"Oh, Sam." I touched his sleeve. "That's horrible. I'm so sorry."

"I knew they'd think I done something, but I didn't." His features burned with grief and fear.

A classic Catch 22. He didn't expect to be believed, so he ran, heightening suspicions. And no doubt if he were interviewed, his nerves would make him sweat and squirm, more signs easily interpreted as guilt or dishonesty.

"Sam, do you know why Doc wanted that corner so badly?"

He shrugged. "Tips is good. People walk by from the bakery and coffee shops. They got loose change. Sometimes they give me bread or an apple, or summit for the dog."

So he hadn't figured out that Doc was there to talk to his daughter.

"You ever see Tory talking with him?"

He thought a moment. "No, ma'am. I don't think so. That's what's so strange. I know you said Tory's his girl, but why they think she'd poison him?"

"Sam, did Doc have a cup of tea that morning? Spice tea? Did Tory bring him one?"

"She do that sometimes, for all of us, but not that morning. No offense, Miz Pepper, but I were hoping she wouldn't. It don't sit so well with me."

I smiled. "That's okay. It is pretty strong. I wondered if maybe he had a cup that she'd given him before you came along."

"He had a cup, now that you say so. I thought it were for begging. 'Cept he didn't beg much. Took what people gave him, but he didn't ask. He were a strange one."

He were indeed.

"Sam, I've been hearing that Tory gave you help when you needed it. Now she needs your help. If I go with you, would you tell the police what you told me?"

He ratcheted around, one huge hand grubbing for the granite block behind us. "No, ma'am, Miz Pepper. Don't ask me to do that. They'll put me away for sure."

Arf bounced up and began to bark the moment Sam moved. Without my shop apron, I had no treats to quiet him.

"No, ma'am," Sam repeated, struggling to get to his feet. "She innocent, but she don't need me. Girl like that, nobody want to put her away just 'cause they can. Not like me."

I stood, extending a hand to help him. He ignored my offer. On his feet now, he picked up Arf's leash and shambled out of the Square, muttering and shaking his head.

Nothing to be gained by following him, pestering him to talk. I believed his description of the incident with Doc, but I also knew that as much as Sam might want to believe me "one of the good guys," he didn't.

He couldn't.

And there are some things we just can't make ourselves do.

Twenty-four

Much virtue in herbs, little in men.

—Benjamin Franklin, *Poor Richard's Almanack* (1734)

I SAT IN THE PARK A FEW MINUTES LONGER, HALF LISTEN-
ing to the music. A pair of pigeons squawked and scratched
for crumbs, and a seagull sporting gray wingtips swept in
for a stray French fry.

Sam knew something he wasn't telling me. There was
no other explanation for his refusal to talk. I'd made a mistake suggesting the police—I should have known Sam was
paranoid enough to fear the worst.

Would he talk to Tory's attorney? I'd suggest it.

Probably not many doctors' daughters on the Public
Defender's client list, let alone one accused of patricide.
Shivery word. I trekked up to the office, explained myself
to the receptionist, and was told to wait.

Five minutes later, a petite blonde in a charcoal gray
pantsuit approached, shifting her black leather bag to her
left hand and extending her right. "Jordan Schmidt. I'm
headed to the jail right now. We can chat on the way."

For a small woman, Jordan set a quick pace, so I talked
fast, explaining why I believed Tory innocent and what I'd

been doing to help prove it. She shot me a doubting glance or two, but I didn't take it personally. The line between help and interference can be faint at times.

"So tell me that part again, about the tension between Dr. Finch and his daughter."

"He's your classic difficult man. Thinks he knows what's best, and if you don't agree, you simply don't understand. But Tory's strong-willed, too, as determined to be an artist as he was to persuade her otherwise."

We stopped for a red light. "Okay, so he's a doctor. Wants her to be practical, choose a career where she can support herself."

"She supported herself just fine, working for me."

"No offense, but retail isn't the most secure field in the world and the pay . . ."

"I pay a living wage. My assistant manager's worked in the Spice Shop for twenty-two years." Old argument, not relevant right now. "Listen, I don't know all the details, but he drew a line in the sand. If she didn't do things his way, she better not come around and she better not expect any help from him."

"You realize you're making the case for motive," Jordan said. The light changed and she stepped off the curb, half a stride ahead of me. "And he got the mother to cut her off, too?"

"Stepmother. She loved her husband, but feared him a little bit, too, I think. Went along to get along."

I opened the jail's front door for her.

"And this Sam character? What does he know that would help my client?"

"Not sure," I said as we approached the security check line. "But he was there when Doc died, and something he saw has him worried."

Visiting hours had ended—though not for lawyers—and a stream of people flowed past the other side of the screening equipment, toward the door. My eyes were on Jordan, but a face in the exit line caught my eye. Yvonne the flower seller?

I turned to look but the crowd had surged by, and all I could see was a woman her height with graying hair.

Jordan put her bag on the screeners' table. "Okay. I'll ask about her dad, and what she knew about his illness. And the old guy—tell me his name again?"

"Sam. I know you don't have to figure out who did kill Doc, but what about his old partners? Other doctors he forced out, or employees who hated him? Can't you dig into his business dealings?"

"Can and will. But make no mistake. She's in serious trouble." She waved her hand as she stepped through the X-ray machine.

Back outside, I scanned the sidewalk for Yvonne, but she—or her doppelgänger—had disappeared.

I could not deny the truth of Jordan's parting words. Tory would need all the friends she could get—and other than Zak, me, and her neighbor Keyra Jackson, I imagined her guest list was short.

Like the list of suspects.

FABIOLA had worked quickly, e-mailing sketches for the new packaging that afternoon. She promised to work all night, if that's what it took, to rough out the design for the fall tins—front and back labels, plus artwork for the recipe inserts. "I'm on fire for you!" her message declared.

Glad someone was.

Reed staffed the front counter and cash register while Zak took care of the day's shipping. On the phone, Sandra tried to help a customer identify a spice she'd had in a dish she couldn't name at a restaurant she couldn't remember.

I was working with a woman putting together a basic spice set for a bridal shower gift for her younger sister, a novice cook. Loved the idea. We could develop a checklist and kits for beginning and more advanced cooks. A natural expansion—we already did a brisk business with our salt lovers' gift boxes, cocoa sets, and other theme packs. *Ooh— what about a spice, tea, and cookbook registry?*

We picked out a storage system—a never-ending challenge, and somewhat personal, depending on kitchen space and layout—and discussed the pros and cons of traditional matched salt and pepper shaker sets. I made my pitch for freshly ground pepper, for freshness and the degree of control it gives a cook.

"But then, what about salt?" she said.

"More options. Shakers, mills, or grinders for crystal salt, cellars or unglazed clay jars for flake varieties. We can do a matched set of salt and pepper mills. But this might be your best bet." I picked up an acrylic shaker-grinder combination and showed her the removable saltshaker on top. "Pour your peppercorns in the bottom, pop the top back on, and twist to grind. It's our best seller."

She gave it a practice twist. "I should get one for myself."

"What about tea?" I said. "A pot, strainers, infusers. We've got it all."

"Our other sister drew that. I'll send her in."

We were piling her choices on the counter when the door opened. In walked Alex Howard.

"I've got this, boss," Sandra said, bumping me aside. She grinned wickedly and gave me a wink.

I swallowed a bad word. Had I been too harsh on him last night? But I wasn't going to apologize unless he did. Maybe not even then.

"Hey, Pepper. Got a moment?"

"Just," I said, wincing internally at the unintentional witchiness in my voice.

"I blew it," he said when I left the counter to join him in a quiet spot. "I should have called you the moment my friend showed up. Can you forgive me?"

"Your friend? The beautiful blonde with the blue Mustang?"

He had the grace to color. "Hey, I admit, I'm a sucker for

good-looking women who drive classic sports cars." *Like you,* the movie-star smile implied.

Cripes. Here he was flattering me, not to mention looking yummy in his chocolate brown leather bomber jacket. I ran a hand through my hair, back to its usual spikes. *Are you really ready to torch this relationship—such as it is—so soon?*

"I'm taking the night off. Any chance I can make it up to you?" This time his voice held a note of seduction, mingled with a touch of presumption.

"Tuesday night," I said, shaking my head. "Flick Chicks."

"Don't you get together every week? Skip it this one time."

But I refuse to be one of those women who ditch their girlfriends when a hot guy comes along. Just because a man has an irresistible smile doesn't mean you can't resist.

"No. But give me five minutes and you can walk me home."

Leaving Sandra to close up, I grabbed my bag and Fabiola's sketches. We crossed the street, and I paused at Yvonne's stall to drink in the floral scents and thank Alex again for last week's bouquet.

"We should source more of our flowers for the restaurants locally, don't you think?" he said.

"Absolutely."

He beamed that *GQ* smile at Yvonne. "Big arrangements for the hostess stands. Small bouquets or individual stems for the tables. We'd need a wholesale rate, but we'd give you plenty of volume. What do you think?"

Yvonne eyed him warily. "No greenhouse. I'm strictly seasonal. March to November." She glanced at me, brows furrowed in a doubting expression, then turned her attention back to Alex, chin raised defiantly.

"Small problem. Not insurmountable." He slid a dark brown leather card case out of his jacket pocket and handed her a card. She wiped her fingers on her apron before taking it. Scrapes and scratches covered the back of her hand and the side of her chin. Hazards of the garden trade. "Call my operations manager and tell her we've talked."

He put his hand on my low back to guide me away. I called out over my shoulder, "Thanks for going to see Tory. I'm sure she appreciated the visit."

A shadow crossed her face. I understood. The jail was only a few blocks from the vibrant, bustling Market, but with all that it represented, with all the sadness and pain it held, it might as well have been in another galaxy.

Twenty-five

Seattle's Lake Union houseboat community nearly died out in the 1960s, pressured by urban renewal, monopolies on moorage, and city officials scratching their heads over the unconventional properties. From loggers' shacks on rafts to million-dollar "floating homes," from city scourge to movie sets, the Seattle houseboat's come a long way.

"LAST DINNER ON THE DECK," SEETHA SAID, SETTLING into a chair on Laurel's rooftop deck. Behind her, pots of red, yellow, and orange flowers bloomed next to planters of parsley, chives, tarragon, and rosemary.

"No!" the three of us cried in unison.

Laurel set down a tray of oven-toasted parchment paper packages, exuding the distinctive aromas of salmon and cilantro. I'd already brought up a wooden bowl of salad greens tossed with creamy Parmesan dressing flavored with one of our new spice blends, and a basket of warm bread. She plucked a flute of Prosecco from the tray Kristen held and raised it high. "But it *is* the last of my basil and tomatoes. Cheers!"

People not familiar with houseboats picture two extremes:

Artistic hippies camping on rusty barges with limited space and even more limited utilities, or the classy, glassy palace where Tom Hanks lived in *Sleepless in Seattle*. In reality, Seattle's houseboats, or floating homes, have all the comforts of landed living, but less square footage and a terrific sense of community.

Laurel's rooftop offers a panoramic view of Lake Union, Gasworks Park, and Queen Anne Hill. All manner of boats and birds pass by, and people, too. After Patrick's death, it had been the perfect refuge. Now, two years later, I couldn't imagine her living anywhere else—and neither could she.

"We bundle up, but we sit out here all year round," she told Seetha. Our newest Flick Chick had moved to the Emerald City a few months ago from Boston.

"Brrr." Seetha gave a mock shiver in anticipation.

Laurel passed me the Caesar. "How was your date with Alex?"

I wriggled in my chair, feeling a flush rise up my neck. I took a belt of Prosecco and told the story.

"Poophead," Kristen said.

"Scumbag," Laurel said.

"She might really be an old friend," Seetha said.

Laurel and Kristen snorted. I didn't want to explain about Tag and the sore spot I should be over by now, according to most people. But betrayal has a long tail. "We're going to try again next Sunday."

"What I want to know," Laurel said, "is what's up with Tory."

Not easy to relate all the details between bites, but I did my best.

"You can't impose your will on your children," Laurel said when I finished. "If you do, you lose them. Simple as that."

"But you want to influence them," Kristen said. "Guide them toward the right choices. This salmon is heavenly."

"Teach them how to make good choices," Laurel said.

"What's right for them is up to them. You can't control the outcome."

Next to me, Seetha stirred uncomfortably. "Need a sweater?" I glanced southwest-ish, where the Space Needle stood in silhouette against the Olympics beyond, the sky a graphic of light blue, deep gray, and that orange-pink that occurs nowhere else in the world.

She wrapped her arms around herself and shook her head.

"I think the wife did it," Kristen said. "Or she hired a hit man. Hit poisoner."

I gestured with my champagne flute. "But what poison? That's what's driving me to drink." Admittedly, a short trip.

"Darned if I know. But you said they have a killer garden. Ooh. What if it was something he grew himself?"

What about that? I'd seen no yellow caution tape or other remnants of a law enforcement visit, or anything else suggesting that the storybook Tudor was a gingerbread trap. But surely the cops were taking a close look at Marianne—and their home and flower beds.

"Remember that movie *Black Widow*?" Kristen went on. "Theresa Russell marries all these rich guys and kills them, but she changes her appearance so nobody realizes it's her, over and over, until Debra Winger, who's a cop, gets on her trail. It's super scary."

"Marianne could be the killer," I said, "But not a black widow. Why kill him after fifteen years? Who's coming to the funeral with me?"

"Can't," Laurel said. "We're catering a private party at SAM."

Seattle Art Museum, not Sam the man. I hoped his fears had eased. Maybe I should seek out Jim, ask what he could do. Maybe I should forget about it all until tomorrow.

Fat chance.

"I would," Kristen said, "but I already offered to work for Zak."

"I can see Tory not wanting to talk to her father. Despite him tracking her down."

The change of subject surprised us all, and we turned to Seetha.

"When a parent is that controlling, it forces the kid— even if they're grown—to see everything as an attempt at manipulation. Because it usually is."

Laurel stretched out a hand. "Is that why you moved to Seattle?"

Seetha brushed her long, layered hair away from her face. She had to be a good ten years younger than Kristen and me, and twenty years younger than Laurel, who'd brought her into the group. "Not me. My parents. My mother's parents refused to accept their marriage. They didn't come to the wedding, and they never came to visit."

Kristen's brow wrinkled. "Why? Isn't your father Indian, too?"

"Yes, but American-born. They hated that she chose her own husband and started a career here. They were afraid that she would never return to India to live if she married him. And they were right. When I was five and my brother three, my grandmother faked a heart attack so my mother would come back to Delhi, and bring the kids. She thought she could get us to stay, but my mother tumbled to her tricks and we left after a week. When she really did have a heart attack a few years later, my mother hired a doctor friend from convent school to make sure it wasn't another con. It wasn't and she went, alone."

Had Tory suspected Doc of faking, like Seetha's grandmother?

"So your grandmother destroyed what she wanted most—her family—by trying to hold on to it so tightly." Kristen squeezed Seetha's hand.

We sat in silence until the sun disappeared.

"Movie time," Laurel said. She piled the plates and silver on a big tray.

"Change in plans," she said once we'd reassembled in the living room, a second bottle of wine uncorked and a pot of decaf scenting the air. "We need a major comfort movie. Nominations are open!"

"*Love Actually,*" Kristen said. "I don't care if Christmas is months away."

"*Ruby Sparks,*" Seetha said.

"Oh, the girls and I loved that," Kristen said. At Flick Chicks, no one minds watching a movie we've already seen. Plus, some nights, the movie is beside the point. We'd been inspired to start the group by the Senior Señoras, a group my mother belonged to before the move south. But we didn't care about improving our Spanish, or improving ourselves at all. We just wanted to hang out with good friends and talk and eat.

We ended up watching *Chocolat,* one of my personal faves, eating salty oatmeal cookies and ginger ice cream, and dipping into a bowl of glazed spiced nuts. Right about the time the mayor broke into the shop to eat the chocolate window display, Gabe wafted in, lured by the warm cookies. Hugs all around, then he settled on the floor in front of his mother with a bowl of cookies and ice cream. Snowball, the fluffy white dock cat who'd adopted them, curled up in his lap.

I passed the bowl of nuts around. Because when our secrets cause us pain, nothing soothes the soul better than good friends and good food.

Twenty-six

Seattle. You've got to love the rain.

—Mark Knopfler, "Seattle"

WEDNESDAY MORNING DIDN'T EXACTLY DAWN. IT SLUNK in, wet and soggy, reeking of diesel fumes and that faint ocean smell of salt water, decayed fish, and seaweed. And seagull poop.

A rainbow of colored umbrellas punctuated the black bumbers favored by the suited class. I opted for a purple hooded rain jacket.

"You're sure in a good mood," I told Sandra after she'd been in the shop ten whole minutes, whistling while she worked, and hadn't groused once about Kristen being late for the Wednesday morning staff meeting. "Mr. Right feeling frisky last night?"

"Hot and spicy," she said, "like our fall mixes."

Zak choked back a laugh.

"I just feel better when it rains," she said. "You know?"

It meant hiding my pink shoes in the closet until spring. "It's nothing magic—just a change in barometric pressure."

"Right. Burst my bubble. Thanks."

Moments later, Kristen stood in the doorway, shaking

out her black raincoat. I let her in, and we all gathered in the mixing nook. Even Sandra's mood dimmed a bit as the reality of Tory's absence sank in.

"Zak, wanta ride with me to Doc's service?"

"I thought I'd go see Tory instead. They won't let her out." He studied his hands, then raised his head. "On top of losing him, she gets the blame. Sucks big time."

Yep.

I'd have to crash the funeral alone. Okay—easier to eavesdrop that way.

"Sandra will be out making more tea this afternoon, so Reed and Kristen, the shop is yours." They nodded solemnly. "That's a figure of speech, not a gift. Hey, we all feel like rotten eggs, but we have to perk ourselves up, for the customers."

I cleared my throat and went on. "I hate to say this, but we need somebody to fill in a few days a week. Until Tory gets back. Any suggestions, let me know."

An uncomfortable silence followed.

"What about the new labels?" Reed asked.

I tried wiggling my eyebrows, but had never mastered the trick. "Soon. And you'll love them, I promise."

"Oh, goodie!" Kristen clapped her hands. "I love Fabiola's designs."

"Just you wait and see."

BY midmorning, the rain had stopped, and I headed out to make a few deliveries. On my way back to the shop, I glanced in the window at Starbucks and did a double take.

It hadn't changed much since 1971. Packed as usual with tourists paying homage to the shop that launched coffee as we now know it, the place radiates a kind of golden glow, richly scented with coffee, steamed milk, and a hint of vanilla. And today, wet wool.

"Gentlemen." I greeted my friends.

"Fine day out, Ms. Reece." Hot Dog said.

"For a fish. May I join you?"

Jim offered me his stool and moved over one, so that I was flanked by the two men.

Hot Dog whipped out a Starbucks gift card. "Got this in my hat one day. Figured it were a joke, it wouldn't have nothing but a few pennies on it, but she said everybody needs a treat, so here we are. What may we get you?"

I started to protest, not wanting them to spend their treat money on me. But everyone likes to be generous now and then. "Double shot nonfat latte, a dash of cinnamon."

"Grande?" he asked. I nodded. He bowed and left to place my order.

I turned to my other companion. "Good to see you, Jim. Keeping dry?"

"Oh, yes. I'm not homeless, you know. I've got an SRO in the Market." Single room occupancy. "But walls make me antsy. I'd rather walk than sit around with the old folks, playing cards or shooting the breeze."

Easy to imagine. "I'm afraid I scared our friend yesterday. I suggested he might tell the police what he saw, and he took off."

"Hot Dog and I met up with him last night." Jim raised a hand. "Please don't ask where. But I don't think it's the police he's afraid of."

"Social workers?"

He tightened his lips. "They call 'em psych wards 'cause they make you crazy."

Hot Dog reclaimed his stool, buttoning the gift card safely into the breast pocket of his wool shirt, a classic brown-and-gold Pendleton plaid, slightly frayed of collar and cuff. "Ms. Reece, I sure am sorry those police arrested Miss Tory. She be the sweetest, most generoustest girl. I was plum shocked."

The light dawned. "Hot Dog, I respect your privacy, and you don't have to tell me if you don't want to. But it might help Tory."

The barista called my name and Jim slid off his stool to fetch my coffee.

"Did she take you to the doctor? To her father's clinic?"

"Yes, ma'am, she did. I got a hole in my heart. Cut my boxing career short." He thumped his chest with his forefinger. "That's why Jim keeps an eye on me, why he and the fellas make sure I don't let my mouth get me into trouble."

I remembered "the fellas" holding him back when the suburban teenagers came spoiling for a fight.

"The docs in the Market clinic do a good job, but it were acting up and she thought I needed a little exter attention. So she took me up to Pill Hill. Paid for the cab and all."

Proof that Tory managed to support herself in retail while keeping her heart open.

"Which doctor did you see?"

"Ken Griffey." His eyes twinkled. "Not *that* Ken Griffey. She talked with him private, then he saw me. Listened to my ticker. Ran some tests. Checked me out good, and din't charge me a dime. Din't charge her, neither—I made her promise he were doing this outta the good of his heart."

Or to get into her graces. But why? Did Griffey not realize how little influence she had over her father? "Did you know Dr. Griffey was her father's partner?"

"No, ma'am. Not till we left. It got late and the place were shut down. This old guy stormed in. Not so old, I guess. Same eyes, but they be a sight prettier on her. They shared some—unpleasant words."

Jim set my latte and the cinnamon shaker on the bar in front of me.

Hot Dog went on. "He said something like, 'You wanted nothing to do with me or medicine, until some freeloader needs help.' And she got mad. She said, 'What good is it if you don't use it for the people in need?' Now I know that was Doc, and he were her daddy. I felt real bad, I did, being the reason they argued."

The argument Robbie the cabdriver had witnessed. "It

wasn't your fault, Hot Dog. It was an old argument, and I don't think it was really about medicine."

"He yelled at Dr. Griffey, too. 'You can't get to me through her. Don't even think about it.' Last thing I want to do now is make things worse for Miss Tory by saying how angry she were at her daddy, but it's the truth, and if anybody asks me about it, I'll have to tell."

I cradled the hot cup, hoping it would warm the chills running laps on my spine. Hot Dog feared he was pointing the finger at Tory, and it was true, Tracy and Spencer would think his story proved their theory. Proved it twice over: Not only did she nurse a grudge against her father for attempting to squash her dreams, but he had also stomped on her charitable spirit.

Too bad "he had it coming" is no defense to premeditated murder.

How did Ken Griffey, MD, fit into this deadly tangle? Had he been trying to get something from Finch, through Tory, not realizing that was a dead end?

Without realizing it, Hot Dog may have given me the clues that would get both Sam and Tory off the hook.

The physical muscle might be defective, but there was no hole in his true heart.

WHEN I left the corporate world, I donated my suits and heels to a "Dress for Success" program for women entering the job market. It felt a little strange, helping women find jobs in the world I couldn't wait to leave, but I like to think of it from an HR perspective as one last supportive gesture.

Besides, they were great outfits. Not their fault my job evaporated.

But I'd stashed a couple of favorites in the back of the closet, just in case. After my coffee break, I dashed back to the shop, then down to the loft, and Presto! Chango! Transformed from funky-chic shop girl to Urban Professional.

I zoomed out of the parking garage and up to Broadway, then worked my way to the Episcopal cathedral. Used to seem like anybody who was anybody in Seattle, if they weren't Catholic or Jewish, was buried from St. Mark's—the default church for the undeclared. But times change, and it's acceptable to be secular in public now.

Designed in the 1920s as a grand cathedral in the European tradition, the partially finished building fell victim to foreclosure in the early 1940s. Local lore says it served briefly as a military training center—the airmen even left behind a mural in part of the crypt, or so the story goes—reopening for services before the war ended. Somehow, it acquired a famous organ and still hosts choral and organ recitals.

But while Brother Cadfael would be baffled by the Book of Common Prayer—not to mention modern English—I'm sure he'd feel at home in the place.

Its calm grace enveloped me the moment I stepped out of the Mustang.

Inside, the church glowed. The pews gleamed in the soft light made evanescent by the stained glass.

It's a cliché to say your heart twists—if it does, you seriously need a cardiologist—but mine made some pretzelish movements. With sorrow not for Doc, although I supposed he deserved some sympathy, but for Marianne, who did seem to love him.

And mostly for Tory, deprived of a father's support and shown his scorn. Now wrongly blamed for his death.

I hoped the jail staff would take pity and give her an extended visiting hour. Maybe one-on-one, so she could touch Zak's hand. So he could clasp her to his broad chest.

After what I'd heard about Damien Finch's sharp tongue and hard heart, the size of the crowd surprised me.

I slid into a rear pew, the better to see who was there. And perhaps, to avoid being seen.

Near the front, behind Marianne and two tall men I judged to be her sons, sat Ken Griffey and a blonde, no doubt his wife. Three other couples filled the row—probably more doctors and spouses. (Shouldn't the plural be spice?) And behind them, several women, including Stephanie, the job-hunting receptionist.

"Nice to see you honoring the dead."

I sat bolt upright, eyes wide, then glared at Detective Tracy. So much for not being seen. "You scared the parsley out of me."

He grinned. "That's a new one."

"We're in church. Where's your partner?"

He pointed with his head and I spotted her, sitting a few rows in front of us on the far aisle.

In the movies and on TV, police go to funerals to spy out the killer. But these two thought they had their man—or woman. "Why are you here? You've got your suspect in jail."

"Never hurts to keep your eyes open."

"Lot of people here, considering how many of them disliked Damien Finch."

The organist changed hymns and the congregation rose.

"Grief means different things to different people," Tracy said.

I considered that as I watched the celebrant process up the center aisle. For some here, grief meant genuine sorrow. For some, a job search. For others, relief. And for someone, if I dare say this in a church, satisfaction.

It was, as nearly everyone connected with Damien Finch liked to say, complicated.

But when I turned to suggest as much to Detective Tracy, he had disappeared.

"I feel like I should go," the receptionist said to another woman outside an hour later. They were standing near the Mustang.

"Not me," came the reply. "Graveyards give me the creeps."

"Need a ride?" I said. "Pepper Reece. We met the other day at the clinic."

"I remember you. Thanks, yeah." She waved good-bye to the other woman and opened the passenger door. "Nice car."

"Thanks. I'm a friend of the family," I said, stretching the truth and sliding into reverse. "How long did you work for Dr. Finch?"

"Stephanie Niehaus. Too long." Her left hand flew to her mouth. "Sorry. My mother raised me better than that."

"She did. That's why you went to the funeral, and now you're going to the burial." I turned off Tenth onto Blaine, headed for Lake View Cemetery. "Don't worry about it. I'm guessing he wasn't any easier on his staff than on his family."

"Half the time, he acted like we weren't there. But when he needed something, it was crack the whip, hop to it, why didn't you know what I was thinking and have that file or form or whatever it was ready for me."

"So why'd you keep working there?"

"Needed a job. And he paid well—he had to, to keep everybody from quitting."

"What about the other doctors? The clinic partners?"

"He drove them away, too. Of course, they weren't actually partners, so when they didn't get what they wanted, they quit or got fired."

One more reason to pay your staff well and treat them nicely. If you don't, they lose their manners and loosen their tongues when you die. "Aren't all doctors in a clinic partners?"

"Some clinics run that way, but Dr. Finch hired them as employees so he could fire them. That's how it struck me anyway. He was always in a tussle with somebody."

I eased the Mustang into a parking space. "Dr. Griffey managed to hang in there."

"He wanted to buy the clinic. But Dr. Finch decided to

sell it to somebody else." She gave me a quick sidelong glance. "I hear things."

Now we're cooking with gas, as my grandfather used to say. Had that person sped up the process a bit by offing Finch? "Who?"

"Not sure. But you know, he seemed different somehow, before he died. He came in regularly and I got the sense that he was trying to—oh, I don't know. Change his ways. Probably my imagination."

We walked up the sidewalk, following a stream of men and women in dark suits or raincoats, umbrellas in hand.

Like other Capitol Hill kids, I'd spent hundreds of hours playing and hanging out in Volunteer Park or riding my bike through this cemetery. In eighth grade, our Washington history class made a field trip here to see the graves of Princess Angeline, daughter of Chief Seattle; pioneer families; and the Nisei War Memorial to the Japanese-American veterans of World War II. My mother had enjoyed walking here, especially in spring when the budding trees framed the view of Lake Washington. My dad had stopped by now and again to pay respects to Bruce Lee and, later, his son Brandon.

But I'd never attended a service here. Among the weathered angels, saints, and other monuments dating back to the 1870s, the most striking has to be the woman seated in a chair, a young girl standing before her. Moss and algae stained the pedestal, and behind it, willow branches stood stark against the gray sky.

I shook off the melancholy it always gives me and told myself to pay attention.

We neared the Garden Mausoleum and I hung back, not sure I belonged. The man I'd known—Doc, the mysterious street man—hadn't actually existed.

Griffey, his wife—sporting a baby bump—and other doctorly types stood behind Marianne and her sons, along with two women I presumed were their wives. Stephanie joined a clutch of women at the group's edge. I glanced around, expecting to see Tracy or Spencer lurking behind a tree. But if they were here, they were well hidden.

The mourners bowed their heads and the priest began to speak, though I was too far away to hear clearly. The service was short, and when it ended, everyone drifted away, speaking in low tones.

I approached the mausoleum and read the names on the plaques. Several generations of Finches were buried here. Damien's name and date of birth had been engraved on a plaque that bore his first wife's name and dates. I'd never understood why people do that, but it wasn't uncommon. How creepy it must have been for him to visit her—assuming he did—and see his own name already in place. And how strange for Marianne, when she visited her friend. Where would she be buried when the time came?

But none of that mattered right now. I stretched out a hand and brushed my fingers over Carolyn Finch's name. How often had Tory come here?

"Your daughter is a lovely young woman. You'd be proud of her—her big heart, her artistic talent. Her determination. You don't know me; there's no reason for you to believe me. But I'm doing everything I can for her."

And then the sky broke open and the deluge began.

Twenty-seven

Rule No. 2,119: Never speak ill of the dead. Save your venom for the living.

—Steve Brewer, *Rules for Successful Living*

"YOU GOING TO THE RECEPTION AT THE HOUSE?" STEPH-anie said when we climbed inside the Mustang, her tone hoping I'd say no and let her off the hook.

"For a bit," I said. "For the family." Not a pretense, really—Tory was still part of Doc's family.

I put the Mustang in gear, looked left, then slammed on the brake, killing the engine in the process. Dang. Not getting enough sleep—my eyes were playing tricks on me.

"Sorry," I muttered to Stephanie, and restarted the engine. She didn't respond, instead leaning forward, staring past me.

"Something wrong?"

"I just thought I saw—no." She sat back, brow furrowed. Something *was* wrong, but what?

"HE lived here?" My new pal's voice rose in amazement. "It's like, straight outta Disneyland."

On the drive north, I'd pressed, but it was clear that

Stephanie not only didn't know who Damien Finch planned to sell his practice to, she didn't have a clue why he had decided to retire. Had Dr. Griffey known the real reason?

Impossible to say. Nothing anyone had said suggested that Finch made a habit of lying—except maybe those broken promises to doctors that both Tory and Stephanie had alluded to. But he certainly had made a habit of withholding the truth when it suited him.

I parked and hesitated, feeling guilty about crashing a funeral lunch. Though Marianne had spoken to me willingly. In private.

"Come on," Stephanie said, car door already open. "It's pouring."

The picture of Tory rotting in jail for a murder she didn't commit lodged in my mind and my promise to her dead mother rang in my ears. We dashed to the house.

Inside, Marianne Finch stood in the dining room, pointing out features of the soggy backyard to Mrs. Griffey. No surprise that the clinic receptionist hadn't been to the good doctor's home, but his partner—or whatever the relationship—and spouse?

I took refuge in the living room. No charm spared here. Oriental carpets lay scattered on the oak floors, and a chair and sideboard were either genuine Stickley or excellent reproductions.

Arched niches built into the plaster walls, a classic Craftsman touch, held a striking collection of antique American art pottery. I recognized a Roseville pitcher and a blue apple blossom wall pocket, a graceful Rookwood vase, and a white ringware vase. I'd whistle if I knew how.

A niche next to the tiled fireplace held a small oil painting in a pale gilt frame that drew me like—well, like forbidden sweets drew the mayor in *Chocolat*.

A close-up of a red brick building, a single window lit for the evening. A lace curtain draped to one side. A small boy at a piano. The rich color, the moody contrast between light and dark, the artist's obvious tenderness toward the boy all marked it as an exceptionally fine slice of life.

In the lower-right corner were the initials VF.

I tried to picture Tory's personnel file. Her paychecks were made out to Tory Finch, and I didn't recall seeing Victoria on the few documents in her file.

And this exquisite oil bore no resemblance to the work I'd seen in her apartment.

"Stunning, isn't it?"

I hadn't heard Marianne approach.

Seeing my consternation, she raised a graceful hand. "My son said you were a spy and I should toss you out, but I'm glad you're here. As Tory's representative."

"Thank you."

"There's more you should see." She beckoned and I followed her up the curving staircase to a second-floor sitting room. On a corner table beneath the slanted ceiling, a hand-blown glass lamp glowed. Modern art glass is popular in these parts, inspired by Dale Chihuly and his Pilchuck School, though this piece could have been genuine Tiffany. Another Oriental rug, in soft reds and golds with blue accents, lay on the floor. A loveseat twin to the one in Tory's apartment and two matching chairs had been upholstered in cranberry velvet.

"Carolyn's?" I asked.

"Tory didn't have room for all the pieces, so I promised to hang on to them for her. I told Damien they had belonged to my friend and we were keeping them. He didn't like it. But I know he snuck in here from time to time."

She was braver than I had suspected. And Damien—had he been that callous, or that wrecked by his first wife's death and his daughter's estrangement?

Marianne gestured at the walls, at oils and watercolors by the same sure hand I'd witnessed downstairs. "This is why my husband became a doctor, and why he was so determined that Tory choose something else—anything else—but art."

More cropped landscapes, several portraits, a few tentative abstracts. I studied the landscapes on the nearest wall, then turned to Marianne, filled with questions.

"VF. Victoria Finch," she said. "Damien's mother. Widowed young, with one child. She struggled constantly to make a living, working for minimum wage as a waitress and a hotel maid. Day jobs. And every night she painted. She's buried in the same mausoleum where he is."

"I always thought those belonged to wealthy families."

"The burial rights were paid for decades ago, back when the Finches had money. Money they later lost. Victoria had to make it on her own."

"Like Tory." I took a closer look at the portrait of a boy with golden brown eyes—the same boy as in the piece downstairs. Damien, at seven or eight. Beside it hung the image of a young woman in her early thirties with the same eyes, though hers held a deep weariness. A self-portrait? "She never mentioned a grandmother."

"She never knew her. Victoria died when Damien was a junior in high school. He managed to win a scholarship and put himself through college and med school. Then he created the life he hadn't had."

I faced her. "He resented the sacrifices his mother made so she could paint."

Marianne nodded, lips tight.

"Okay, so Victoria struggled," I said, "but who can deny her talent? Or Tory's? Have you seen her work?"

"She had a gift." Marianne spoke softly. "And so does Tory."

"You never told her? Tory never knew why her father was so opposed to her plans, her dreams?" Marianne had been between a rock and a hard place, but I couldn't understand why she'd helped her husband keep such a terrible secret.

"She managed, you know. Beautifully." And had enough money to help her friends on the street.

"Damien didn't see it that way. Better for her to give up art altogether than suffer in its clutches, especially if she had children. I'm not saying he was right, but that's how he felt."

I sat on the antique walnut chair, processing it all.

She perched on the settee across from me. "I found out a couple of years ago, when I cleaned out the attic and discovered all these paintings."

My heart ached, and that was no metaphor. "Such pain, all because he insisted on keeping the past hidden."

"Because he loved his daughter. He wanted to spare her."

What had Laurel said last night? You can only trust that you've taught your children to make good choices, then let them make those choices. From the outside, it looked like Damien, Carolyn, and Marianne had taught their daughter well. But Tory's father, scarred by his own childhood, didn't trust her. Or more likely, himself.

"There you are, Mom." A tall man in his late thirties, in dark suit pants, a white shirt, and a sky blue tie stood in the doorway. He glowered at me. "People are asking for you."

Where had I seen him before?

"Pepper," she said. "My son, Dr. Kevin Ripken."

He nodded curtly and extended his arm, a wedding ring glinting on his hand. At the top of the stairs, Marianne paused. "Please tell Tory I will visit, but it's still too soon. Give her my love."

The clinic, Monday afternoon. Kevin Ripken had emerged from his stepfather's office and kissed his mother tenderly, but radiated tension toward Ken Griffey.

Rivals for the clinic ownership?

Recognition must have shown on my face. Ripken's eyes narrowed. In warning, or worry?

Twenty-eight

SEATTLE RAIN FESTIVAL—SEPTEMBER TO MAY ANNUALLY.

—Bumper sticker

I GLANCED OUT THE WINDOW AT THE TOP OF THE STAIRS before following Marianne and her son down. The rain had stopped and the gray gloom had lifted. Dare I hope for brighter days to come?

In Seattle in September? Nah.

In the kitchen, Stephanie chatted with a nurse from the clinic, who promised her a ride home. I handed her my card—still the old design, but not for long.

She read the card, then raised her wide eyes. Obviously, she had not connected me to her employer's daughter, the suspect in custody. They'd be whispering before I cleared the threshold.

I paused on the front steps to check my phone. No messages from the shop, but one text from Fabiola. *Looking good, girlfriend!* she wrote. The designs in progress, I presumed. I smiled at the screen.

A text from Callie the librarian read, *No recent partnerships on record. I'll keep digging.*

That made sense, after Stephanie's comment that Finch preferred clinic arrangements that he could change at will. I dropped the phone back in my bag.

"You have to talk to her. Sooner, not later. There's too much at stake." A woman's voice.

"She isn't going to want to talk to me. She's going to want to help the kid," a man replied. Dr. Griffey? Or Dr. Ripken?

"Tell her if she won't honor his promises, you won't keep yours. You'll take the patients and the staff and start over on your own."

I peeked around the hedge. A pregnant blonde and a man with sandy graying hair. Griffey.

"Marianne, I'm showing Kenny your garden," Mrs. Griffey called out in a perky voice, although I hadn't heard her mention the plants or the view. "So lovely."

Marianne Finch came into view, careful to stay on the turtle paving stones. Her heels would sink right in to the ground.

What promises did Mrs. Griffey mean? Promises made on Monday, when Marianne and her son dropped in to see Griffey, promises relating to a deal Finch had reneged on?

Did that make the son a suspect—and cast Marianne in a different light?

Did I need to rethink my assumption that no one would kill a dying man?

Did I need to get out of here before I charged back in and asked more questions that got me tossed out on my keister?

Three maybes and a definite yes.

I'D driven three blocks when I remembered why Dr. Kevin Ripken had looked familiar when I saw him in the clinic. Last week in the shop, I'd taken him for a tourist and sold him spice tea for his wife. But he was the stepson of a murdered man, visiting the scene of the crime. Wondering how his stepsister, enough younger that he didn't know her well, could have done such a thing.

I pulled the Mustang over and fished out my phone. Google said Dr. Ripken was a cardiologist and surgeon, in a group practice in Seattle. Photos on the group website showed the same man I'd just met.

Had Kevin Ripken hoped to take over his stepfather's practice?

But what did any of this have to do with Tory?

Talk about complicated.

SINCE my first taste of teenage freedom, whenever I need to get away and think—or just get away—I hop a ferry. Used to be, you could buy a one-way walk-on ticket for seventy-five cents and ride as long as you wanted. I'd buy a cup of cocoa and lean on the railing, letting my worries drift away in the ferry's roiling wake. No matter that they were usually waiting for me back at the dock.

But 9/11 changed security permanently, so now you have to get off on the other end and buy another ticket before getting back on. Fares rose, too. But what could be more comforting on a gray day, post-funeral, than riding the waves of an old habit? I dropped the car at my loft and headed for Pier 52.

Along with my black pantsuit and heels, I'd donned a black wool gabardine raincoat, my favorite coat ever. I cinched the belt tight across the double-breasted front and carried my cocoa out to the rails.

It always feels about ten degrees colder on the water. I closed my eyes and let the breeze spritz salt air on me—though with all the goo in my hair, only a gale could blow it free.

What a day. What a week. Everyone I had talked to seemed to think Tory had killed Damien Finch, but no one seemed to blame her. Not even Marianne, who'd loved him.

I opened my eyes and sipped my cocoa. The ferry system had gone green and switched from insulating white foam to paper cups like we use in the shop. Cold stung the backs of my hands; heat stung the palms.

Nearly fifty years after his mother's death, Damien Finch had still resented her choices. I expect every child feels like a part of his parent is outside his grasp. But that distance had wounded him, and he blamed it—and her early death— on her need to paint.

Had his rigid dictates been an effort to protect his daughter, or an attempt to keep her, too, from falling prey to the evils of artistic ambition?

We might never know.

Damien Finch had been dying. Was that a key fact, or a red herring? (Never mind that the herring in the Market fishmongers' stalls are a bright, shiny, slithery silver.)

So who knew? I ticked off the names. Marianne and, presumably, her son Kevin and his anonymous brother. And their wives.

Tory. Though she may not have believed him.

Ken Griffey and his wife? I couldn't be sure. Griffey had known of the retirement, but not necessarily the reason. Finch might have enjoyed keeping that bit to himself.

Clinic staff? The receptionist had been clueless. What about the nurses and the office manager?

Patients? Mr. Franklin had said Finch was retiring, but I suspected that if he knew why, he'd have said so.

Robbie the cabbie? He'd said one puzzling thing: Dr. Finch didn't like to drive, "not since months." And then he'd described the argument between father and daughter. Months since the fight, or the diagnosis? Robbie was easy to talk to. Finch might have told him.

Wait a sec. I shivered inside my coat and moved closer to the observation deck, where banks of windows on each side offered wind protection but didn't block the view of Bainbridge Island and the Winslow docks. Griffey's wife had mentioned Finch's broken promises. What if Griffey thought that he could pull an end run? That if Finch died before he sold the clinic to someone else, his estate would have to carry out his contractual obligations and sell to Griffey?

If there was a contract.

Marianne would hardly tell me, and Tory wouldn't know. Stephanie?

Could I convince her to let me prowl through her dead boss's office? Talk about violating confidentiality six ways to Sunday.

And hadn't I heard, back at the law firm, that contracts don't have to be written to be enforceable? You just had to be able to prove their terms. Not so easy, when one party was dead.

Beneath us, the big engines shifted gears and the decks vibrated as we slowed our approach. Once home to many farmers who supplied the Market—the prewar Japanese farmers' strawberry fields were legendary—Bainbridge Island had gradually become a wealthy bedroom community. Midafternoon on a Wednesday, commuter traffic was light. A dozen or so cars and a few delivery trucks had driven on in Seattle.

Okay, so the hypothetical contract obliging Finch to sell to Griffey might have given him a motive for murder. That still left the question of means. How could Griffey have gotten poison into the tea, or the cup?

The engines downshifted again and I moved up to the foredeck, pausing to watch a bald eagle bank above the harbor.

I headed through the empty viewing area to the stairs down to the car deck. We were a few minutes from the dock, but walk-ons are first off.

Halfway down the long flight, the heavy steel door slammed above me. The sound echoed in the craterlike space. Footsteps thudded on the metal treads.

Between steps, I heard a woman say, "She'll figure it out."

I froze, one foot suspended, one hand on the rail. *No. Impossible.*

"Don't worry," her companion replied. "I'll do whatever it takes to protect our future. For all of us." The engine noise drowned out the rest of his words.

The Griffeys, or the Ripkens?

They were following me. They had plans, they wanted Tory to stay in jail and take the blame for her father's murder, and they were following me.

To the left, a wall and a handrail. To the right, an open railing, and below, the car deck. Nowhere to go but down. I just needed to get there before he—whoever he was—got to me.

But with my tote bag on my shoulder, the cocoa in my hand, and the unfamiliar high heels, I could only move so fast.

"We have to stop her."

A few more steps. A few more.

The big engines chugged and the ferry shifted forward ominously. I grabbed the metal rail, my foot swinging free in midair. Between the rails, I saw only the steel decking and the car roofs below. The ferry stuttered and swung to the side, and I heard a shout. Beneath me? Behind me? Or from my own throat?

My foot scrabbled for purchase on the metal treads. Found it. Lost it. Found it again. I shifted my weight, struggling for stability. My belt came untied and the long coat flaps twisted around my legs.

Three steps to go.

My left leg collapsed. A hand grabbed my coat from behind, jerking me back against the open railing. The metal rail struck me mid-back, knocking the breath out of me. One more shove, one more unexpected movement of man or boat, and I'd go flying.

I wrenched away and stumbled down the next step, caught in my own coat.

The hand reached for me again, fingers grasping at my shoulder, my collar, my neck.

My right foot touched the level surface of the car deck. I spun around and flung the cup of cocoa up the steps.

And into the face of Sunny Jim.

"YOU followed me. Ow. That hurts."

"We had no idea, Pepper. I swear. We must have left the Finches' house right after you did."

"If you weren't following me, why were you on the boat?" I stifled a yelp as the first mate pressed another spot on my ankle. After my near-crash and twisted ankle, the ferry staff had bundled me into a wheelchair and escorted me and the Griffeys into the terminal. The ferry had unloaded its passengers and vehicle traffic and chugged back to Seattle without its first mate, the officer charged with handling medical emergencies.

"I wish you'd let me take a look at that. I am a medical doctor." The remains of my cocoa had been too cool to cause Ken Griffey any damage, beyond making his face and suit jacket a chocolatey-syrupy mess. But the shock had slowed him down.

"My heart is fine. Except that you half scared me to death, grabbing me like that."

"You stumbled. I thought you were going to fall down the steps, or slip through the railing."

Hearing his voice had thrown me off balance. But I'd have gotten down safely if he hadn't threatened to stop me.

"We were heading home. We live on the island." Mrs. Dr. Griffey's first name remained a blank.

"Let's elevate this ankle." The first mate gently raised my leg and rested it on the seat of a chair. "I've got to hunt up some ice and call my safety officer." He stepped out, leaving the door open, and began muttering into a large, black hand radio that crackled in reply. Communications technology on the ferries lags eons behind the Seattle Police Department.

"You said, 'We have to stop her.' And at the house, you"—I pointed at her—"you talked about 'the kid' and broken promises. I thought you meant stop Marianne from helping Tory. But you didn't. You meant me. You wanted to stop me from finding out what you'd done."

"No," Griffey's wife said, shaking her head furiously. "Tell her everything, Kenny. It's time."

Griffey pried two chairs from a stack and set them facing mine. I wondered whether to call the first mate to witness a murder confession.

Griffey looked like the peanut butter boy after the factory burned. "We—we wanted Marianne to do what was right, even though her husband hadn't. She always was his better half."

That rang true—she'd kept Carolyn's memory alive by keeping up a relationship with Tory against her husband's wishes. She'd even kept Carolyn's furniture for the girl.

"It had nothing to do with Tory," his wife said. "We barely knew her. We were horrified when she was arrested."

"Instead of you. Because you killed Doc. Dr. Finch." Sharp pain shot up my leg.

At his doorway post, the first mate pivoted, radio in hand, eyes darting from me to the Griffeys and back.

"No!" they both said.

I shifted in the hard chair, careful not to jostle my ankle. "Let me see if I have this straight. When you came to work for him, he promised to sell you the clinic when he retired." They nodded. "But then, he changed his mind. He decided to bring in a new owner to take his place." Heads bobbed again.

"I admit, I was furious," Dr. Griffey said. "I may have said stupid things. Stephanie may have heard me. The cabbie may have heard me. But I would never violate my oath. 'Do no harm.'" He put his hand over his heart.

It sounded genuine. But then, sincerity is easily faked. If he could kill someone, he could lie about it.

"So 'the kid' you talked about wasn't Tory at all. It was Kevin. Dr. Ripken, Marianne's son."

"Finch liked to leave things dangling, throw people off their stride, so he could manipulate them into doing what he wanted." Hurt and betrayal wracked Griffey's voice.

"We thought," his wife said, "that if the deal with her son wasn't done yet, we could get her to see reason. Sell the clinic to Ken, as Finch had agreed years ago. Ken had talked to them both, before Finch died. He thought she was on his side."

If that was true, then the Griffeys had no motive for murder.

"And after he died? When she came to see you at the clinic on Monday?"

"I showed her the contract. But she said Finch had always intended to bring in her son, after he got experience elsewhere. She wanted me to agree to that, to try to work together. A compromise, instead of a lawsuit."

Unless I missed my guess, she'd been trying—to use the phrase that kept cropping up—to make things right. Damien Finch had promised his wife to bring her son into the clinic, at the same time as he'd promised Griffey to sell to him when he retired.

Hoist by his own petard. Caught in his own trap. Snared by his own shenanigans.

And killed. By one of the dueling doctors, to prevent a compromise over the clinic?

Or by someone else for a reason I hadn't yet discovered?

"But you couldn't accept that?" I said.

"It sounds reasonable on the surface," Griffey said. "But I have a family to provide for. I've spent years building up that practice. I needed the security of ownership, of knowing Marianne and her son couldn't toss me out on a whim."

The first mate knelt beside me and repositioned my foot

on a bag of ice and a small pillow. I gritted my teeth. Even if the Griffeys were lying about the contract renegotiations, how could they have gotten poison into a Spice Shop cup in Doc's hands early in the morning on a street corner in the Market?

Look for the simplest explanation. Much as I hated to admit it, Tag might be right.

On the other hand, even if they were telling the truth now, the Griffeys could still be killers. So could Dr. Ripken. But I couldn't place any of them on my shop corner the morning Doc died.

I couldn't place anyone there but Tory and Sam.

"Did you know why Finch decided to retire? That he was dying?" I asked.

"He didn't tell me. But I recognized the signs—weight loss, jaundice, enlarged lymph nodes in the neck. One day I found him vomiting in an exam room. He left the office for appointments during the day—something he'd never done before."

"You said his mood changed," his wife prompted.

"Yeah." He let out a humorless laugh. "He'd always been secretive and demanding. Manipulative. But he seemed—torn. Anxious. Burdened."

"Who wouldn't be, knowing what he knew?" I asked.

"Then his lab reports got mixed in with a patient's by mistake. Pancreatic cancer."

Just as Marianne had said.

"I'm taking you back on the next ferry," the first mate told me. "It'll be here in a few minutes. If you want to press charges against these people, I'll have to call the authorities."

"Where were you last Wednesday morning?" I asked the doctor. If he said surgery, I'd know he was lying.

He colored, as even prematurely graying redheads do, and reached for his wife's hand. "We went for an ultrasound, here on the island. It's our first baby."

She reached for her purse. "I have the picture in my bag. It might have a date and time."

No wonder he'd been smiling when he came in, late, to see his elderly patient. "They can go," I told the first mate.

Through the window, I saw that bald eagle swoop in and chase a seagull off a pier. I hoped he was having a better day fishing than I'd had.

Twenty-nine

I know my herbs. They have fixed properties, and follow sacred rules. Human creatures do not. And I cannot even wish that they did.

—Brother Cadfael, *St. Peter's Fair*, by Ellis Peters

"I CAN WALK," I TOLD THE FIRST MATE AS THE FERRY docked on the Seattle side—smoothly this time. "I only live a few blocks away."

"No, ma'am," he said, tilting the wheelchair back and pushing me forward.

My grumbling worsened when I saw who waited for me.

"What are you doing here? How did you know?"

"The safety officer is an old SPD buddy. He recognized your name and called me," Tag said.

I thanked the first mate for the first aid, and hobbled into the ancient black Saab as Tag stood on the curb, grinning. Nice as it is to have people take care of you occasionally, it loses its charm when they're so pleased with themselves.

I leaned back, eyes closed, images from the screwy afternoon whipping through my battered brain. "Oh, wait," I said as Tag signaled a turn onto Western. "We need to run by the shop and drop off a key."

He grunted and flicked off his signal, rewarded by a beep from the car behind us. As he drove up the hill, I gazed out the window. The patches of blue that had teased me on the return ferry trip were gone, the sky once again a leaden gray.

I saw the dog before the man. Arf and Sam, lumbering down the alley. Even at a distance, he looked forlorn, the ball cap so not his style.

Tag drove up First past the entrance to the Market, then turned down Pine. Bumping along the cobbled slope did not help my aching heart or my sore ankle.

But what nagged at me was the image of that blue Mustang thundering down this very stretch into traffic—if it hadn't hit the curb first.

"What did Olerud find in the street the other day?"

Tag's brow furrowed, but he said nothing.

"He found something," I said, "where the winemaker's car was parked. He called to you and you dashed up there. You took pictures and pulled out an evidence bag."

His jaw tightened almost imperceptibly. Before we got married, a coworker told me a square jaw signaled a hard-headed man and to think twice about the wedding.

"Don't deny it," I continued. "I saw you."

At the corner, he put the car in neutral and held out his hand. "Give me the key."

I dug out the spare and he marched into the shop, returning a moment later with Reed at his heels. Tag hopped in and I rolled down my window.

"Long story," I said. "Short version, twisted ankle. Need you to close up. You know the routine?"

Eyes wide, Reed stood a little taller. "Course I do, Pepper. I've been watching you."

"Suck-up," Tag muttered as I rolled up the window.

"He's solicitous. It can be an attractive quality. You might try it."

He glowered and gripped the wheel.

At my building, he insisted we take the freight elevator,

and I didn't object. The prospect of hobbling up all those flights of stairs made my whole leg ache.

By the time we reached my door, the pain had worsened and I accepted Tag's help getting settled on my soft, welcoming couch and prying those nasty heels off my feet. I didn't even wince when he tossed his damp jacket over a wicker chair instead of hanging it on the hall tree by the door. *Relax*, I told myself. *He'll be leaving soon.*

But then he brewed two cups of spice tea and sat in the red paisley armchair in the corner, a serious look on the face I still found endearing. And, heaven help me, sexy.

If I wanted to solve this crime, if I wanted to find the real killer and get Tory out of jail, if I wanted to help Sam and get back to focusing on my shop and my own life, I needed Tag's help.

And if I wanted him to leave, I had to ask for it now.

"When we turned on First, I saw—" I said just as he said, "You got off lucky this time. Haven't you figured out yet that sticking your nose into other people's business is dangerous?"

"I can take care of myself."

"Obviously not."

Why did it always come back to us scrapping like cats and dogs?

I guess I'm kind of opinionated, too.

He blinked first, letting out a long sigh. "Brake fluid and tiny steel shavings."

I nearly dropped my tea mug. "Holy moly. Someone cut the brake line? She could have been killed. The owner, I mean. Are you guys investigating? Who had it in for her?"

His china blue eye softened and I suddenly understood. "Ohmygod. You think someone had it in for me. They thought that was my car."

He didn't speak. He didn't have to.

I stared, openmouthed. "But if they want me off the case,

they—he, she, whoever—knows Tory is innocent. And doesn't want me to figure out who the real killer is."

Tag looked so miserable I almost felt sorry for him.

"Have I put her in more danger? Is that why Tory is still in jail, so Spencer and Tracy can keep investigating without tipping off the real killer?" *And why you hopped right to it when you heard I'd been hurt?*

He stood and began pacing. "Pepper, you know I can't tell you anything."

"But you can tell me if I'm on the right track. Damien Finch was not a popular guy. His wife went behind his back to stay in touch with the daughter he'd cut off. His partner— or whatever Griffey is—feared he'd lose his chance to take over the clinic. His stepson—"

Tag's phone rang and he snatched up his jacket and fished it out.

Blast the man. I'm begging for info and he takes a call. The current meter maid?

"Be right back," he said.

I wasn't sure whether I was angrier at him or myself as I heard him dash down the stairs, my loft door ajar. I cocked my head, listening, and heard the soft swish of the building door opening and closing.

The ice bag slid off my foot and I wriggled it back in place. The loft door opened and Reed walked in, followed by his father, carrying a worn black medical bag. Behind him came Laurel and Tag, lugging a basket of familiar white take-out bags.

"Am I throwing a party and didn't know it?" I asked.

Bags were set down, kisses exchanged, inquiries made.

"My son said you needed help." Ron Locke gestured toward my ankle. He had the same unruly black hair as his son.

Reed shrugged. "Can't have you on the sick list. Not while there's a killer on the loose."

Five minutes later, I was pinned down good, acupuncture needles ringing my ankle. In the kitchen, Tag and Laurel unpacked her bags and opened wine. A tossed salad and penne rigate with shrimp, asparagus, and a sesame-chile sauce. Warm, herby aromas drifted through the loft.

Laurel took pity on me and brought me a salty, crusty Parmesan breadstick, one of my very favorite foods, and a glass of white wine.

"And salty oat cookies for dessert?" I said, hopeful.

Tag made a noise like a seagull when it finds a cache of abandoned French fries.

"Sorry," she said. "Sold out."

The seagull squawked pitifully.

Tag and Laurel don't exactly hate each other. It's more like disdain. She considers him a two-timing, self-indulgent playboy who thinks he's God's gift to women.

And he sees her as an interfering, self-righteous snob.

They've each got a point. And yet he'd called her, and she'd come.

"Brother Cadfael," Ron Locke said a few minutes later, when we all had full plates and drinks. "Love those books."

"What's in the salad dressing?" Reed asked Laurel.

"My secret blend." She winked at me. One of our new blends.

They'd all come here to take care of me. Reed and Laurel wanted me to keep helping Tory, Tag didn't, and Ron Locke had no dog in the fight. But they all wanted me back on my feet—no pun intended—safe and sound.

It's enough to make a grown woman's eyes sting.

And it did.

Thirty

THE LA SALLE HOTEL—FRIENDS MADE EASILY.

—Sign on a long-gone Market brothel

YOU NEVER REALLY APPRECIATE YOUR PARTS UNTIL THEY don't work. But I had a newfound appreciation for the miracle of acupuncture, and the white cream Dr. Locke had given me. Conjuring up the scents of Brother Cadfael's herbal formulas and fermenting potions, I'd given it a good sniff. "How can it work if it doesn't smell?"

"It's a homeopathic remedy—a European system rooted in herbalism, but developed centuries after Cadfael's time. Safe and effective. He was open to all traditions, and so am I."

But good as my ankle felt Thursday morning, long treks in search of clues and suspects were out. Driving might not be too smart, either, with a manual transmission and Seattle's hills.

Definitely an elevator day.

I limped through the Market, deflecting questions from the orchard girls, Yvonne, Misty the Baker, and others. Despite its bustle, the Market is a small town in many ways, with its interconnections, its rumor mills, its lightning rods, and its whiners. Its friendships and romances, its feuds and petty jealousies.

Safely tucked in my tiny office, I checked the till and ran yesterday's numbers. Everything balanced. We'd rebounded beautifully from the wee hit our sales had taken the day of the murder. But I still didn't know the long-term impact.

Or who the killer was.

I opened a file drawer and rested my foot on it. Had I been impulsive yesterday, as Laurel suggested when she heard the story? Laurel, who had practically shoved me into investigating in the first place. Or foolish, as Tag said. At worst, a bit of both. At best, I had misunderstood the Griffeys' actions and their conversations in the garden and on the ferry, leaving me only myself to blame for my injury.

At least my mistakes were honest ones.

Was there the teeniest chance that Spencer and Tracy were right? That Tory really was the killer? From their perspective, it made sense. She had motive, means, and opportunity.

And no one else did.

No. I refused to believe it. Plus, if she'd killed Doc, who wanted to warn me off the case? I swung my foot off the file cabinet and started to stand. Searing pain tore up my leg and thrust me back into the chair.

"No," I said out loud. Tears flooded my eyes.

I would keep on doing everything I could to free Tory and get her back here where she belonged.

In the absence of any brilliant investigative plans, I threw myself into the busywork of running a retail shop. Never any shortage of that. Despite my attempts to spread the word, no serious prospects for our temporary job opening had come knocking while I was out yesterday. So I called the cooking schools, the state job center, and an employment agency I'd used with good luck in the olden days.

I caught up on e-mail, Facebook, and Pinterest. Bummer

that Callie the librarian had not found any leads. Called her to check in, and left a message.

Truth be told, I was going a little stir-crazy, cooped up in my shop. I like getting out and about. My bad ankle meant I couldn't drop in on Marianne Finch and pry into the story the Griffeys had told me.

Besides, pestering a new widow the day after her husband's funeral is bad manners. And I do have some.

I thought back to my clinic visit and the old man I'd met in the lobby. What about former patients? Marianne had said doctors had to protect their assets from potential liabilities. But how to identify them? Stephanie might talk, but such prying was better done in person than by phone.

My old law firm had done some medical malpractice defense. In fact, it was a med mal case that backfired and blew the place apart. Jennifer, paralegal-turned-bookseller, had worked in that group.

I reached for the phone and it rang.

"May I speak with Tory Finch?" the caller said.

"Uh, she's with a customer. May I take a message?"

"King County Superior Court Clerk's Office calling. Please tell her the files she requested are available now."

I'd just hung up when the phone rang again.

"Pepper, it's Jordan Schmidt. Any chance you could swing by today? We got the tox report on Damien Finch. We'll retain a toxicologist, but it raises some questions I'd like to ask you."

For that, I was willing to endure a little pain.

After lunch, I hobbled out of the Market and nabbed a southbound bus. The streets ticked by. If the founders had a system for naming downtown's east-west streets, it's lost to time. The names run in pairs, from south to north: two Js, two Cs, and so on. Some people use the mnemonic "Julius Caesar Made Seattle Under Protest." Since the early Romans didn't get this far west, I prefer my own version:

"Jesus Christ Made Some Unusual People." It's certainly true, and a good number of them were riding the bus today.

First stop, Clerk's Office. I took the elevator to the sixth floor. Waited in line, willing my palms to stay dry, keeping my pleasant HR smile on my face.

"Records pickup, for Tory Finch." Putting it that way meant I wasn't lying to an officer of the court. Sort of.

The clerk drew a short stack from under the counter and handed it to me. I paid cash, said thanks, and stuffed the bundle into my tote. *Nonchalance, that's the ticket*. But the sooner I got out of there, the better I would feel.

Next up, Public Defender's Office.

"So the preliminary tox screen came in. Autopsy report isn't done yet, but I called the ME and got some good info. Wait a minute, where did I put it?" Jordan prowled through the papers on her desk, a surface about as densely covered as an anthill. She shoved books and files aside willy-nilly, nearly knocking over three of those ubiquitous white paper cups. While she searched the top of her credenza, I snatched up two cups within reach—both half-full of cold coffee—and set them on the floor by my chair. At least if one fell over there, it wouldn't ruin any files. And the stain would blend in nicely with the carpet.

"Where is it?" she repeated. "Oh, I wanted to tell you. I got a call from Mrs. Finch. The victim's wife, the suspect's stepmother." She sat up, a thick stack of paperwork in her lap. "She said you went to see her . . ."

I held my breath while she flipped through the files.

"And she said . . ." Flip, flip, flip. Next time I run into one of my old employees hunting for a law job, I'll tell them if you can file, the PD's office needs you.

"Here it is!" Jordan thrust a report in the air like a drill team leader raising the flag. "Mrs. Finch said you have her half convinced that Tory's innocent. She wants to meet with me and the prosecutor. The sooner, the better, she said."

Thank you, I silently told the heavens. "Have you talked

with the detectives on the case? Spencer and Tracy?" I told her about the vandalism to the blue Mustang and the theory that the real killer—or a confidant—had meant to warn me off the case. I did not tell her that information had come from Tag.

She scribbled notes on a yellow pad. Would the pages ever find their way into the file? They say a disorderly desk is the sign of a brilliant mind. For Tory's sake, I hoped so.

"Apparently the blood tests weren't much help. They showed therapeutic levels of several drugs, pharmaceutical drugs."

"He was being treated for pancreatic cancer," I said.

"But they also tested his stomach contents, as well as the paper cup he'd been holding. The results are consistent with the physical findings from the autopsy. Seems our victim died almost instantly from acute aconite poisoning. The chemical signature indicates a plant-based poison, rather than a chemical synthetic. That's one reason why they've focused on Tory. If they are still focused on her. And why I hoped you could shed some light." She tossed the report onto a stack on the floor.

"It's not a culinary herb," I said.

"Well, no," she said. "It's toxic."

"Some edible plants have toxic parts. Rhubarb leaves can kill. Other plants are safe if they're cooked but toxic if they're eaten raw, like morel mushrooms." I'd taken *Brother Cadfael's Herb Garden* out of my tote the other night, so I found my phone and started searching.

The first two references to aconite were on pharmaceutical sites, crammed with polysyllabic words only a doctor would understand. Two doctors were on my radar screen, Ken Griffey and Kevin Ripken. "Ah, here we go. Chinese medicine uses the plant to treat arthritis. European herbalists and physicians used it until synthetic substitutes were developed. Grows in the mountains, in the Northern Hemisphere."

An image pixelated into view. I strained to make it out.

"Holy marjaroly." I didn't recognize the sketch or the photograph slowly coming into view. But the common name of aconite gave me the shivers.

Monk's Hood.

I called Ron Locke's clinic for a consult. The doctor of acupuncture and Chinese medicine could see me in an hour.

Meanwhile, I limped over to Fabiola's building and up the stairs to her studio.

In the text and Tweet era, actual phone calls seem to have gone the way of the dodo bird, but this was obviously Call Somebody Day in Seattle. Fabiola pinched her thumb and forefinger together to indicate she wouldn't be on the phone long.

I sat on a work stool and rested my foot on another, massaging the cream Ron Locke had given me into my swollen ankle. It brought nearly instant relief.

They must not want you to know what's in this stuff, I thought, squinting at the tiny type on the tube. *Calendula officinalus*, I knew—the flowers are edible. *Hamamelis virginiana, Arnica montana. Aconitum napellus.*

Ohmygosh.

But Ron Locke had promised the cream was safe.

And I wasn't dead yet.

I dropped the tube back in my bag and withdrew the fuchsia folder. Despite its humbling end, my ferry ride and the lovely hour alone this morning in my delicious little shop had convinced me we'd found the right theme.

Fabiola scrunched up her face, her free hand making the universal "talk, talk, talk" motion. Today, she wore a black jumpsuit with flared legs and jet beading on the broad lapels. The plunging neckline exposed a lacy gold camisole. Her subdued Elvis look.

I pulled out the court files Tory had requested. They

related to three different lawsuits against her father. A five-year-old suit by another medical doctor, alleging breach of contract for, if I understood the legalese, failure to convey partial ownership in the clinic.

In other words, a disgruntled doctor promised a partnership he didn't get. Like Ken Griffey.

But the final document in that file eliminated any motive for murder: a stipulation that the dispute had been settled and should be dismissed, signed by the parties, lawyers, and judge.

Likewise, the second file, a ten-year-old claim by a nurse for wrongful discharge, had been settled and dismissed. Nobody who sues for money and gets it—whether it's all they wanted or not—is likely to come back years later bearing a grudge and a cup of toxic tea.

The third suit, a claim by A. Y. Anderson, asserted malpractice by Damien Finch, MD, causing permanent physical damage, loss of income, and pain and suffering. And loss of consortium, a ten-dollar word I gathered meant the marital relationship.

"I am so sorry. I thought he would never shut up." Fabiola tossed her phone on her desk. "That calls for a double shot. You?"

I nodded and Fabiola fired up her commercial-grade espresso maker, a gift from a client with a very profitable business repairing espresso machines. In moments, the grind, puff, hiss, and drip of beans, hot water, and steamy milk infused the air.

She set two white porcelain heart-shaped espresso cups on the worktable.

"I heart these cups. They would fly out my door."

"Gift. I found these labels, for your jars. For the tins, we can echo the theme." She handed me a sheet of four round labels, the images and fonts exactly what I'd pictured. "I used the historic photos you sent and your suggestion to add a little color."

"Like those old hand-tinted photographs. And the salt-shaker. Oh, wow." She'd captured the fifties' diner style I adore perfectly, in a simple line drawing.

"I did a grayscale version for the recipe inserts and hand-outs. We can use the same image on your new business cards and recipe cards. On everything printed." She splayed samples before me.

"Fabiola, you are fabulous."

She raised her cup in a toast and flashed her bright white teeth. "Pepper, my pal, you're not too shabby yourself."

VISITING hours had ended, leaving me no chance to consult Tory about the files today. Meanwhile, I needed a translator. And I knew just where to find one.

I wandered the bookshop while Jennifer perused the documents. The Tea Shop Mysteries by Laura Childs. For Sandra, for Christmas? The White House Chef Mysteries by Julie Hyzy. I'd had no idea there were so many food-related mysteries. The Domestic Diva Mysteries, the Coffeehouse Mysteries, even a Key West Food Critic series.

My stomach growled.

"The plaintiff alleges he—or she, we don't know—was a patient of Dr. Finch. He had a femoral arterial bypass, which means inserting a graft to bypass a blocked artery and restore blood flow to the lower leg and feet. Right here." Jen stepped out from behind the counter and drew an artery on her pant leg with a finger. "They usually use synthetic grafts, but in this case, they harvested an artery from the lower leg."

"Ughh." I shuddered.

"If I read this right, the patient alleges that Finch should not have done that, and that in the process, he nicked a nerve, causing permanent damage."

"Don't nerves regenerate?"

"Sometimes yes, sometimes no."

A customer asked for mysteries set in Ireland. "Light or

gritty?" Jennifer asked. "In between," came the reply. Jen led the way to the Foreign Settings shelves, recommending Sheila Connolly's County Cork Mysteries and an Erin Hart novel set on an archeological dig.

Had I been right to wonder about a vindictive patient? Who was this person? And how had Tory known?

"Where was I?" Jennifer had left the customer to browse. "Oh, right. The failed bypass. Case dismissed."

"Settled?" Like the other two.

"No. I think the judge is saying that the plaintiff couldn't find an expert witness to testify that Dr. Finch breached the standard of care."

"Meaning?"

"In a med mal case, you need another doctor in the same field to testify that the defendant doctor screwed up. A bad result isn't enough. You need evidence of an actual error."

The customer set a stack of paperbacks on the counter, including the Connolly and Hart books, and two in another series. "You'd love these, Pepper," Jennifer said, flashing a cover at me. "Sister Fidelma, seventh-century Irish nun and legal advocate. When you finish Brother Cadfael. Planning a trip?" she asked the customer.

I gathered my files as they chatted and Jennifer rang up the purchase. "Thanks, Jen."

"Wish I could be more help," she replied.

She'd been more help than she knew. But what I really needed was to know why—or even if—any of this mattered.

Thirty-one

If you use an electric coffee grinder to grind fresh spices, be careful not to overdo it. Heat destroys the volatile compounds that give a spice its aroma and lighter flavor notes. To keep your coffee from tasting like fennel—or your cloves like French roast—grind a tablespoon of rice to a fine powder. The grit cleans and sharpens the blades, and absorbs any residual oils. Or try a mortar and pestle—toning your arms at the same time!

I WAS BEGINNING TO FEEL LIKE AN ABSENTEE SHOP owner. I'd hailed a cab on First to cart me up to Ron Locke's clinic. Patients jammed the small waiting room.

"Mercury retrograde," the receptionist said ruefully. "Everybody's running late, or their appointment's running long."

As good an explanation as any. I scribbled my cell phone number on a message slip. "Ask him to call when he's got a moment."

I limped down Pine, thinking that we ought to carry a few reference books on medicinal herbs. I'd ask Ron for suggestions when he called me back.

Meanwhile, why not ask a plant expert?

"Hey, Yvonne. How's business?"

She scowled, her dirt-stained fingers gracefully arranging a bouquet of statice. "Nobody buys flowers in the rain."

Trust Yvonne to find the hole in every doughnut.

"This is a long shot, but you know so much about flowers. Do you know aconite?"

Her fingers hesitated, then got back to work. The scrapes were healing nicely. She tied a ribbon around the bundle and stuck it in a bucket. From another, she withdrew a long, slender stem with multipronged leaves, topped with a cluster of lovely purple flowers. Bell-shaped.

Hooded.

I hesitated before taking it. "It's beautiful. Is it poisonous?"

She gave me a withering look. "Would I sell it if it were?"

"Right. Don't forget to call Alex's office. He's serious about buying flowers from you."

A customer asked for pink and white dahlias and Yvonne returned her attention to her flower buckets.

I crossed Pike Place and stepped up on the curb. It had been a week since Doc's death, and the memorials had long vanished. The handwritten notes were safely tucked in an envelope in my desk.

A whizzing sound caught my attention. Tag stopped his bike, balancing on one long, lean leg. The weather had to be pretty nasty before he changed from bike shorts to long pants.

"Shouldn't you be inside sipping tea with your feet up?"

"Shouldn't you be off-duty? Your shift ended hours ago."

"Subbing for a buddy who wanted a long weekend for his wedding anniversary." As usual, Tag's eyes were hidden by his sunglasses, but a slight flush crept up his neck. "I was wondering—"

A delivery truck clattered by, behind him, drowning out his words. "What?"

His radio squawked and he shifted his weight to keep his

balance, one gloved hand gripping the bike's handlebar. "Umm, I was wondering if you'd like to, maybe, go out for dinner Sunday. There's a new place on Capitol Hill I've been hearing about. French bistro."

Dang those sunglasses. But the stuttering and nervous gestures gave it away. Tag Buhner was seriously asking me, the ex-wife who left after catching him with another woman, out for dinner. A dinner date.

"Unless you have other plans," he said, glancing around as if hoping a crime would pop out of nowhere and save him.

"Actually, I do. But thanks. It's a sweet invitation. Another time?"

"Yeah, sure." He hopped up on the bike. "Take care of that ankle," he called as he spun away.

A sweet, strange invitation. I smiled, shaking my head, and walked into my shop.

In the office, I braved another application of the herbal cream. It honestly did tone down the pain.

Out front, the staff had business well in hand. Reed reshelved jars while Zak packed up a few mail orders and Sandra helped a customer in search of the perfect chile powder. I straightened a display and answered the phone. The Middle Eastern restaurant on the lower Hillclimb had used the last smoky Aleppo pepper—key to a signature dish—and was running low on several spices needed for the weekend. I promised to drop off the order on my way home, and enlisted Reed to give me a hand packing it up.

Sandra rang up her customer, and the staff and I were alone in the store.

"When are we going to get to see those new labels, boss?" she said, but her heart wasn't in the jibe. "Kristen and I went to the jail. That poor girl. Place gives any decent person the willies."

I wrapped my arm around her shoulder. "We'll get her out soon."

"There's still a killer out there. I mean, this is a big city. Bad things happen. But . . ."

Tough on the outside, soft in the middle—that's my second in command.

The front door opened and a woman entered, carrying a large market basket and a list. I squeezed Sandra's shoulder. She dabbed at her eye, raised her chin, and marched forward.

Meanwhile, my thoughts drifted back to Tag. The public nurses a lot of misconceptions about the police, and doesn't always realize that most officers are good people who care deeply about the community. Tag had shown his tender side last night, calling my friends to bring food and medicine.

Did he finally understand that I was making a good life for myself, by myself? It intersected his only because we both work downtown. He'd been watching me last night with a wistful expression on his face—it vanished when he realized I'd seen it.

Was he wondering if we could make a place for each other in our lives again?

Was that why he had told me about the cut brake line?

How bizarre that a car so similar to mine had been parked up the hill from my shop. I'd left the Mustang outside the shop for a few minutes on errand days a few times. It's distinctive. People might have noticed it.

I don't believe coincidences happen to teach us lessons—not a big fan of the micromanager theory of God—but I do think that when strange and scary things happen, we have an obligation to learn from them.

What I was supposed to learn from this, I had no idea.

Almost closing time. I carried the pots to the sink and dumped out the remaining tea.

But I did know. Alex's explanation about the Mustang and the winemaker might be true, or a bit of careful bluffing.

Either way, it made me uncomfortable, and that was all that mattered.

I wasn't going to get involved with Tag again.

But I wasn't going to get involved with Alex, either.

Mr. Right might be out there, or he might not. But I was right where I needed to be.

Thirty-two

The Market's Gum Wall—a colorful bit of psychogrunge started by movie goers who stuck their gum to the bricks while waiting in line.

—No. 1 on TripAdvisor's list of the germiest tourist attractions in the country

THOUGH THE SEASON WOULDN'T OFFICIALLY CHANGE until next week, the air already felt different. A little cooler, a little damper.

The last light off when we closed was the twinkling fake-crystal chandelier. The first piece I'd hung after buying the business.

I could hardly wait to show off the new labels. To celebrate a full year of owning this surprising, maddening, magical place. A full year of my new life.

Life might begin at forty, but it really gets rolling at forty-two.

"Chin up," I told Zak as he, Sandra, and I walked out. "Good news soon."

"You keep saying that. I wish you would tell me why."

"Soon." I patted his broad shoulder. "See you in the morning."

"Night, boss," Sandra called, and they took off in opposite directions.

Elevator or stairs? I debated briefly as I crossed Pike Place, crowded with trucks and vans as the daystallers tore down and loaded up. My ankle felt pretty good—whether it was the aconite or another ingredient, that herbal cream worked miracles. Brother Cadfael would approve. Taking the ramp and stairs might be easier than wending my way through the chaos in the street and the Arcade, dodging traffic and shoppers attempting to negotiate last-minute bargains.

My tote, heavy as ever, on one shoulder and the delivery box in both hands, I squeezed between a big-bellied butcher and a rolling storage crate, and headed Down Under. No late shoppers here. Most businesses had already closed, the overhead lights in the central hallway making me a ghostly reflection in the shop windows.

A single light glowed in the import shop, and I paused to peer inside. In places like this, and antique and vintage stores, some merchandise flies out the door while other items hunker down on the shelves for years. You never know when you'll find the perfect thing you didn't know you needed.

The light emanated from the back corner. A mannequin draped in a turquoise-and-gold sari blocked my view and I craned my neck to see around her. The small lamp, a red silk shade on a brass base, might be the perfect accent piece for my Chinese apothecary.

A dark shadow crossed in front of the window as someone bustled by.

"Tomorrow," I promised the red lamp. "I'll be back."

I shifted the bag on my shoulder and continued down the ramp, rounding the corner where the haunted bead shop used to be. Some Market folks swear they feel a draft here, a breeze blowing through an open window in the solid wall.

I'd never noticed it—until now. My steps slowed and I glanced around in the dim light. A scuffling sound—smaller than a person, bigger than a rat.

It stopped. I paused, then kept walking.

The odd sound started up again. More than two feet. More than one person.

I picked up the pace. The long, steep Market steps weren't far away, beyond the open steel double doors.

Thwack! Something hard but hollow hit me in the mid-back, and I staggered forward. Pain shot through my left leg. The tote slid off my shoulder and the weight of it tugged me sideways. I landed on my knee, a sledgehammer working on my ankle.

But there was no one in sight.

I breathed deeply. A sharp, tangy whiff of spice hit my nostrils, and I squeezed back a sneeze. In my twisty-turny fall, I'd managed to hold on to the delivery box. But a bag inside must have burst open.

Gritting my teeth, I pushed myself up, weight on my right foot, testing my left. The stabbing had reduced to a throb, but I still felt like swearing. Now I could get out of here.

But first, I dug in my bag for my phone.

C'mon, c'mon—I know you're in there.

Finally, my fingers found the smooth plastic cover. I slipped the phone into my pocket and picked up the box, hoping my delivery wasn't completely ruined.

I took a step toward the doors that led to the wide outdoor landing and the stairs. My right foot was midair when that same hard, hollow object hit me.

But this time, I was ready. I spun around, ignoring the twisting and grinding in my ankle, and reached inside the delivery box for the open bag of smoked paprika.

Pulled it out and flung it in the face of my attacker.

Who sneezed loud enough to bring down the Viaduct.

I dropped the box and my tote. Yvonne sneezed twice

more, doubled over by the force of her allergic reaction. I grabbed the five-gallon flower bucket she'd used to attack me and, when she rose up to sneeze again, took a mighty swing.

Down she went, on hands and knees. I sat on her back and she collapsed to the floor.

I reached for her left hand and yanked on it. "Give me your other hand."

Her right hand flailed.

"*Give it to me.*" I snared it and pinned it down with my knee, then untied her apron strings and wrapped them around her wrists. She yelped.

"I don't care if it hurts. You killed Doc, didn't you? And you cut the brake line in that car, thinking it was mine." Her husband—ex-husband—had been a mechanic. "That's how you scraped your knuckles and your chin."

She sneezed, the sound ringing off the concrete, glass, and metal surrounding us. I scooted forward, my butt on hers, my left knee pinning down her elbow to keep her from loosening the apron-string handcuffs. My tongue found a dab of paprika on my lip. My ankle screamed.

"You planned the poisoning, but the car was spur-of-the-moment, wasn't it? You've got a knack for spotting openings—I'll give you that. You could have killed dozens of innocent people. Where is my phone?"

In the melee, it had gone flying. I whipped my head around, panicked, seeing nothing.

Then, a soft breeze. Feet scrabbling.

A wet nose. A big hand.

"Here it be, Miz Pepper," Sam said.

"Call 911, Sam."

"Can't, Miz Pepper. You gotta call." Terror rattled his voice. The dog stood beside him, a faithful guardian.

"Okay. You dial. Hold the phone and I'll talk. Shut up," I told the whimpering Yvonne.

"Pepper Reece," I said to the dispatcher. "I'm sitting on

a killer. Literally. Down Under in the Market, behind the big doors between the Mezzanine level and the Hillclimb."

"Hold the line, Ms. Reece. Help is on its way."

But I couldn't hold the line. I needed both hands to hold Yvonne. The phone lay where Sam had left it, cradled in her back, on speaker so I could hear the dispatcher calmly, quietly setting help in motion.

"What did you think you were going to do—kill me and stick me on the Gum Wall?"

"I only had to knock you out." Yvonne's words came out thin but angry. "Drag you to the steps and throw you down. Or push you through the rail. Like almost happened on the ferry."

I shuddered. My own stupidity had given her the idea. "You killed Doc. Dr. Damien Finch. You sued him for malpractice but the claim got tossed, so you had to find another way to get revenge."

"Damien Finch made my life a living hell. If he'd have paid up—you're hurting me." Her breath came in short, ragged bursts.

But I didn't dare let up the pressure. Yvonne might live in constant pain, as the malpractice claim alleged, but all those years running a flower farm had made her strong.

"My husband left—he couldn't take it anymore."

"Right. Anderson was your married name. You use your middle name instead of your first, and you took back Winchell after your divorce." Her grunt sounded like agreement. "You saw Doc in the Market. You recognized him—oh, I know when. He bought flowers for his daughter. He bought them from you."

Last Wednesday. The flowers Tory had thrown into the trash.

"He didn't even recognize me," she said, angry tears shattering her words.

"You found a Spice Shop cup." She made a snorting sound, and I realized my own inadvertent complicity. "You got the cup and the tea from me. You brought him hot tea, poisoned with aconite. You gave it to him and watched him die." That's what Sam had seen. "Tory had nothing to do with it. So why go see her in jail?"

"For justice."

I jabbed my knee into her twisted arm, glad for the freedom of movement my stretchy pants gave. Wondering if Brother Cadfael had ever had to resort to grade school wrestling moves. "Why? What did you want from her?" Outside, footsteps pounded closer and closer. A minute, at most, to get the truth.

"Wanted her to—pay me—" She was gasping now. "For what I suffered. Pay me from her inheritance. Then I'd say I saw what really happened. That she didn't kill her father like I hinted to the police at first—that old bum did it."

Sam. Yvonne had gone to the jail to try to blackmail Tory into paying her off, by threatening to frame Sam for Doc's murder. A murder she had committed herself. I jammed my knee deeper into her back.

"Damien Finch was dying of cancer," I said. "Everything he had went to his wife. Even if Tory had the money, she would never have let you hurt Sam."

She groaned—in mental or physical agony? I no longer cared which.

"That was you at the cemetery, wasn't it?" Stephanie had seen her, too.

"We got her, Pepper." Tag's hands lifted me up gently. Olerud stood ready to grab Yvonne.

Other officers moved in. Tag wrapped a strong arm around my shoulder. Someone handed him my pink phone.

"Good job," he whispered into the spiky hair he hated. "You got her."

I'd had help. But Sam and Arf were gone. In the shadow of the concrete column where Yvonne had hidden—waiting after she'd followed me Down Under, waiting while I mooned over the red lamp in the import shop window—lay a worn brown leather wallet. I wriggled free, picked it up, and flipped it open.

Winfield Robinson III, the ID read, followed by an address in Memphis, Tennessee.

"My guardian angel," I said, handing the wallet to Tag.

Detective Tracy huffed into view and surveyed the scene. His eyes narrowed when he spotted me. I grinned.

And out of nowhere, and everywhere, voices began singing a medieval chant.

Thirty-three

The bluest skies you've ever seen are in Seattle.

—"Seattle," words and music by Hugo Montenegro,
Ernie Sheldon, and Jack Keller

I TRACKED DOWN SAM'S SISTER IN MEMPHIS AND CALLED that night.

"Oh, thank the Lord," she said. "I've prayed every night, on my knees, that Win was safe and warm out there. You are a true friend. You are the answer to my prayers."

"He's got a dog," I said. "Arf. They were my guardian angels."

She laughed, a rich, bell-like sound. "That figures. When we were kids, my daddy dragged home a mutt for us. It needed a name. So Win called it Arf, after Little Orphan Annie's dog."

"Wasn't Annie's dog named Sandy?" I didn't remember the comic strip, but I'd seen the musical.

"Sure was. Arf was the sound the cartoon dog made when he barked, in that little balloon they draw, for the words?" This time, she laughed in pleasure and relief. "He loved that dog, my brother did."

I explained how Sam—Win, she called him—had found

a hidden door in the wall near the import shop and taken refuge in the space behind it. A handful of those semisecret spaces still exist in the Market, created by decades-old renovations long forgotten. Mostly Down Under, Market tales often associate them with ghosts. Happily, this ghost had been a helpful one.

"Win has a place here if he wants it," she said.

I'd steered Detectives Spencer and Tracy to Jim and Hot Dog, who agreed to help them find Sam and Arf. I got the impression that Jim had been letting Sam stay with him in his SRO, a strict violation of the rules. In fact, that may have been where Sam went the day I lost him in Post Alley. I didn't say anything, though. Jim believed in rules—failure to respect them had been part of his gripe with Doc—but I'd begun to understand they were a code of conduct rather than a set of laws.

And sometimes, you have to bend the rules to help a friend.

They were resourceful men, and kindhearted. I knew they would try to help Sam understand that he was no longer under suspicion, and that the police wanted to know what he'd seen not to trap him, but to bring the true killer to justice.

Spencer had promised me Tory would be released sometime Friday. In Yvonne's stall, they found a Thermos bottle buried in the bottom of her storage cart, and sent it off to test the residue for aconite.

Tag offered to escort me to the loft and keep me company, but I turned him down. "You'll need that overtime if you're inviting women out for fancy dinners."

Brother Cadfael and a bottle of wine were all the company I needed.

The restaurant owner had half fallen over himself, apologizing for putting me in danger, despite my insistence that he hadn't. And he wouldn't think of letting me apologize for messing up his delivery and sending his spice order to the police evidence locker instead. He insisted on sending me home with freshly baked pita bread, tzatziki, dolmas, and falafel.

While he bustled around packing up my dinner, I'd called Zak and given him Friday off. With pay.

I wasn't badly hurt, though the incident had revved up my adrenals. But after I got home and took a long, hot shower to rinse off the paprika, I did rub on a whole lot of Dr. Locke's magical herbal cream. Aconite and all.

FRIDAY morning, the sun shone on a city brightened by rain. I should have known something was up when my friendly barista at the base of the elevator wouldn't let me pay and insisted on giving me a box of warm, fragrant cinnamon rolls for my staff.

When I stepped off the elevator, the morning din paused. It turned to applause as I limped my way into the Main Arcade and through the Market. Misty the Baker hugged me tenderly, and the orchard girls kissed my cheeks. The cheese maker, the dim sum seller, Herb, and the honey man all beamed.

At the end of the first row of daystalls, near the space Yvonne usually occupied, the Market Master stood, grim-faced. "We are so sorry," he said. "And so grateful."

And I was so speechless.

The shop lights glowed and Sandra greeted me with open arms. Behind her, Kristen waited impatiently.

"Wow. So this is what it takes to get you to work early."

Tears streamed down her face.

Minutes before we opened, Jim and Hot Dog came to the door. At their request, I joined them on the sidewalk, where Sam and Arf waited.

"We wanted to bring you flowers," Hot Dog said. "But under the circumstances, it din't seem like the best of taste."

I tried to suppress my laughter, and failed.

"Sam. Oh, Sam. What would I have done without you?"

"You'da been all right, Miz Pepper. You always gonna be all right. But I sure am glad me and Arf could help."

He'd spoken to his sister last night, and accepted her invitation to return home. She and her husband ran a storage facility with an apartment for an on-site caretaker—work Sam could do. And it would keep him close to family, "but outta her hair," as he put it.

"But this dog, Miz Pepper, he's a Seattle dog. He belongs out here, with you and the men." His big hand cradled the top of Arf's head. "They's bought him this new collar. See, you can adjust it like so. It's got lights. They're bright—you can even see them through this ratty old fur."

Nothing ratty about Arf's fur, silky-smooth from regular brushing. I stroked the dog's ear.

"Plus they're LED. And waterproof." He handed me the leash, tears in his eyes. "In church when I was a boy, we sang this song about how the world's one big circle of hope. It hasn't been that way for me for a long time, but I think the circle's turning. Don't you, Miz Pepper?"

Arf's leash lay loose in my hand. He sat patiently, tail extended, eyes bright.

"Yes, Sam, I do. Hold on. I have something for you."

I slipped into the shop for the item I'd gotten that morning from one of the Market craftswomen. Back outside, I handed him the black beret and he tried it on, checking his reflection in the Spice Shop window. He preened, grinning.

"Sam, a question before you leave. If your name is Winfield, why are you called Sam?" His sister hadn't known, either.

"They say I look like that actor, Samuel L. Jackson. It's the beret. Without it, he ain't near as handsome as me."

I kissed him on the cheek, and watched as the three men strolled down Pike Place. Arf sat tall, watching them go, but when I said his name, he raised his head and wagged his tail.

Apparently, I now owned a dog.

The shop bustled all morning, a good thing. Thank goodness for customers and deliveries and all the other Friday distractions. Otherwise, I might have sat in my office bawling.

Midmorning, the detectives dropped by. "As predicted," Tracy said, "Ms. Winchell's Thermos held remnants of your tea and aconite root."

"She repeated the confession she gave you," Spencer said. "She recognized Dr. Finch when he bought the flowers, realized he was Tory's father, and decided that if the court system wouldn't give her compensation, she'd get it her own way. Those unidentified fingerprints on your paper cup and the partial prints on the wall turned out to be hers. She'll be charged for attempted blackmail as well as murder. "

Tracy cackled. "Wanna bet her lawyer moves to suppress the confession as the result of an allergic reaction? Acting under the influence of paprika."

"What about Tory?" I asked.

"Prosecutor's doing the paperwork to dismiss the charges right now," he said. "Contrary to what you might think, Pepper, we don't want to blame the wrong person, either."

"Your samovar came back clean," Spencer added. "You should have it back soon."

They had barely cleared the door when Tag dropped in. He took off the glasses, eyes bleary from the double shift and early call.

"Thanks for your help," I said. "And for the offer last night."

He nodded and spoke quietly, staring at my feet. "Pepper, I am so sorry for everything I did to hurt you. I will never stop loving you, and I will never stop being your friend. I understand that you don't want anything from me—"

"Except the occasional response to a 911 call."

He laughed, then scanned the room, turning serious. "You have done wonders here. You are an asset to the

Market. And you were absolutely right—I didn't think you could pull it off. I have never been so happy to be so wrong."

"Apology accepted. Even if it is coming from severe sleep deprivation."

He kissed my forehead, put the mirrored glasses back on, and strolled out, his bicycle shoes clicking.

Two TV reporters called, and a newspaper reporter dropped in. I told them all I'd be happy to talk later, after things got back to normal. I didn't tell them that might be a very long time.

But we took a big step closer to normal when Zak walked in, right after the lunch rush, Tory by his side. Exhausted but radiant, my ordinarily restrained employee hugged, cried, blew her nose, and cried some more. We ate the sandwiches the Italian deli sent over and the cookies Misty the Baker delivered, and tried to hold it together in front of the customers. We mostly failed, but I didn't care—the news had already spread, and the Seattle Spice Shop was Ground Zero for the curious as well as those in need of parsley and thyme.

"Tory, a moment?" We stepped out the side door. "After your father was killed, what prompted you to look up the court records for cases he was involved in?"

Sorrow darkened her golden brown eyes. "The day before, when he followed me to the bus stop, he said something about the past coming back to haunt him. I didn't know what he meant, but I knew he'd been sued a few times, so I took a stab at that."

Ah. So he had recognized Yvonne after all. "But you never saw the records, and you wouldn't have connected A. Y. Anderson with Yvonne the flower seller."

She shook her head, her eyes filled with regret.

"One more question. Why didn't you tell me she came to the jail to try to blackmail you?"

"I told my lawyer, and she was working out the best way to take that to the police. But I still wasn't positive that

Yvonne had killed my father, and I needed you on the case. Besides, if she knew I'd told you, she'd have come after you again. I couldn't have lived with myself if you'd gotten hurt because of me." Tory brushed away a tear. "Hurt worse than you already had been, I mean."

I didn't tell her she'd be surprised how much she could live with. Instead, I drew an envelope containing a full paycheck out of my apron pocket. "Go home. Rest. Eat good food. And call your stepmother. She does love you."

"One more thing. You're the first to know," she said, and I tilted my head, questioning. "I said yes."

Took me a moment to realize what she meant.

My cheek muscles were sure getting a workout.

Shortly after Tory and Zak left, my phone buzzed. A text from Alex, replying to the phone message I'd left. And no, it's not okay to break up by voice mail, but we weren't really together—which had been the point of my message. I never had found out what dirt Tag thought he had on Alex. Didn't matter. I'd found out for myself that I valued reliability, trust, and honesty more than a flashy fling—and that I trusted my own judgment.

So sorry, the text read. *But it's probably for the best.*

No argument there.

Thirty-four

*I thank the Lord that I'm not a poor man. I'm not a sad
man, no, not me. I've got the sun and the moon and the
wind and the rain. And I never lack for good company.*

—Traditional American folk song

three weeks later

THE STREETLIGHTS IN PIONEER SQUARE GLOWED AS EVE-
ning descended on the city. Laurel, Gabe, Fabiola, Arf, and
I picked our way across the cobbles toward an abandoned
storefront. No more heels for me—I wore my magic pink
flats.

Make that formerly abandoned. Tonight, as part of the
Seattle Storefronts project, the space teemed with color,
music, and motion. Heart, and soul.

Outside the entrance stood a tall metal piece. I recognized a bicycle fork, chain, and gears, hotel silverplate, and
a pair of surgical forceps, among other metal detritus. It
waved like a tree reaching for the sky. A paper tag hung
from a leafy shape that looked suspiciously like a grapefruit
spoon. THE GUARDIAN, it read. KEYRA JACKSON. NFS.

Blown glass forms filled the front window of the storefront

turned temporary gallery and studio for the artists calling themselves "The Twelfth Avenue Collective"—tenants from Tory's apartment building and friends and neighbors.

Inside, I filled the small water bowl I'd brought along. "Sit, Arf." Arf sat, and Gabe sank to the floor beside him.

Along one brick wall hung light sculptures and masks made from bark, fabric, and metal. Sturdy cases in the middle of the space held pottery. Keyra's found-object art hung everywhere, even from the ceiling.

A temporary stage held the setup for a band.

But what drew me was the exhibit on the opposite wall. Titled "Two Generations," it was anchored by two oils: the small, sweet portrait of young Damien at the piano that I'd spotted in the Finches' living room. And Tory's fairytale painting of house and garden, now complete.

To one side hung the paintings Marianne Finch had shown me, from her secret sitting room. On the other were the pieces I'd seen in Tory's apartment, and a small grouping I'd seen in the conceptual stage, titled simply "The Spice Shop Series."

Tory had not come back to work since her release. I'd found a part-timer to start next week, and this time, I was determined to get to know my employees from the beginning.

But Tory and her pen and sketchbook would always be welcome.

"Isn't it wonderful?" Marianne handed me a glass of champagne. "I only wish Damien had lived to see it. To see his mother and his daughter as the amazing artists they truly are."

"I've been saving these for you." I drew the envelope of notes from my pocket. Her eyes dampened as she read them.

"Thank you," she whispered.

A drumroll sounded. The chatter stopped and all eyes focused on the stage. Resplendent in a red-and-black plaid sweater dress and black tights, Keyra wrestled the microphone from the stand.

"So much to celebrate tonight. This space, this art!"

We all cheered. Sandra and Mr. Right had arrived, as had Seetha, Kristen, Eric, and the girls, and Reed and his parents. Jane, rhinestone-studded bobby pins tucked into her white crown, wound her way past clusters of people and looped her arm through mine.

"The Twelfth Avenue Collective will occupy the space until it's leased," Keyra said. "We'll keep regular gallery hours. Collective members will work here, and we'll be open for studio visits. Thanks to the Storefronts project, rent is one dollar a month. Even we can afford that." Another drum roll.

"Music tonight is by the Zak Davis Band. Happy thirtieth birthday, Zak." Drums plus cymbals and loud cheers.

I glanced back at Arf, his big head in Gabe's lap.

Keyra raised a champagne flute. "And congratulations on your engagement, Zak and Tory."

Cheers arose, and the spotlight picked out the happy couple. Zak, a black sport coat over his black T-shirt and jeans, beamed down at Tory, his arm around her waist. She glowed—no other word for it—in a shimmering red lace dress. They kissed, and we all clapped.

"But wait. There's more."

The lights dimmed, a single spotlight on the stage. Fabiola took the mic and images flashed on the wall. For once, the setting outshone her outfit, a simple navy coatdress from the 1940s.

"We are also celebrating the first anniversary of the new ownership of a Seattle institution, the Seattle Spice Shop," she said. "All the food tonight is seasoned with the Spice Shop's fall spice blends. And here to unveil the new logos and labels is Pepper Reece."

Truly, I'd had no idea. I stepped onto the stage and Fabiola handed me a small remote.

"Oh, my gosh. Thank you." I clicked through the slide show she'd created. First, the vintage labels we'd chosen for the jars: creamy white with a double red border, a classic midcentury design. For teapots and other accessories, paper tags on strings, evoking vintage retail. Plus she'd found a source for the red-and-white-striped mailing labels I remembered from packages my grandparents sent.

Our tins featured historic Washington State ferries and their crews, black-and-white photographs tinted with shades of blue, forest green, and that blushing pale pink. A different boat for each blend: the *Klickitat*, the *Walapa*, the *Klahanie*, and the *Tyee*.

"Great art, music, friends. Not to mention good food. Let's celebrate!" I snapped the microphone back into the stand and stepped down, my ankle not even giving a twinge.

"Good dog, Arf." I took his leash and we made a quick circuit on the cobbles, stretching our legs and drinking in the fresh air.

Back at the entrance, I paused to study Keyra's sculpture. Tory and Marianne joined me, arm in arm. Tory's fingers reached for the dog's floppy ears.

"We were wondering," Marianne said. "If you might find room for this piece in the shop."

I stared, wide-eyed.

"He isn't eligible for a leaf on the *Tree of Life*," Tory said, referring to the sculpture in Victor Steinbrueck Park erected to honor the county's homeless after their deaths. "Since he wasn't actually homeless. But for all his faults, my father never forgot that his first obligation was to protect me. He died watching over me. And we were hoping . . ."

"Yes," I said. "Yes. I know just the spot, by the tea cart."

Because everyone needs tea. And everyone needs a guardian, now and then.

Recipes and Spice Notes

The Spice Shop Recommends . . .

CHANGE OF SEASONS BLEND

A comforting combination with a hint of heat, good any time of year.

- 1 tablespoon or more chopped dehydrated bell peppers
- 1 tablespoon dried oregano
- 1 tablespoon dried garlic granules
- 1½ teaspoons sea salt (kosher or crystal)
- 1½ teaspoons Aleppo pepper
- ½ teaspoon ground black peppercorns or tricolor peppercorn blend

Adjust the spices to your own taste, remembering that sources and freshness vary. The heat and any sharpness you taste will mellow after a few hours, and the blend will take on its own distinct flavor.

Makes 4 tablespoons.

For a dip: Mix 2 tablespoons spice mix with 1 cup sour cream or yogurt. Yummy with chips or raw veggies, or on a baked potato.

For salad dressing: Make an infusion by adding 1 cup olive oil to 2 tablespoons of spice mix. Allow to sit at least a few hours; overnight is even better. For a basic vinaigrette, whisk half a cup of infused oil into ¼ cup balsamic vinegar, adding the oil slowly to create an emulsion. Or add the oil to the vinegar in a jar with a tight-fitting lid and shake to emulsify. Balsamics can vary in strength and flavor, so adjust amounts to your taste.

The infused oil is also a wonderful addition to sautées.

HERBES DE PROVENCE

A savory touch, to transport your taste buds.

  2½ tablespoons dried oregano
  2½ tablespoons dried thyme
  2 tablespoons dried savory
  2 tablespoons dried crushed lavender flowers
  1 teaspoon dried basil
  1 teaspoon dried sage

Mix spices in a small bowl. Store in a jar with a tightly fitting lid. Makes just over half a cup.

As with all herb blends, experiment with your own touches. Let your taste be your guide. Other frequent additions: rosemary, sweet marjoram, or fennel seed. (Marjoram and oregano are distinct herbs but closely related and can be substituted for each other in some recipes.) Try a blend with whatever combination of the suggested herbs you have on hand. Then, next summer, grow a pot of lavender on your deck or in a sunny window!

Herbes de Provence are spectacular sprinkled on sautéed potatoes, rubbed on chicken before grilling, or best of all, in roast chicken and potatoes. Add them to a lamb or a vegetable stew—think eggplant, tomatoes, and zucchini, maybe some cannellini (white beans). Use them to season homemade croutons or tomato sauce.

Wrap a teaspoon of Herbes de Provence in cheese cloth and tie with kitchen string to make an herb bouquet, also called a *bouquet garni*. Drop it into a small jar of olive oil for a few days to make an infusion for salads or sautées.

At Home with Pepper

GRILLED CITRUS CHICKEN WITH ORANGE YOGURT DIPPING SAUCE

FOR THE MARINADE:

- ¼ cup olive oil
- 2 tablespoons lemon juice
- 2 tablespoons fresh oregano, chopped, or 2 teaspoons dried oregano, crumbled
- ¾ teaspoon salt
- ½ teaspoon fresh ground black pepper
- 1 pound boneless, skinless chicken breasts, sliced into ¼-inch-thick strips

FOR THE DIPPING SAUCE:

1 cup yogurt
1 teaspoon orange zest
2 teaspoons fresh orange juice
1 tablespoon fresh oregano, chopped, or 1 teaspoon
    dried oregano, crumbled
½ teaspoon minced garlic
½ teaspoon cumin

Combine marinade ingredients; add the chicken strips and marinate for about 20 minutes.

Meanwhile, combine the ingredients for the citrus dipping sauce in a medium bowl; cover and refrigerate. (Pepper uses a glass bowl with its own sturdy cover, so she can reuse any leftover sauce.)

Heat the grill to medium. Thread the chicken onto skewers for even grilling. Grill about 4 minutes, then rotate and grill until completely cooked, about another 4 minutes.

Serve the skewered chicken with the yogurt sauce. Or remove the chicken from the skewers, using a fork to slide the chicken onto a bed of greens, and dress with the yogurt sauce.

POTATO AND BROCCOLI FRITTATA

Pepper drew inspiration for this recipe from the potatoes and broccolini in the Market. A hybrid of traditional broccoli and gai lan, also called Chinese broccoli or Chinese kale, broccolini has long, slender stalks with small florets and kale-like leaves, and a peppery taste that holds up well when cooked. If you can't find it, use traditional broccoli or broccoli raab. Traditional broccoli can be hard to find with the stalks intact, but the search is worth the effort. Use a paring knife or vegetable peeler to cut out any knots and peel off the tough skin. Those stalks carry a lot of flavor and vitamins and minerals.

If you don't have a chance to pop into the Spice Shop for Herbes de Provence, make your own with whatever you have on hand. And don't skimp on the Parmesan! If you need to cut it because you're watching sodium—Parmesan is naturally low in fat— reduce the amount that goes in the egg mixture. The cheese on top broils to such lovely salty, crunchy perfection—you don't want to miss that!

For dinner, serve with a green salad and crunchy bread, and a white wine—a light non-oaky Chardonnay, a Pinot Grigio, or any white with a clean, crisp touch.

    8 to 10 small white potatoes (about 10 ounces total),
        scrubbed and quartered
    1 cup vegetable broth
    ¼ cup olive oil
    8 ounces broccolini, trimmed and chopped into
        ½-inch pieces
    1 small red onion, thinly sliced
    1 tablespoon Herbes de Provence
    8 large eggs
    1 cup grated Parmesan cheese
    ½ teaspoon salt
    ½ teaspoon freshly ground black pepper

Place the potatoes and broth in a large (10- to 12-inch) ovenproof skillet. On the stove top, bring to a boil and simmer for 10 minutes, turning the potatoes often, until almost all of the stock has been absorbed and the potatoes are tender.

Preheat your broiler. If yours has variable settings, use the high setting and leave the rack in the middle of the oven. If your broiler is not particularly hot, raise the rack.

Add the olive oil, broccolini, onion, and Herbes de Provence to the potatoes in the skillet. Continue cooking on the stove top on medium heat for about 2 minutes, turning frequently, until all the vegetables are coated with oil and herbs. Reduce heat to medium-low and cover the skillet, cooking about 3 minutes, until the broccolini has become mostly tender.

Beat the eggs with half the Parmesan and the salt and pepper. Check the heat in your skillet; you may need to turn it way down to avoid frying the eggs in the next step. Pour the egg mixture over the vegetables. Cover and cook on the stove top over medium-low until the eggs are lightly set, about 10 minutes.

Sprinkle the remaining Parmesan on top and place the pan under the broiler, until the top is bubbly and golden, and the eggs are just set throughout, about 5 minutes.

Let cool slightly before slicing into wedges.

Makes 8 servings. Wedges reheat beautifully for breakfast or lunch.

PENNE RIGATE WITH ASPARAGUS AND SESAME-CHILE SHRIMP

No caterer on call? No matter! At Ripe, Laurel makes this with penne rigate, the short, ridged tubes, but the thicker-ridged rigatoni or farfalle, better known as bow ties, also work well.

This is an easy salad to serve warm or at room temperature, and requires very little shopping. Pepper keeps a small jar of grated ginger in her fridge for emergency cravings. If you like a little more heat, use hot sesame chili oil.

¼ cup white or brown sesame seeds, toasted
1 pound penne rigate
1 pound asparagus, trimmed and cut in ½-inch pieces
 (if asparagus isn't available, substitute broccolini)
¼ cup peanut butter (chunky or fresh-ground)
¼ cup rice wine vinegar

¼ cup soy sauce
2 tablespoons sesame oil
2 tablespoons brown sugar
2 garlic cloves, pressed
1 tablespoon minced fresh ginger
½ teaspoon red pepper flakes
¼ cup hot water
1 pound medium shrimp, tail-off, cooked
1 red bell pepper, seeded and cut into thin strips
    ("julienne")
4 green onions, thinly sliced and cut into 3-inch pieces
½ cup chopped fresh cilantro (divided use)

Preheat oven to 300 degrees. Spread the sesame seeds on a baking sheet and toast about 10 minutes. Don't overbake; they will continue to brown a bit as they cool.

Cook and drain the pasta. During the last minute of cooking time, add the asparagus. Drain in a colander and rinse with cool water to stop the cooking.

While the pasta is cooking, make the sauce. Combine the peanut butter, vinegar, soy sauce, sesame oil, brown sugar, garlic, ginger, and red pepper flakes. Add the hot water and stir—a fork or small whisk works best—until the sauce is smooth, breaking up any chunks.

Pour the pasta into a large bowl for serving. Add the shrimp, red bell pepper, green onions, and ¼ cup of the cilantro. Add the sauce and mix to combine all the ingredients. Top with the remaining ¼ cup cilantro and the toasted sesame seeds.

Serves 6 to 8.

Spice Up Your Life with Pepper and the Flick Chicks

SALMON IN PACKETS

A tasty combo. The parchment wrapper steams the salmon and veggies, and makes for super-easy cleanup!

FOR THE PESTO:

1 cup washed cilantro leaves
1 clove fresh garlic, peeled
¼ cup raw pumpkin seeds
kosher or crystal sea salt, to taste
dash of cayenne
½ cup olive oil

OTHER INGREDIENTS:

2 salmon filets, skinned
1 carrot, cut in thin matchbox strips ("julienned")
1 zucchini, julienned
2 green onions, cut thin lengthwise and cut into 3-inch
    lengths

Preheat oven to 350 degrees.

In a small food processor or blender, blend the cilantro, garlic, and pumpkin seeds. Add the salt and cayenne to your taste. Slowly pour in the olive oil, a little at a time, and blend to a spreadable consistency; add more if the pesto is too thick.

Cut a piece of parchment paper for each filet, large enough to wrap it. Place one filet in the center of the paper. Spread the filet with a thick layer of pesto. Layer a few carrot and zucchini sticks and onions on top. Fold the parchment ends in as if you were wrapping a package, and secure with a toothpick. Repeat with the second filet.

Bake for 20 to 30 minutes, until the salmon is done. Time will vary depending on the thickness of your filet; it's okay to unwrap one packet to check doneness.

CREAMY PARMESAN SALAD DRESSING

Two variations: one with fresh herbs, and one with Pepper's Change of Seasons blend, which Laurel served the Flick Chicks.

BASIC INGREDIENTS, FOR BOTH VARIATIONS:

1 medium shallot, coarsely chopped
1 cup nonfat or low-fat plain yogurt
¼ cup shredded Parmesan
2 tablespoons olive oil
2 tablespoons lime juice

FOR A FRESH HERB DRESSING:

2 garlic cloves, peeled
1 tablespoon fresh oregano leaves, chopped
1 teaspoon freshly ground black pepper
1 teaspoon salt, or more to taste

FOR LAUREL'S VARIATION:

1½ tablespoons Change of Seasons blend

Mix all ingredients in a small food processor or blender until thoroughly combined. Chill at least 1 hour, to let flavors meld. Adjust seasonings to your taste.

Makes about 1¼ cups.

It Wouldn't Be Movie Night Without Tasty Treats . . .

SALTY OAT COOKIES

¾ cup (1½ sticks) unsalted butter, at room temperature
1 cup light brown sugar
½ cup granulated white sugar
1 teaspoon baking powder
¼ teaspoon baking soda
¼ teaspoon ground cinnamon
2 large eggs
1 teaspoon vanilla
1¾ cups all-purpose flour
2 cups rolled oats (not quick-cooking)
sea salt, for sprinkling (small crystals are best)

In mixer bowl, beat the butter on medium-high until light and fluffy. Add the sugars, baking powder, baking soda, and cinnamon, and beat until well blended, scraping down the sides of the bowl as you go. Reduce speed to medium and add the eggs and vanilla, mixing thoroughly. Add the flour and oats, mixing on low and scraping sides of bowl just until incorporated. Cover the bowl and chill the dough for at least 1 hour; this allows the oats to absorb the eggs and vanilla and to soften, which is important for the texture of these cookies.

Preheat oven to 375 degrees. Line a baking sheet with parchment paper.

Roll the dough into large balls, about the size of a golf ball. Place about two inches apart on the baking sheet and flatten slightly. Sprinkle tops of balls generously with sea salt. Bake about 15 minutes, until cookies are puffed and beginning to turn golden. Cool on a wire rack.

*Makes 18 to 20 cookies about the size of hockey pucks, with
a chewy exterior and a soft interior. They pair beautifully
with ginger ice cream. If you plan to eat more than one,
protect your stash from teenage boys.*

GINGER ICE CREAM

*Ginger ice cream is fabulous by itself, or with Salty Oat Cookies.
This recipe makes a quart, using a Donvier ice cream maker.
You may need to adjust amounts and method for your own ice
cream maker. Crystallized ginger may be found packaged or in
bulk at your natural grocer's, with other dried fruits or in the
herb and spice section.*

2 eggs
⅔ cup sugar
1¾ cups milk
2 cups cream
½ teaspoon vanilla
¼ cup (roughly) fresh gingerroot, finely grated, plus
    any liquid left by grating
½ cup crystallized ginger, finely chopped

Beat the eggs and sugar with an electric mixer until thick and
cream-colored. Add the milk, cream, vanilla, and fresh ginger,
along with any liquid left by the grating. Mix well. If your grated
ginger has any stringy fibers, pour the mixture through a
strainer at this stage. Stir in the crystallized ginger.

Freeze according to your ice cream maker's directions. As
with many homemade ice creams, it will be soft at first, but will
harden if stored in an airtight container in the freezer. Keeps
about 1 week.

SPICED GLAZED NUTS AND PRETZEL MIX

2 cups mixed raw nuts: any combination of cashews,
    whole almonds, Spanish peanuts, pecan halves, or
    hazelnuts
1 tablespoon unsalted butter, melted
3 tablespoons brown sugar
½ teaspoon ground cinnamon
¾ teaspoon cayenne pepper
1½ tablespoons maple syrup
1 teaspoon flaky sea salt, kosher salt, or other
    coarse salt
2 cups mini pretzel twists; if you can't find mini
    twists, break up larger twists or sticks

Preheat oven to 350 degrees.

Mix the nuts in a large bowl. Spread on a baking sheet and toast in the oven for 10 minutes, stirring once. Leave the oven on after you remove the nuts.

Melt the butter, either on the stove top or in the microwave, and pour into the large bowl. Stir in the brown sugar, cinnamon, cayenne, and maple syrup.

Add the toasted nuts, still warm, to the bowl and stir until coated. Mix in the salt and pretzels, and stir until the nuts and pretzels are completely coated. (Adding the salt after the nuts and sugar mixture is stirred keeps the salt from dissolving.)

Spread the mixture on the baking sheet and toast in the oven for 15 to 18 minutes, stirring twice during cooking. Remove from the oven and cool completely. The mixture can be stored in an airtight container for up to a week.

Makes about 4 cups.

When the mixture first comes out of the oven, you may taste a sharpness and fear that you overdid the cayenne. Remember Pepper's advice on giving blends time for the edges to wear off—these flavors mellow beautifully in just a few hours.

Save Room for Coffee but Not Sure About Dessert? Two in One!

MEXICAN COFFEE

FOR EACH DRINK:

½ ounce tequila
½ ounce Kahlúa
1 cup hot, strong brewed coffee
¼ to ⅓ cup vanilla ice cream
dash of cinnamon, optional

Make the coffee. Use clear glass serving cups if you can, for presentation.

Set out the ice cream. You want it partially melted.

Combine the tequila and Kahlúa in the serving cup. Pour in the coffee, add the ice cream, and add a dash of cinnamon. Serve immediately. Enjoy!

M7G0610

P.O. 0005229963 202